Judy Astley was frequently told off for day-dreaming at her drearily traditional school but has found it to be the ideal training for becoming a writer. There were several false-starts to her career: secretary at an all-male Oxford college (sacked for undisclosable reasons), at an airline (decided, after a crash and a hijacking, that she was safer elsewhere) and as a dress designer (quit before anyone noticed she was adapting *Vogue* patterns). She spent some years as a parent and as a painter before sensing that the day was approaching when she'd have to go out and get a Proper Job. With a nagging certainty that she was temperamentally unemployable, and desperate to avoid office coffee, having to wear tights every day and missing out on sunny days on Cornish beaches with her daughters, she wrote her first novel, *Just for the Summer.* She has now had ten novels published by Black Swan.

AWAY FROM IT ALL

Judy Astley

BLACK SWAN

AWAY FROM IT ALL
A BLACK SWAN BOOK : 0 552 99951 2

First publication in Great Britain

PRINTING HISTORY
Black Swan edition published 2003

1 3 5 7 9 10 8 6 4 2

Set in 11/12pt Melior by
Kestrel Data, Exeter, Devon.

Black Swan Books are published by Transworld Publishers,
61–63 Uxbridge Road, London W5 5SA,
a division of The Random House Group Ltd,
in Australia by Random House Australia (Pty) Ltd,
20 Alfred Street, Milsons Point, Sydney, NSW 2061, Australia,
in New Zealand by Random House New Zealand Ltd,
18 Poland Road, Glenfield, Auckland 10, New Zealand
and in South Africa by Random House (Pty) Ltd,
Endulini, 5a Jubilee Road, Parktown 2193, South Africa.

Printed and bound in Great Britain by
Clays Ltd, St Ives plc.

For Maureen
(Checkout no. 39, St Clare's Sainsbury's)

One

Elvis was in Sainsbury's again, browsing in the cat-food aisle. He'd been there the previous Wednesday too, but in the café that time, eating fried eggs with baked beans and reading the *Daily Mail*.

Alice Perry, who had lost her virginity to a French exchange boy called Marcel on the day the real Elvis had died, shoved a twelve-pack of Felix Fish Favourites into her trolley, watched him pick out two boxes of Go Cat (chicken and tuna flavours) and put them in his basket. He looked like a man who lived alone: unkempt, tatty round the edges, uncared for. His studded denim jacket had been bought when he'd been many kilos lighter and his pointy black cowboy boots had unevenly worn-down heels, as if he'd been struggling to strut the famous Elvis swagger and had angled uncomfortably to the right. Arthritis in his knees, Alice guessed. This Elvis had come a long hard way down from the Vegas glory-days; it would be hard to imagine him thrusting his creaky pelvis at anything more gruelling than a British Legion karaoke night.

She wondered about a suitable cat for him – perhaps a huge, white, bad-tempered creature, extravagantly fluffy and sporting a leopard-print collar spangled with chunky rhinestones. She hoped its fur was in better nick than its owner's lank, thinning hair. No-one else in the store seemed to have noticed him, as if long-dead stars often strolled the aisles of the Richmond Sainsbury's doing their celestial shopping. Possibly John Lennon was sometimes in, checking the sell-by dates on the fresh pasta sauces, and maybe Jimi Hendrix could frequently be spotted filling a trolley with frozen pizzas and herbal tea.

'S'not really 'im.' A skinny teenage shelf-stacker, hanging up flea collars, was eyeing Alice with blatant scorn. He nodded in the direction of Elvis who was now making his way towards the frozen peas, adjusting his aviator sunglasses and scratching his ear.

'He's in most weeks. He's a nim-per-son-a-tor.' The boy pronounced the word clearly and slowly, as if Alice might be unaccustomed to words of several syllables.

'Yes. I thought he probably was.' Alice gave him a bright, broad smile, one that usually gave people an impression of a thoroughly nice woman, and left the boy to his pet products. She heard him mutter 'Stupid cow', not quite under his breath.

'Mum! Can we go? Like, now?' Alice's daughter Grace, who'd been stocking up at the Pick 'n' Mix, caught up with her by the breakfast cereals. She stood close, shimmying in between her mother and the Weetabix, making sure she was the sole object of attention. Her pale bare arms had a typical London lack of muscle tone. That afternoon Grace should have been at the school sports day, psyching herself up to win the 400m hurdles, not trudging round a supermarket. She could certainly do with the exercise and fresh air, Alice thought guiltily. Like so many London children, especially the cosseted, ferried-

8

everywhere-by-car ones, she looked pallid and limp like a plant raised in dim light.

'What's the rush?' Alice asked. 'Is your headache coming back?' It was a sly question, they both knew it. Grace rarely had headaches but when she did they neatly coincided with school events that she wanted to avoid, such as today's end-of-year grand athletics finale. Alice on her own would have been hard on her, told her to take a couple of paracetamol, go to school and see how she felt later. But the girl had deliberately and speedily got to Noel as he was leaving for work, knowing quite well he was a far softer sympathetic touch. Alice raised her hand, aiming at Grace's forehead to check her temperature and Grace stepped quickly backwards, just beyond reach, leaving her mother looking as if she was hailing a Nazi leader.

'I'm OK. It's just freezing in here. And I'm mega bored.' Grace was gazing round with an expression of astonished disappointment, as if she'd expected the shelves to be stacked exclusively with items desirable to a fourteen-year-old girl of sophisticated tastes.

'Well you didn't have to come. You could have stayed at home and made cups of tea for Mrs Pusey.'

'God no, anything but that,' Grace groaned, reaching across behind her mother's head for a pack of Pop Tarts. 'But why couldn't we have gone somewhere more fun than here? There was a skirt in Warehouse I wanted to try on.'

'I always do the shopping on Wednesday afternoons. It gives Mrs Pusey a clear run at the cleaning. If I'm in the house she spends hours telling me about her latest cancelled hospital appointment.'

'You always say that. "I always do this, I always do that." ' Grace glared at her mother.

'And besides,' Alice said, 'you're supposed to be ill.'

'Yeah, well.' Grace started rooting through the contents of the trolley. 'Have you got the Monster Munch?'

'If they were on the list,' Alice told her, looking through the selection of muesli in search of one without added sugar.

'List! That's another thing you always say: "Is it on the list?" like the world would end if you bought something you hadn't actually written down.' Grace was now bored to exploding point. 'Why can't you just grab what you think we'd all like and be . . . oh . . . *thing* . . . like you do things just when you feel like it . . . for bloody once! You always have to plan your whole life out on paper, like you can't even breathe without a book of instructions!'

'Spontaneous. That's the word you were looking for,' Alice told her, at the same time acknowledging how rarely that word could be applied to herself. Alice's near-paranoid reliance on routine and order was a frequent source of domestic teasing – 'Oh look, it's ten thirty, Mum will be having camomile tea and one rich tea biscuit' – but this wasn't the time to argue about it. Two elderly ladies, who'd been discussing the unfamiliar array of creatures offered on modern-day fish counters, suspended their debate to stare brazenly at Grace and Alice, anticipating a good loud row that they could talk about later in the coffee shop.

'Leave it, Grace, OK? I've just got to get the bread then we can go.'

'Five loaves of organic wholemeal, two French sticks, one pack of crumpets, potato cakes and . . .' Grace chanted in a sing-song voice, not needing to look at Alice's list.

'Yeah I know, and a partridge in a pear tree,' Alice added, accepting her daughter's mockery.

10

'Not if it isn't on the list. Your kind of shopping is just sooo boring.' Grace grinned.

'Oh I don't know, didn't you notice Elvis Presley back there?'

'*What?*'

'El . . . Oh never mind, just someone I saw,' she said, thinking suddenly of French Marcel, sharp beach pebbles digging into her back and the cool tingle of his fingers sliding down across her naked stomach. 'He was a long, long time ago.'

Nearly three hundred miles away, close to the far end of Cornwall, in what an estate agent with fingers desperately crossed for a sale would describe as a mature rambling garden, Alice's brother Ariel Lewis (who had long preferred to go by the less whimsical name of Harry) was in the biggest of his three poly-tunnels mending a tear in the fabric. He didn't much mind about the elements gaining access to his plants, or the ever-encroaching nettle jungle taking root inside. He didn't even mind foxes wandering in for some night-time warmth, but that side of the tunnel was visible from the footpath down to the cove and he didn't want nosy, law-conscious hikers peering in and identifying the thriving crop as top quality guaranteed-female cannabis. This year he was trying two varieties: Durban Poison and Trance, twenty plants of each. If the local Plod copped knowledge of this little lot, Harry could be looking at the wrong end of a five-year stretch, however much he pleaded (not entirely untruthfully) that it was grown for the relief of his mother's arthritis.

Harry tried not to think of his mother as he sealed the polythene split with gaffer tape. Jocelyn Lewis wasn't at all well. The doctor hadn't seemed too fussed about it, but it was all right for him – he didn't have to deal with any of it. He'd said she'd only had a minor stroke ('only'? Where did 'only' come into it?) and that with a bit of care and attention she'd be fine, might never have another, could live another thirty years. But she might not. She might drop dead tomorrow, or she might have stroke after disabling stroke and dwindle away to a helpless shell of a human. Joss would need watching: she could have another at any moment, that was the bottom line. And a much more serious one, a real life-cruncher for all of them. The whole business was making him jumpy. Harry's wife Mo wasn't much help: she kept saying things like, 'Well she's on the downward slope now,' and other such cheerless comments that set him thinking along the depressing lines of stairlifts, waterproof mattress covers, small pale meals on trays and the creeping stench of gradual bodily decay. Mo had had an unfamiliar stubborn, set look on her face these last days since Jocelyn's brief episode of faintness and disconnection, as if she too sensed the same deteriorations on the way and would viciously mutilate anyone who dared to suggest that any of the resulting burdens should fall on her.

'You should get Alice to come down, see for herself what's happening to the mad old bat. Take a bit of the load off. It's all right for her, swanning about in London in her swanky house with her posh-school kids, scribbling silly children's stories and calling it work. She should try skivvying for the sodding B and B trade down here in this rotting, run-down dump as well as chasing around for *your* mother.'

Harry had been shocked to hear Mo speak so fiercely. She'd never expressed anything so combative before. She tended to drift around Penmorrow in slow mellow calm with little sound but the swish and rustle of her velvet skirts. She was usually smiling in a mildly amused, mysterious way, as if she had secret inner powers that let her mind bypass trivial day-to-day problems, such as were there enough towels without holes in them for next week's visitors.

What she'd said was true though, the house was crumbling more than a bit and not just around the edges. The top windows desperately needed replacing, especially in Harry and Mo's bedroom where the splintering wood was so patched with filler that you daren't let out a trapped butterfly in case the whole rickety casement fell out and landed in the pond. And the pond too, that was choked with weed and the stench of putrid mud, and the slope down from there towards the beach was eroding, so the tree roots were up and arching over the path. His twin sons, nearly thirteen and pretty much strangers at their school, seemed to be running wild and beyond his control, like honeysuckle that's grown too far into a rambling rose. And then there was The Ghost, as he and Mo called him, Jocelyn's resident writer, Aidan ('helping me put my own words in the right order'), ensconced without charge in the best Bed and Breakfast room, the only one with a decent en suite. Jocelyn didn't consider that 'an expense'.

'He's needed. My publisher is getting impatient,' she insisted grandly. 'How else am I to put together my autobiography?' Harry lacked the necessary spirit to suggest that as she had been famous as a novelist (just the one book, long, long ago), she could reasonably be expected to scribble down her life story herself. He'd be countered with many good reasons as to why not. Joss had a limitless supply of justifications for whatever she chose to do – it seemed to come with the territory, a lifetime of being the one in charge, with years of practice at getting her own way.

Harry sighed to himself and tried to concentrate on hunting out stray snails from among his plants. It didn't do to get too deeply into considering the dilapidations of the place. It was a thought train with no terminus and too many branch lines. Every single problem led to a host of others, and you could only do what you could do. For him and for Mo this meant keeping the pair of cottages (Cygnet and Gosling) along the lane in a condition just about passable for undemanding holidaymakers who put Location way above Luxury. Those few who booked a room ahead of their holiday were attracted by the once-famous element of Penmorrow, too. They wanted a piece of its past hippy wackiness, the whiff of notoriety. They wanted to see the Arthur Gillings statuary – Big Shepherd on the front lawn (with his few remaining sheep), Jesus Erect in the hallway, the silver shark leaping from the pond. Visitors liked to go home and tell of the many paintings, wall-hangings, pottery and sundries left behind by the former illustrious housemates. There were unexpected things: the delicate Andy Warhol flower sketches, Joe Orton's underpants, Marc Bolan's pink feather boa (both items adorning Jesus to salvage his modesty), the Bailey prints of Jocelyn young, pregnant and naked in the orchard with storm clouds looming in the vast sky around her.

The bedrooms and bathrooms in the main house were kept more or less functioning for the bed and breakfast trade, who were often so glad to have found somewhere not sporting a smug 'No vacancies' sign that they didn't take much notice of the shredded carpets, chipped tiles and the blue water stains in the bath. There was neither time nor money left over for

14

the rest of it. And there was such a very, very big rest of it.

Jocelyn Lewis sat in her old cane peacock chair close to the hexagonal alcove window that looked out over her terrace and down through the trees towards the beach. She liked to look down, pretend she was viewing the world from a far-off tower. She loved seeing how people moved, the shapes they made with their bodies as they picked their way over wet sand and shingle, how they arranged themselves into their family groups, setting up little personal territories bounded by windbreaks and lilos and chairs and cool-boxes. They behaved so differently on the beach. No woman of late middle years would ever normally hitch up her skirt in front of strangers and sit right down on the ground in the middle of a crowd. But on the sand below Penmorrow she saw chubby pale thighs being exposed, underwear tumbling to the sand beneath skimpy beach towels, plump breasts being hauled unhurriedly back into place after escaping from unreliable bikini tops. Altogether, beach scenes amused her. The clumsiness of humans on sand reminded her of seals lumbering on shore. Man's natural elements were now only ones he'd constructed himself: the shopping mall, the street, the sofa. Given a purely natural landscape to deal with, people could only struggle.

Beside Jocelyn in her hexagon sat her own solid image in the form of a life-size bronze statue, gazing out at the sea like a companion spectator. This bronze Jocelyn, immortalized by Arthur Gillings over forty years previously when she'd been in her mid-twenties, was forever lithe and slender, naked and half crouched as if picking up shells, her head up and smiling as if

15

she listened to the seabirds, or to a lover calling. More than one male visitor to the house had been caught thinking he was alone, stooping to stroke the smooth gleaming figure, running a curious hand over the strong thigh, finding his fingers inevitably exploring between the rigid legs as if magically the sculpted folds there might feel soft and tenderly damp.

Jocelyn patted the statue's cold hard head. If the young bronze Jocelyn could have turned to look up at her older self, she wondered what her thoughts would be: perhaps, 'Who is this worn-out creature beside me?' Or, 'Poor woman, why does she look so pathetic?'

For Jocelyn did feel seriously under-strength. This was new to her, this sensation of mild but perpetual difficulty. Never before, except in the most pleasurable ways, had she been so aware of her body. Its new limitations, the unpredictable unsteadiness, the un-reliability of the legs, made themselves clear at every pre-dawn waking. The nightly trek to the bathroom to deal with an ever-weakening bladder had to be thought through carefully. She'd lie in the middle of the sagging mattress on the tarnished brass bed and contemplate negotiating the high drop to the floor. First she had to switch on the bedside light (there could be shoes to trip over, a cat to tread on). Then she had to sit – slowly so the blood didn't get a chance to rush, next to swing her legs over the bedside, then place her right hand in the very centre of the marble table beside her to get her balance ready to drop down to the floor. She had to hope that light bulbs had been replaced (Harry was hopeless, you had to tell him a dozen times at least), that the two creaking steps to her bathroom wouldn't have fatally succumbed to rot.

Sometimes, when she'd made it safely back to bed and was thanking the gods for that small survival, she thought of old lovers. Counting through them, trying to remember their names in the right order was her version of counting sheep, and she sent up more thanks to her spirit gods for the long-ago delights they'd given her in that same soft, high bed.

Alice gave the risotto a final stir, scattered chopped flat-leaf parsley over the top of it then cursed her forgetfulness. She should have left the parsley separate in its bowl for those who wanted it to help themselves. Now they'd have to endure the sight of Theo picking all these green bits out and laying them in a neat circle round the edge of his plate. When he'd got them all (and he'd spend a good while poking around with his fork to make sure), he'd move them round and shuffle them apart till they were as perfectly equidistant from each other as his mathematical eye could judge.

'Possibly a mild case of obsessive-compulsive disorder?' Alice had once suggested to Noel after Theo had arranged tomato seeds in groups of five on the black ash table so they looked like a row of domino faces. Noel's eyes had gone narrow with anger and he'd denied, with curses and vehemence, the possibility of any such thing in *his* family. For Theo was his son, not Alice's, just as Grace was Alice's but not Noel's. Noel's wife Helen had died in a car accident when Theo was nine. Alice's former husband lived in Los Angeles with a tiny blonde ex-gymnast who gave pet-bereavement counselling and either knew better than Alice had how to avoid being thumped around when the mood took him, or feisty LA-style, gave back as good as she got.

Alice, in her recently remodelled steel and cherry-wood kitchen, ignored the phone when it rang. Beyond the door she could hear the usual scramble as both

Theo and Grace leapt to answer it. If the call was for Alice a cross weary voice would inform her of the fact, as if the phone was teen territory, out of bounds to grown-ups. Both teenagers spent hours tapping out text messages on their own mobile phones, sometimes to each other in the same room. Alice occasionally wondered if the conversation skills of an entire generation would eventually atrophy and die.

'It's for you Mum; it's Harry.' A flash of Grace's face and hair appeared and disappeared from the doorway. Information imparted, she wasn't about to miss a second of *The Simpsons*.

Alice picked up the kitchen extension. 'Harry! How's everything down there? Weather good?'

'Same as ever when the wind's easterly. Bloody freezing. Mist. Can't see the end of the beach.'

'I suppose I shouldn't tell you we've got a bit of a heatwave here then!' Alice always felt compelled to display excessive jocularity when talking to her brother, as a way of counteracting his habitual low-key semi-gloom. She thought it made her sound faintly ridiculous: Noel had once said that in conversation with Harry she sounded like a children's TV presenter.

'Joss isn't well.' Harry, quickly bored with the social niceties and mindful of his telephone bill, stated this bluntly. 'The doctor thinks she's had a mild stroke.'

Alice, shocked, grasped the edge of the translucent blue glass worktop. 'What happened? Is she in hospital? I'll come down . . .'

'No, she's fine. She's here at Penmorrow. There's no panic, but maybe you could come and stay for a while? Mo's finding it tough. And there's The Ghost, this man from some publisher, writing her life story and getting in the way. We could use a hand.'

Alice thought quickly. 'Well Grace and Theo have

18

only got another ten days of school. I could come then, and bring them. We've not booked for Italy till late August . . .'

'Can't you come sooner?' Harry sounded more angry than disappointed.

Alice counted to five and gathered her thoughts. Her mother was ill. Perhaps she was dying – perhaps all those years of drink, cigarettes and hippy-trippy drugs had caught up with her. Joss wouldn't admit to feeling scared, worried or needing anyone's company but she might be terrified inside.

'OK, I'll come tomorrow. I'll bring Grace and then Theo can join us at the end of term – I doubt Noel will want him missing school. Have you got room for us or shall I try and get into a hotel?'

'We've got room. There's no-one in Gosling – the cooker's only got two rings working so we're not booking it out.' Alice bit her lip: Gosling was a crumbling, draughty, tumbledown cottage close to the beach path. The salt spray had rotted most of its thatch over the years and the only heating was a sulky log fire that blew smoke into the sitting room at the slightest breeze. Noel thought it merited nothing more than immediate demolition but Alice remembered it from her childhood when Arthur Gillings had lived there, creating his mad (but world-famous) sculptures and telling her stories of Cornish wreckers and his own (not entirely invented) smuggling adventures. With enormous patience, he'd helped her to read the whole of *Peter Pan* out loud, waiting while she struggled with difficult words and as delighted as she was by how much she learned on the way through the long volume.

'That cooker's needed replacing for ten years!' Alice said to Harry. There was silence and she could have bitten her tongue for the lack of tact: Penmorrow's

19

finances had been bordering on desperate for so very long. There was no way that Harry, Mo and Jocelyn could do what she had so casually done: simply flick through luxury kitchen brochures with a specialist designer and pick out the best of everything, scarcely stopping to check on prices.

'Gosling will be fine,' Alice said, making a mental note to take extra duvets. 'I'll see you very soon. Love to Joss and Mo and your boys.'

'Look, why don't I take Theo with me as well tomorrow, seeing as there's only a few days of term left?' Alice suggested to Noel after supper. She'd sent the children to watch TV so that she could discuss her trip with him. He sat silently at the table, refilling his wine glass and looking disgruntled. She picked up Theo's plate and took it to the dishwasher, pausing to rinse away the tidy garland of parsley that she'd predicted he'd leave. 'And it's not as if they do much during the last week of term.'

'It'll make them unsettled. They'll think it's all right to take off from school on a whim . . .' And this, she thought, was the man who'd only that morning so easily accepted Grace's 'headache'.

'A whim? My mother is *ill*, Noel! A stroke, even a mild one, is a very serious thing.'

He said nothing, but raised a quizzical eyebrow.

'And don't look like that!' She was angry now. 'You know Joss would be the last person to fuss about nothing. It could be that things are worse than she'll admit. She must at least be pretty shaken, she's not even that old. I think she saw herself going full steam into serious old age, like a true *grande dame*, and then simply dying on the bench in the afternoon sun under the old beech tree.'

'People who smoke as much as she does don't often see old age. Frankly she's lucky to have got this far.' Noel drained his glass and started pouring another.

'Neither do people who drink as much as you do,' Alice warned, shoving knives hard into their dishwasher slots. 'Anyway, apparently there's a man staying there, asking her about her life. He's doing her autobiography. Harry's worried that it's all too much for her.'

'Autobiography, my arse!' Noel's voice was full of scorn. 'She only ever wrote one book!'

'Yes but what a book. *Angel's Choice* was a groundbreaker. The film is probably still showing, somewhere.'

'I know, I know, it's had more TV showings than *The Great Escape*. A cult classic, book and film both,' Noel interrupted, sounding as if he was reading from a review of all-time cinema hits. 'And of course there's the Penmorrow hippy-commune aspect. I expect the great British public will love that. Lots of salacious free-love revelations there.'

Sometimes, just sometimes, Alice could understand her mother's early objections to Noel. The first time she'd brought him to Penmorrow, Joss had taken one amused look at him and declared, her voice rasping with mirth and Marlboros, 'Darling you can't possibly marry him! A man with a *tie*!' It hadn't been the best of introductions. Noel, used to the effortless charming of women, had kept a cool and rather disapproving distance after that and so it remained, five years on.

Alice wiped her hands on the tea towel and flung it onto the worktop. 'Look Noel, I wasn't asking permission. I'm going to Cornwall tomorrow and I'm taking Grace with me, stuff school. I'm happy to take Theo too but if you think he'll miss some vitally

21

important maths lesson or something, well *you* can sort out arrangements for looking after him. OK? Now I'm off to pack.'

Noel, conceding defeat, gave her the lopsided grin that had first secured her attention at a school parents' meeting six years before. It was a long way from an Elvis-leer but was equally calculated to attract. Alice thought of the man she'd seen in Sainsbury's that morning. He and Noel couldn't be more different. Noel had a decidedly well-tended look, sleek and scrubbed and ever-ready for inspection, like someone who lives in the perverse hope of being run over, purely for the opportunity to be given top marks for their pristine underwear by ministering medics. For his whole life, first by his adoring mother and then by his two wives, he'd been as carefully nurtured as a specimen orchid. Perhaps a short time home alone would remind him, Alice thought, that even a lifelong Golden Boy, maybe even Elvis in his day, sometimes has to carry the garbage out to the bins.

Two

Alice had been born on Penmorrow's front verandah steps on a searingly hot June night at the beginning of the 1960s. Jocelyn, after many hours of dire pain, felt she had turned into a she-wolf, howling at the moon. The current four adult females of the household had attended her, one of whom irritated her enormously by groaning along in sympathy throughout the labour. She had viciously punched another who'd been insistent that squatting over a mushroom ring on the lawn would soothe the agony and bestow magical fairy qualities on the baby. Jocelyn had also felt cheated to find that in spite of lavish doses of raspberry leaf tea and months of protracted daily yoga, as per instructions in an ancient tome on natural remedies, she did not feel anywhere near as harmonious with Mother Nature as she had anticipated. Nature and God, too pleased with themselves after putting Adam together, had completely bodged the job of creating Eve and had left her with obvious design faults. She would happily have agreed to being whisked off to the local cottage hospital for a major input of pain-busting drugs if the menfolk of Penmorrow hadn't been banished in the only functioning car to do their ritual waiting in the Mariners pub around the headland in Chapel Creek, well out of speedy summoning distance.

That long hot night, across the small sandy bay, the residents of the village of Tremorwell had turned up the volume on their televisions to drown out Jocelyn's primitive keening and had wondered anew about the sanity of those who lived up at Penmorrow. One or two crossed themselves and offered up prayers for the survival of mother and child. An ambulance was called (it was never discovered by whom) and a midwife arrived in time to find Jocelyn drinking celebratory elderflower wine, and her birth companions anointing baby Alice's head with a concoction of sage and comfrey for health, happiness and wisdom. Contrary to local rumour, the placenta had not been cooked in a pie and eaten (along with the fairy mushrooms). It was buried beneath the sunny strawberry patch where it would, if a fox hadn't scrabbled it out of the ground and stolen it, have enriched the land and symbolically completed the circle of life for that small community.

Penmorrow was accepted locally as both a rich source of gossip and as a harmless enough household of assorted Bohemians and artistic oddballs, and villagers relished casual name-drops when a well-known artist or musician was seen at the pub. Although a nervy few twittered amongst themselves about 'goings-on', generally the Penmorrow folk were welcomed as long as they didn't get offensively drunk on the beach, indulge in unwelcome molesting or feel the need to know where the stocks of French-labelled spirits behind the counter in the shop came from.

The cast of characters living at Penmorrow was an ever-changing one, and Alice's childhood was punctuated by departures and arrivals. Arrivals delighted her. When someone new was about to join the household there would be a big cleaning session in whichever room or cottage was currently spare. Jocelyn would bring in great bunches of wild flowers from the garden, or long fronds of pussy willow and cherry blossom. Milly, a frail and edgy painter who brooded about the faithless husband she'd left behind in Liverpool, would donate a couple of moody compositions that had proved unsellable, and Arthur Gillings (the one person, other than her mother, that Alice remembered as being there for her entire childhood) would wheel in, on a porter's trolley, his elegant bronze statue of a sly-faced Pan that always greeted new inhabitants. 'It's only on loan,' he would warn as they were shown to their quarters, as if in the night they might up and off to London with it and enter it into a speedy, profitable auction.

The Penmorrow furniture was originally heavy and old and gloomy – massive Edwardian wardrobes and chests of drawers the colour of treacle toffee, all salvaged cheaply by Jocelyn as a job lot from a clearance warehouse. Residents were encouraged to decorate any available surfaces, to leave their mark on their rooms in whatever way they wanted for as long as they occupied them, so over the years the treacly furniture gained layer upon layer of thick oily paint.

'So very Bloomsbury,' Jocelyn had once said to her daughter, twirling round in a room that had walls clumsily daubed with massive tulips and fat parrots. Alice, ten years old and hypercritical, hadn't liked it at all – it didn't look finished. The artist had run out of red paint for the flowers and had given up halfway along one wall, leaving the rest covered with scrappy splodges of green. The parrots were too big and had silly smirks on their faces. No-one ever painted the ceilings in the house, either: they were too high and

25

too big and there wasn't a proper ladder. Alice minded this: the ceilings didn't match and in a household where disorder was the rule she very much preferred things that did. There'd be exciting walls painted with big primary-coloured shapes, or midnight black with galaxies of silver stars or covered with pale mauve hessian, but above would be a sad, cracked, buff-coloured expanse of old plaster patchily stained from nicotine and long-ago oil lamps, and with untidy chunks flaking off.

Communal areas, the sitting rooms, kitchen and hallways, were painted in rich glossy purples, orange, deep jade green and the brown of bitter chocolate, and stayed much the same forty years on. Visitors would occasionally comment (daringly) that a few coats of magnolia would brighten the place up, but Joss liked her moody jewel colours. A wide-ranging collection of artworks hung everywhere. One of Joss's lovers, in spite of being rejected, had given her an Alfred Wallis painting. Peter Blake had stayed for a while and left behind his early sketch ideas for the Beatles *Sergeant Pepper* cover. There were works by Cornwall painters John Miller and Patrick Heron. Bernard Leach pottery was scattered about on the kitchen dresser, one jug holding a flourishing collection of biros, and an abandoned page of David Bowie's handwritten song lyrics languished in a drawer.

On the days new people joined their household, Alice would hang about in the hallway and sit on the stairs for hours, ears alert for the sound of tyres on gravel, hoping for a new friend of her age, someone she could make camps with in the wood, read school stories (secretly) with and who would join her in building pretend sand-cities on the beach below. When a car pulled up, she'd run to lurk shyly behind

26

the coatstand and peep out from under Arthur's musty black velvet cloak, breathing in the scent of old cigars and a hint of rum. Sometimes a family in a ramshackle van would arrive, but more often it would be a disappointingly solitary person in the station taxi. Once she'd heard a big argument as the cab driver had tried to charge too much extra for having to transport a loom and two sacks of assorted yarn. She'd been afraid then, only six years old, thinking this new person was fierce and monstrous. She'd never seen anyone really angry, not shouting mad. Penmorrow was full of people smiling; grown-ups claimed all the time that they adored children, revered them for being truly natural beings with secret knowledge from prebirth. Sad Milly called Alice the 'prettiest child of the flowers' which terrified and alarmed her. The prettiest flowers were the ones you picked in the gardens, taking them from their plant families and sticking them into vases, deprived of fresh rain and air and true sunlight, where they died too quickly and were forgotten and thrown out to rot on the compost. She didn't want that to happen to her.

Alice took a last loving look into her impeccable sitting room and felt like giving it a goodbye hug. Four shades of meticulously selected white (Kelly Hoppen range from Fired Earth) made up the walls and paintwork, and the subtle nuances of depth and tone gleamed in the early morning light at their most delectable. All the buttery yellow sofa cushions were plumped up and ready to be collapsed into. On the long low glass coffee table *Elle Decoration* and *World of Interiors* magazines sat temptingly waiting, as yet unread. The table by the window held a fresh and lavish arrangement of scented stocks, lupins and delphiniums. Such comfort and composure wasn't something Alice was overeager to trade for her mother's collapsing Cornwall domain. The kitchen there would make a health inspector apoplectic and on her last visit only one of the four lavatories in the main house had been working – something had lodged in a crucial pipe.

'Harry will fix it, in due course,' Jocelyn had said airily and carelessly when Alice had suggested calling a plumber. She'd given her that old slow smile, as if Alice was a confused heretic questioning the household's essential tenets. Alice knew what Harry's version of 'due course' was. It would be when he'd figured out that the idle policy of long-term 'wait and see' wasn't going to improve the situation and would probably cost more in the long run.

'You were so lucky that you didn't have to go to school.' Grace stowed the two cat baskets into the back of Alice's Ford Galaxy and stroked the noses of the occupants – one fat old tabby cat, one white rabbit. The cat miaowed crossly and the rabbit snapped at her finger. 'Behave!' Grace warned them and then climbed into the front seat beside her mother. Theo was sprawled across the back seats. Noel had decided (overnight) that in spite of missing school, an absent Theo was a lot more convenient than one on the premises. Theo would need to have his picky but enormous appetite regularly stoked; he would need to be prised from his bed each morning and would push his luck over drink and squalor in his room and have hordes of huge, noisy, grubby friends tramping in and out. With Theo many miles away Noel would be free to play golf in the sunny early evenings and do something about getting his handicap down to the competition level he'd need to be at if his retirement days were going to have any edge to them. He could also take Paula, the firm's recently employed receptionist, to Le Caprice and try to persuade her that her feckless eternal-student husband didn't deserve her. The preamble to seduction was a skill for which he liked to keep in practice, and which he considered very much on the same relaxing and battery-charging par as Alice's visits to her aromatherapy masseuse.

'There's nothing lucky about being uneducated,' Alice reminded Grace, as she did every time her daughter came out with this envy-statement. 'I *longed* to go to school. I didn't even know what it was till I was about eight and worked out where all the village kids disappeared to in the daytime. And once I'd found out I wanted the whole thing, a uniform, dinner money, homework, playtime milk, skipping rhymes, the lot.'

'Yeah but no exams,' Theo sighed. 'Awesome. No SATs, no GCSEs, no having to decide between chemistry and biology when you hate them both. No pervy games teacher nudging your arse in the showers.'

'Do they?' Alice gave Theo an enquiring look by way of the rear-view mirror.

'No they don't. He just says that because it's the kind of thing parents take notice of,' Grace said sharply, turning round and glaring at her stepbrother. She wasn't glad he was coming with them, not one bit. Theo (and Noel) treated the whole Penmorrow set-up as if it was a huge joke, as if Joss and Harry and all of them were ridiculously thick for not living their lives the fast urban way, like they did. When they visited the house, Noel and Theo picked silly, pointless faults all the time. Once, Noel had said loudly in front of everybody that Penmorrow was exactly the kind of house where it would be a terrific idea to say yes to anyone who rang up offering a deal on naff PVC windows. He'd say things to Harry like 'That grass

29

could do with a good cut' when it was obvious Joss just didn't care about that sort of thing. Long grass in London meant you were really carefully growing a wildflower meadow that you'd read about in some Sunday colour supplement. In London you did it, Alice had told Grace jokingly, the expensive way, sending away to smart nurseries to get all the plants delivered ready-grown in special little biodegradable pots. Joss got better results without trying and the whole thing looked right, all overgrown and woven through with cornflowers and ox-eye daisies and ragged robin and little bee orchids. Everything at Penmorrow grew plump and luscious, like the apple trees in the orchard, where their branches came right down to the ground and you could hide away underneath them with a book. The solitary apple tree in their Richmond garden had been pruned and shaped so drastically it looked like a depressed, amputated thing. And it only produced about six scabby apples a year.

Last time they'd all been to Penmorrow, for a few freezing days after Easter (typically, the heating oil had run out), Grace remembered there'd been a row about money. Noel was keen on money, she'd noticed: he was always talking about 'financial arrangements', which made her think of vases of flowers. He had chosen to catch Joss at a bad moment, just as they were finishing supper and the grown-ups were all a bit pissed, and told her it was high time she should 'sort out her affairs'. Grace had laughed because she thought it sounded as if Joss should make lists of all her lovers – and she knew there'd been plenty of them; at bedtime when Grace was little, Joss used to tell her tales of her past loves the way other grandmothers would read Beatrix Potter and Winnie the Pooh.

'I take it this is solicitor-speak for "make your will immediately and be sure not to leave the moolah to a cats' home",' Joss had mocked. Noel had smirked at her and said that surely she didn't want to donate her property to a system of government she'd never supported, and that it was a good idea to be prepared.

Joss had snarled, blown a cloud of blue cigarette smoke over him and enquired loudly and slowly, 'Good for whom exactly?'

Grace had thought she sounded like royalty. Another bottle of wine later she'd called Noel a 'bourgeois cretin', flung an overripe mango at him (a sticky mess on his shirt) and told him to fuck off. She'd informed him all lawyers were shit and the fact that he'd married her daughter didn't make him an exception. Noel had sniggered in a really patronizing way as if she was just an arrogant old peasant, too dim to understand that his Cambridge degree meant that what he said must be right. Grace wondered now how Joss would be when she and her mother turned up with Theo, whom she considered a dopy clone of his father. Perhaps she wouldn't mind. Most likely she'd have forgotten. She might even be too ill to notice who was in the house, or who they were. It was a sad thought – she loved the powerful, stroppy Jocelyn just the way she was.

As they headed west on the A303, Grace looked round to check that Theo was safely under his head-phones, out of hearing range. His head was nodding to some tick-a-tick beat.

'Mum? Is Joss really very ill?' she asked Alice. She didn't want Theo to hear the reply. If it was yes, he'd start on about who was going to inherit Penmorrow, just like his dad did. It was obscene, talking of people only in terms of their cash value. You expected it from

Noel; Alice laughed it off and said it was just a habit from his job. Theo was different though – at sixteen, what was his excuse?

'She's had a stroke and she's a bit confused and upset, but she might completely recover and be perfectly all right. Or at least, that's what Harry said.' Alice didn't sound too convinced. Grace wasn't surprised. Harry sometimes didn't seem to be part of the world at all, as if life was a sort of circle game like a hokey-cokey and he was still waiting for someone to notice him standing by the wall, to take his hands and show him how to join in. He reminded her of a troll or a gnome, someone who lived a completely parallel existence, finding it a perpetual struggle to pretend to be a real live human. Grace remembered when Alice had first taken Theo and Noel to Penmorrow and they'd met Harry who hadn't spoken at all for two days. He'd smiled a lot at his sister's new people but hadn't shown any curiosity or even polite interest about them. Theo, about twelve at the time and used to a vocal babble as a background to his life, had asked Alice what was wrong with him, why was Harry 'like that'?

'He's not "like" anything,' Alice had snapped rather defensively. 'He's just himself. An individual.' Noel had chuckled and commented, 'Well he's certainly that.'

The day was hot and dusty and the windscreen was splattered with dead insects. With the sunroof open, Alice could smell a mustardy mixture of oilseed rape and recently cut silage. Remembering the old festivals that Penmorrow had celebrated, she worked out that they were two weeks past Litha, the summer solstice. She wondered if on that day, Joss had still hung her quartz crystal necklace in the hexagon window to harvest the peak of the sun's power. She'd be needing that extra strength, now that she'd reached a frail point in her life.

Alice drove on past fields full of something that was a soft, hazy lavender blue. Lupins, she guessed, wondering at how little she knew about what the countryside currently grew. In her early teens she could have identified every crop between Tremorwell and Plymouth and named a dozen breeds of sheep. She'd hardly travelled beyond Cornwall then, although at the age of nine she'd spent a couple of months with Joss and Harry in a primitive mountain cottage on Ibiza, at a time when the drug culture there had nothing to do with all-night clubbing. Harry, who was five, had caught measles very badly and Jocelyn had wanted to come home, fast. It was the only time Alice had seen her mother close to real fear and panic, as at the airport the check-in girl had noticed that his name was 'Ariel' on his mother's passport and not the 'Harry' that Arthur Gillings, who had organized their trip, had put on the tickets. It had been Alice who had stayed calm, explaining to the girl about the confusion over names, lifting her feverish brother's tee shirt so that the livid scarlet spots and the urgency of the problem could be seen. This had secured them a section to themselves on the plane and an ambulance waiting at Heathrow to take them to Ashford Hospital for Harry to be checked over.

It had been then that Alice had realized that if she wanted a completely responsible, unfalteringly capable person in her life, she herself would have to be that person. She had relished, at that time, Enid Blyton's Magic Faraway Tree books. Like her, the fictional children were allowed to roam out of sight of home all day and enjoy whatever fanciful adventure

33

happened to come their way. What made her ache with envy was that her own mother was nothing like the comfortable homebody in the books. Joss was no roly-poly, aproned figure forever concocting delectable family meals in a clean, bright kitchen. Some of the time she wasn't on the premises at all but was away, either with a thrilling new lover or being interviewed, airing her controversial opinions on child-rearing, on men and relationships to any radio, TV show or magazine that asked her. Her children were left, as per her personal creed, in the care of whichever adults happened to be in the house at the time, for Joss believed that essentially humans were group animals, and that women, left to nature, would live like lionesses, communally raising their cubs and mating with whoever took their fancy as and when hormones decreed.

When Alice wandered back to Penmorrow at the end of a day on the sunny beach or in her camps in the woods, she used to make fervent wishes, hoping that whoever's name was down on the rota to do the cooking that day had managed to get something edible organized. She and the other Penmorrow children never actually went hungry, but unlike the lucky Blyton children, she was more likely to be met by an unappetizing grey-green lentil bake and a failed goat's-milk yogurt experiment than a rib-sticking casserole followed by apple crumble with lashings and lashings of cream.

Harry and Mo's twin sons, Chas and Sam, were waiting on the doorstep of the rundown Gosling cottage as Alice drove up the rocky track to Penmorrow. They lurked under the porch, half hidden behind honeysuckle that had made its way almost across the

34

doorway. Alice felt mildly annoyed: Harry had known they were coming, been insistent that they did. If he hadn't even hacked a way in, did that mean the cottage's interior was equally unprepared to greet them?

'God, look at the state of them. Neanderthals,' Theo commented, glaring out of the window at the two boys. Alice smiled and waved at them, privately agreeing with Theo that they looked very much as if they'd come straight from filming *Lord of the Flies*. Their hair had grown long and matted, as if they'd been aiming for dreadlocks but someone had insisted they comb it out now and then but not too often. They were wearing torn tee shirts that had once been white but which had been smothered with mud and moss to make a pretty good imitation of the camouflage pattern that Grace had on one of her Top Shop skirts. The two boys scowled as the car stopped and Alice wondered why, if they felt that hostile to the presence of their cousin and aunt, they were bothering to hang about.

'Hello you two!' she said cheerily. 'How are you both?'

'Awright,' Sam grunted. Chas said nothing, but stared past Alice to watch Grace taking her pet baskets from the car boot.

'Another rabbit?' he asked, his lip curled into a sneer.

'Yeah. What of it?'

'Nothing,' Sam said swiftly, then asked with some eagerness, 'is it for letting go?'

Grace hesitated, looking for support from Theo, who still lazed in the back of the car as if waiting for a lackey to open the car for him.

'It is for letting go. I always let them go. You shouldn't keep pets in cages.'

35

Grace had been buying a pet-shop rabbit each summer since she was seven, entirely for the purpose of being able to take them to Cornwall and set them free. The hills and woods of Tremorwell and beyond had become well populated with interbred bunnies, a motley mixture of grey, black and white fur, some with ears that flopped down and some with dense reddish coats. Secretly, Alice was pretty sure the newly liberated animals wouldn't survive much longer than it took to mate with the nearest wild rabbit. Pet-shop animals, cage-bred over countless generations, wouldn't have much nature knowledge to contend with wily foxes and sharp-eyed hungry buzzards.

'Harry doesn't like it,' Chas said. 'He says there's too many already. They eat the food he grows. He might shoot it.'

'So I'll let it go up the hill on the other side of the bay then. OK?' Grace told him, swinging the basket past him as she pushed her way into the porch. The rabbit's feet skittered on the newspaper in the basket. Alice caught sight of the twins exchanging sly grins and she wondered what kind of scam they had going.

'Mo says to come up for some dinner at seven,' Chas told Alice. 'And she says Joss is having a rest.'

'Sodding great,' Alice said under her breath as the boys strolled off up the path to the main house. 'You drive all this way, summoned like it's some kind of mad emergency, and you have to wait for a royal command. A cup of tea would have gone down well.'

Jocelyn was alone, sitting at the end of the huge oak table that might once have graced a monastery. The chairs had come from a church and were complete with slots in the back for hymnbooks. Alice remembered those as every Penmorrow child's crafty repository for sneakily spat-out food. Joss was looking, Alice thought, like an aristocratic character in a TV costume drama who dresses for dinner every night and keeps a full complement of serving staff in defiant face of reduced circumstances. There was no outward sign of her recent illness. Jocelyn, on first glance, was looking much as she always did, wearing her dark green Moroccan dress with pink embroidery round sprinklings of tiny mirrors, and her usual rather heavy burgundy lipstick. The table was already laid for nine and Joss, sitting behind an opened bottle of red wine, was fiercely polishing a fork using a turquoise paper napkin, her long white plait hanging over her shoulder and flicking backwards and forwards on the table top as she rubbed at the stubbornly tarnished surface. She was, Alice noticed, wearing her quartz crystal necklace.

'Hello Joss,' Alice said quietly, approaching her mother. Jocelyn looked up with a broad smile and started to push her chair back.

'No don't get up. I'll join you.' Alice sat down beside her mother. 'Mo says supper's nearly ready; the kids are just bringing the plates through.' She leaned forward and took her mother's hand. She was wearing her full quota of heavy silver rings with gems of topaz and opal and aquamarine. Almost tearful with concern, Alice asked, 'Now how are you?'

Jocelyn's welcoming smile vanished. 'I'm perfectly all right,' she snapped tetchily, drawing back her hand. 'I'd feel a lot better if people didn't keep asking me that. I expected better from you and you're just the same: that hushed tone, the implication that I'm keeping a deep secret pain all to myself and that if you press all the right buttons I'll blurt it out and weep copiously.' Joss stabbed the fork into the table top with enough force for it to stand for a second or two, swaying under the blow.

'Bloody kids. I remember when all you children used to fight for the job of polishing the silver. Now look at it.' She flicked her hand at the tarnished cutlery. Alice noticed that the skin on her knuckles was stretched tight and thin, like ancient worn-out linen sheeting. Her finger ends, by contrast, were thick-skinned and plump, stained a shiny tawny like ripe acorns by over half a century of nicotine.

'We only fought to clean the silver because it was better than going out in the freezing rain to clean out the chicken shed or wash the slugs out of a pile of lettuces.'

'At least everyone got their turn at the good and bad jobs. Chas and Sam, they don't seem to . . .' Joss sighed then conceded to Alice, 'You're looking well, anyway. Very London, that haircut, very "Smart Lady".' They both giggled. 'Smart Lady' was a long-ago Penmorrow term, applied to any occasion when it was necessary to dress up to face officialdom and appear suitably neat and tidy. Being summoned to the education authority, a bank manager or a lawyer meant rifling through the communal dressing-up basket in which was kept a supply of neat city clothes. There were a couple of dull grey suits for men, with plain white shirts and an assortment of junk-shop ties. For the women there were plain court shoes in a selection of sizes into which it was always a struggle to force broad splayed feet that were more used to open-toed sandals, and a couple of plain soberly coloured dresses. Best of all by far was the sky blue Chanel suit. This was Alice's favourite. Its skirt was knee-length (though unflatteringly mid-calf on sad Milly) with a low fan of pleats at the back which made it swing jauntily and shift about provocatively on the wearer's hips. The jacket had a nipped-in waist with a slender navy leather belt that could be knotted tight. Alice at eleven, had coveted this Smart Lady outfit more than anything and yearned to be grown-up enough to wear it before it succumbed to moths and was banished to the jumble bag. Of course by the time she was, she wouldn't have been seen dead in it.

'Supper's ready! Sit down everyone!' Mo came bustling through from the kitchen carrying a tray on which sat a pair of plump cooked chickens. She looked fussed and flustered – her lank, prematurely greying hair was stuck in steamy wisps around her face. Harry followed with his hands full of vegetable dishes. Sam and Chas, joshing and nudging each other, shambled in behind their parents and sat together at the far end of the table. Grace and Theo emerged from the opposite doorway, from the sitting room, and stood together looking uncertain.

'Theo, come and sit next to me,' Alice suggested. 'And, Grace, you go the other side of him.' It seemed important that Theo, for at least this first vulnerable day, should be spared any scathing comments from Chas and Sam about his peculiar eating habits. There were courgettes on offer: Theo would probably pile them up in the centre of his plate, arranged like a spiral staircase, then eat only what surrounded them.

'Where's Aidan? Isn't he coming?' Jocelyn, her hand stroking the back of the empty seat next to her, asked Mo. Mo wiped the back of her hand across her brow and glared at her mother-in-law.

'I don't know. He knows what time we eat. Perhaps he's gone to the pub.' Mo snatched Chas's plate out of his grimy hand and started thudding potatoes onto it.

'No I haven't. Of course I haven't. I'm here.'

So this must, Alice realized, be the writer that Harry referred to as The Ghost. He didn't look very ghost-like to Alice, more like an archetypal London Media Man, a species undoubtedly unfamiliar to Harry. Aidan had that blinking, short-sighted geeky look that didn't quite hide a boyish attractiveness even though he must be at least thirty. Alice was amazed at the transformation Aidan's arrival brought to her mother. Jocelyn couldn't have looked more thrilled if Jesus had phoned to say he'd chosen to make Penmorrow the venue for his second coming. Aidan, tall and wearing fashionably narrow, frameless glasses, shimmied across the room and kissed Jocelyn's outstretched hand. He was wearing pale cream crumpled linen trousers and an oversized black tee shirt and carried a slight scent of Alice's favourite Clarins shower gel. Next to her, Alice heard Theo trying to stiffle a giggle.

'Aidan! Sit beside me, sweetie, here. Aidan, this is my daughter Alice. And Alice, this is Aidan. Aidan is helping me with my autobiography and we're only halfway through. He is the reason I cannot die yet.'

Three

Grace sat up in the lumpy single bed and looked down towards the beach through the low window fringed by loose tufts of mossy thatch that the squirrels had scuffed from the roof. The broad window ledge beside her had brown smudgy spots where rain had found its way in. On a rough stormy night, Grace knew she'd have to move the bed out of the weather's reach or she'd be woken by a spattering of cold raindrops. This room in Gosling had the best view in the whole of Penmorrow. Through the gap in the trees where a diseased ilex had fallen in the big storm of 1991, you could watch the day opening up from the sea's edge to the centre of the village. Sometimes there'd be a seal lolloping about to see if any early morning fishermen on the rocks caught anything that they were willing to donate to idle wildlife. Usually there were a few villagers out jogging – occasionally they stopped to talk to each other, other times they just gazed straight ahead and raised a hand slightly as if there was no energy to spare to puff out a hello. Dog-walkers shuffled along the sand, disregarding the 'No Dogs' notice, confident that it referred merely to holiday-makers and to busier times of day. At the far end of the sand, where the sheltering cliffs rose up, the beach café had early surfers in for a bacon sandwich and polystyrene mug of tea before the trippers arrived in search of beach toys, pasties and wetsuits to rent.

The rabbit had to go today. Grace had kept it just that first night in its basket on top of the chest of drawers and it was sitting still and gloomy, staring at her with a decided look of feeling very let down. It couldn't even be bothered to twitch its nose. She didn't blame it – a creature saved from a pet shop's crowded cage was entitled to expect accommodation more palatial than a blue plastic prison. She'd taken Monty the cat's empty basket outside and stowed it under the porch in case the rabbit felt the further unfairness of one animal being out and enjoying itself while he was still imprisoned. Monty, ears up and whiskers at full alert, had rushed off to spend the night outside, reclaiming his hunting territory. Waking in the early hours to the sound of him crunching his kill beneath her bed was one of the very few things Grace wasn't too keen on about country living.

From the sofa bed in the sitting room downstairs, by way of the gaps in the floor where the boards were disconnecting themselves from the rafters below, Grace could hear the beep-beep of Theo texting someone. She was amazed he was awake. It wasn't even eight yet and on a normal non-school day he'd be well deep into whatever turgid teen dreamland boys like him inhabited in their sleep. She could also hear her mother in the kitchen – there were sounds of a kettle being filled and clunking down on the stained and splitting old wooden worktop. Several minutes later the fridge door creaked open and there was a shriek, followed by, 'Shit! Where did that come from?'

Grace climbed out of bed and padded barefoot down

the stairs, careful not to slip on the ancient worn-smooth, sludge green carpet. 'Mum? What was that?' she asked Alice, who was now stirring a teabag furiously round in a mug of boiled water.

'There was a bloody great mouse! In the fridge! Probably living on the mould at the back. You could grow a crop of ice mushrooms in there. This place! No wonder the business side of it is so crap. I mean who'd pay to stay here?' Alice waved her arm round, encompassing the flaking ochre walls, the cupboards with their doors hanging askew and several handles missing, the curtains with grease-splattered hems, sporting an orange daisy pattern that had been Mary Quant's trademark almost forty years before. Grace could see that her mother was close to weeping for her own streamlined domestic universe.

'Perhaps it got in when you put the milk in there last night.'

'It didn't, I'd have noticed. I bet it got in through the drainage hole at the back. Good thing we brought Monty – where is that cat by the way? Did he sleep on your bed?'

Grace shrugged. 'I thought he was with you. He's probably hunting in the woods.'

'Huh. A lot of use he is out there. We need him in here. I'll get some traps. Don't tell Joss.'

Grace laughed. 'Why not? When has she ever minded about killing stuff? You told me she used to wring the chickens' necks, no problem.'

Alice, pouring a year's worth of ancient crumbs out of the toaster and into the sink, said, 'It's not the killing, it's about me being such a wuss that I'm squeamish about sharing the premises with a bit of harmless wildlife. You know what she can be like. Tough doesn't even come close.'

Grace did know. She remembered when she was no more than seven and she'd just learned to swim after a course of weekly lessons at the local pool. Jocelyn had invited her to join her for her daily morning swim in the sea. Grace, conscious of the honour of graduating to being her grandmother's chosen companion, had been scared of the waves and had taken her armbands along, just in case.

'You don't need those!' Jocelyn had crowed at her. 'The sea will hold you up, just trust it!' Too fast, she'd grabbed Grace's hand and hauled her into the crashing grey waves, giving her no time to adjust to the cold and the heavy clinging sand shifting over and under her small, unsteady feet.

'I thought you said you could swim!' Jocelyn had teased her minutes later when she'd pulled the choking child back to the shore and watched, hands on hips and a mocking smile, while the mortified Grace threw up a lungful of salt water. Grace had hated her then, sobbing out the unfairness of it all as she staggered up the hill path back to the house, her barely dried body clammy with damp sand. But then Joss had done the thing she always did when she'd upset someone: she'd soothed and comforted and petted and coaxed until Grace could only love her again. She'd wrapped her in the precious silky patchwork quilt with its golden spiky stitches linking each perfect diamond patch, sat her in the rocking chair by the Aga and given her hot cocoa with brandy and extra sugar and told her it was wise to be wary of the sea, to respect its powers. But not to be afraid, not to fight it – it was a force for the good and did not want to do damage.

Later the same week Grace had silently followed Joss down to the beach again in the early morning and slid into the waves beside her, taking her own time to get used to the cold. Jocelyn, she discovered, hadn't really been wrong, and when she relaxed the sea did support her and she wallowed and bobbed as easily as a turtle. It was only years later that she'd thought about that episode and realized that there was nothing magical about the sea's powers. It wasn't on anyone's side in some kind of war between nature and knowledge. Survival in it was a matter of luck and a well-mastered swimming technique. Her all-powerful grandmother had simply handled the situation with almost dangerous irresponsibility.

Tremorwell's village shop hadn't changed a lot over the years. It stood in a prime position on the seafront beside the Blue Cockle pub, converted in the 1950s from a disused net shed. When the shop was crowded with summer visitors, the very oldest residents liked to show off their credentials as genuine old-time Cornish by wrinkling their noses and declaring that they could sense mackerel in the air. The only fish sold these days were firmly processed into child-friendly shapes, orange-crumbed, packeted and frozen. The electronic till, fierce bright lighting and self-service layout were advances since Alice's childhood but, on her way to pick up a newspaper and a few food essentials, she knew that there'd be the same old bizarrely dated stock on the shelves.

Only in Tremorwell, she imagined with a tweak of nostalgic fondness, could there be such a demand for tinned stewed steak, spam and piccalilli. The TV-cook phenomenon, the organic movement and the pasta revolution had passed the place entirely by. Bacon was the cheapest pre-packaged economy brand and all cream and much of the milk was long-life, in spite of the presence of a thriving mixed farm on the far side of the hill. For the wooing of tourists there were a grudging couple of bottles of olive oil, a dusty shelf of sour bargain-price wine and sumptuous ice cream in fourteen flavours. Outside stood cardboard boxes of misshapen, bruised and fast-softening vegetables which would certainly have been rejected by any reputable supermarket. Mrs Rice, current proprietor and postmistress, complained that the trippers brought boxes of food down from London and only popped into the shop for emergency toilet rolls, the *Guardian* (which she didn't stock) and firelighters for their fancy stainless steel barbecues. And so the supply and demand circle continued to be vicious and barely turning.

Alice, ambling slowly down the hill and along the lane above the beach, almost dreaded going in, wondering which of the three local harridans would be that morning's keeper of the till. She always pictured them as resembling Beryl Cook's famous painting of a seaside landlady: all fluffy mules, Dracula teeth and a ravenous appetite for gossip. Whoever was on the till today would, without fail: a) exclaim at her presence in the village: 'Oh so you're down again!' b) comment on her London pallor: 'You look like you need a breath of country air!' and c) mention whatever was on the mind of the village, in this case: 'Jocelyn, now, they do say she's very poorly m'dear,' which Alice would interpret accurately as an order to give a detailed rundown of her mother's exact state of health with possible estimate as to the projected day of her demise.

It was all normal enough stuff by any community's standards, and Alice recognized that her aversion to sharing personal information wasn't usual or logical. But since the very first days when she'd ventured out alone as a small child running errands, every time she'd entered the shop she'd pleaded silently, 'Don't ask me things, please don't ask me,' in dread of facing these Dracula women with their dribbling eagerness to glean something salacious. With unashamed greed they'd solicit information about What Went On up at the mysterious commune and invent for themselves when disappointed.

'They do say there's witchcraft up at Penmorrow,' was one rumour (largely untrue, though pagan festivals were celebrated.) This could be followed by 'Those children, they run wild like savages and forage on raw shoots from the garden,' (not wholly a lie – mealtimes weren't exactly regular), and 'It's all free love and orgies,' (uttered with more hope than evidence). Alice, having spent all her growing-up years under this inquisitive speculation of the entire village, enormously valued the unintrusive anonymity of suburbia. Only lovely Brenda, mother of her first-ever best friend Sally, had never plied her with sly questions, but she had died three years ago and Alice, clutching a list like a lucky talisman, hoped that today she could fend off the worst of the coming inquisition.

Aidan was outside the shop, reading adverts on the postcards taped to the inside of the window. He was wearing a blue Beach Beat tee shirt and baggy cream Quiksilver board shorts but still somehow managed to look, she thought, very Urban Man Interprets Surf-wear.

'Looking for a handy gardener or a Shape Sorters class? Lost your cat?' Alice asked, peering past him at the sun-faded writing on the cards. Some looked as if they'd been there for decades. There were offers of babysitting, painting and decorating, half-shares in ponies and several bed and breakfast venues. Among

47

them was a bleached-out photo of Penmorrow and an offer of luxury accomodation that was well in breach of the Trades Descriptions Act.

'That must have been a long, long time ago.' Aidan pointed to it and grinned at her. Alice felt defensive suddenly, just as she did when Noel criticized – it wasn't for outsiders to snigger at her family's slide towards dilapidation.

'It wasn't always the way it is now. Harry and Mo have been going through some difficult times,' she said, turning away to go into the shop.

'Hey, wait, Alice.' Aidan followed her in. 'Sorry, I didn't mean . . .'

'No it's all right. Really.' She stopped him quickly, turning to press her hand against his chest to make sure he shut up. Mrs Rice, at the till by the doorway, had already ceased checking off her waiting customer's shopping, and with a box of teabags held suspended in mid-air she stared at Alice and Aidan with a look of expectancy.

'Oh it's you Alice! Here for long?' she said, then went on without waiting for a response. 'The sea air will put the colour back in your cheeks. And how's your mother? Getting better? Not like her to have the doctor in. We were only saying . . .'

'Hello Mrs Rice, it's good to be back. Joss is much better thanks – should be fine,' Alice declared breezily, stepping quickly past to find bread, milk and the *Independent* as well as a restock of basic cleaning material. Mo had asked for help – the best Alice could do for now, she decided, was to sort out the health hazard that passed for a kitchen and give Gosling a complete overhaul. She didn't look back at Mrs Rice's face. She knew that disappointment would be etched in every sun-baked jowl. Like Cilla Black anticipating a *Blind Date* wedding, she'd have been eagerly trimming new magpie feathers onto her best funeral hat.

At the back of Penmorrow, close to where Harry's polytunnels hid both illicit and legal crops, there were many rickety sheds that Noel had once rudely (and ignorantly, Grace had thought) compared to a small Third World shanty town. Some had slabs of corrugated iron patching rotted roofs, others had mismatched chunks of old fencing where whole sides had given way. One was simply a bare skeleton of a structure, covered with a blue tarpaulin as if it had grown itself a protective tent beneath which to decay in private. At least it was rainproof and was where Harry kept the ancient ride-on mower for cutting down the meadow and the orchard twice a year.

Theo and Grace went to see if Alice's old cart was still hidden away among dismantled hen houses, perished goat-tethers and the heaps of ancient compost on which, Alice had said, mushrooms used to be grown for the household. Theo was treading carefully – his new Globe CT-V skate shoes were not really built for accidentally stepping on the sharp side of an abandoned scythe or paddling in spilled chainsaw oil. 'You've got shoes that look like bumper cars at the price of a family saloon,' his father had commented sourly when Theo had first worn them. Oh funny ha ha, Dad, Theo had thought, wondering if Noel had spent his own fifteen-to-twenty years in a deep cavern somewhere in a remote mountain revising schoolwork.

'Can you see anything?' Grace called to him from the far side of a heap of old paint cans.

'Like what? Like just *what* are we looking for?'

Grace didn't snap back. She recognized he was just doing an 'I'm too cool for this stuff' act.

'I told you. A little pull-along cart, bits of wood on pram wheels. Mum said Arthur used to tow her around on it when she was really small. It'll be just what we need: I'm not lugging that rabbit all the way up the cliffs by hand.'

'I don't know any Arthur, who's Arthur? Can't you just let it go in the garden like you always used to?' Theo had got something sticky on his hands. He wiped them down his jeans and hoped it wasn't paint or something that stank.

'You do know Arthur, well you know *about* him – he lived here with all of them. One of Joss's men. Did the statues. There's two in the Tate. He's – was – famous. Oh come on Theo, you heard what Chas and Sam said. Harry's been shooting rabbits. And this one's white – even a crap shot could hardly miss him. He'll look like a fat pillow, sitting on the grass at dusk.'

'You should've got a black one then,' Theo muttered, edging towards the sunlight beyond the door. 'Come on, there's nothing in here.'

As they made their way to the next shed, Mo's chickens in their tatty baked-earth run started up a warning cluck.

'See, they're being watch-hens. Geese are better though – Mum says geese really scare away burglars.'

'So do Rottweilers and burglar alarms and video entry systems,' Theo grunted moodily. Grace always did this at Penmorrow – she went on about her mother's childhood as if she'd been there herself. She was all right in Richmond – she watched telly and wore little cropped-off tops and played computer games and read stupid-girl magazines just like everyone else. It was here she changed. A couple of weeks of this, Theo thought, and she'd be dressing up in hippy beads and going veggie and whittling herself a wand. Just rad. Not.

Alice left the bags of shopping with Mrs Rice, who'd promised that her grandson Jason would deliver them later on his moped.

'It's good to see the traditional village-shop service still going,' Aidan commented as they left the shop and turned off along the seafront towards the beach café.

Alice laughed. 'I think it's more a case of old traditional curiosity,' she told him. 'Penmorrow has always been a great source of gossip. I bet you'll still hear the words "hippy commune" if you hang out long enough.'

'That's what I need for Joss's book – the locals' perspective,' Aidan said. 'Joss has got plenty of fantastic stories about her own life but I need to fill in more background. I need to know how the outside-world part of this village fitted in. Can you help me with that while you're here? Would you mind?'

Alice thought for a moment, stopping to lean on the sea wall and staring out at the incoming waves. 'No I don't mind,' she told him. 'Obviously I don't remember the early years – I was only born six months after Joss bought Penmorrow and she'd already had her book published and got the most out of being famous. But I can remember what growing up here was like.' She frowned and turned to Aidan. 'I bet Joss made it all sound completely idyllic.'

Aidan smiled. 'Yes she did, rather. Lots of waving her arms around and accusing me of having a stifled upbringing, just because I had two parents, one ordinary home and regular schooling. Apparently,

51

I need to be "freed from my imprisoning demons", whatever that means.'

'I think it means "lie back and chill",' Alice told him. 'Which is all very well but you've got a job to do and probably a deadline to meet.'

'And a publisher who's terrified Joss will die and I won't even be halfway through.' He shuffled a bit. 'Sorry, I shouldn't have mentioned the "D" word, not tactful of me.'

'It's OK. It's time I stopped thinking of her as immortal – though she's fairly young really, compared with most who get ill. If it wasn't for all the smoke she's inhaled over the years . . .'

'Not all of it the stuff you can buy at the village shop, I'd guess,' he chuckled.

'Now that reminds me – something I thought of this morning. Come down to the café and I'll tell you,' she said, leading the way to the few steps down to the sand.

The beach café was a long timber shack painted to resemble someone's idea of a Caribbean roadside bar. Dancing figures holding cans of drink cavorted on the sun-faded blue paintwork, with fronds of exotic blooms swagged above them beneath the overhanging rusted tin roof. Outside, sun-paled wooden tables and chairs were filling with a mixture of families and tanned young surfers enjoying the warming sun. It was going to be a good day, profit-wise, Alice guessed. Joss had bought the café years before to thwart the council's proposal to pull it down, and Harry had been installed as manager. These days his only involvement was collecting the annual rent from whoever had applied to take on the lease for the current season, as well as hanging out with the boys who ran the adjoining surf school in the hope that their youth and vitality would rub off on him.

Aidan fetched two mugs of coffee and sat beside Alice facing the sea.

'Surf's a whole culture down here, isn't it?' he commented, watching a girl riding her board effortlessly across the bay. 'It's a language and dress code miles away from up-country cities.'

'Oh I don't know – Grace and her friends wear a lot of stuff made by surf companies. Though I suppose some of them might not realize it. I mean look at you – surf-label man.'

Aidan looked down at his clothes with mild surprise. 'Hey, the cream of St Ives this lot, bought on a sad conformist urge to fit in.' He sipped his coffee and looked at her intently. 'Tell me what you remembered. Do you mind if I use this?' He produced a tiny chrome gadget from his jeans. 'It's a tape recorder, except it's electronic, no tape, too clever.'

'No, go ahead. I haven't got anything profound to tell you though. It's just . . . well this morning when a mouse jumped out of the fridge . . .'

'They're everywhere up there, aren't they?' Aidan cut in. 'I saw Mo step over one, really politely, in the kitchen yesterday.'

'I'll sneak in a few humane traps. Anyway . . . I said something about mushrooms growing in the fridge and I remembered a time when Joss and Milly cooked some that none of us kids were allowed to eat. We thought they were mad – especially as they didn't eat them either, they just strained off the juice and made a kind of tea with it. All the grown-ups drank it. But we had a cat called Brian who sneaked onto the table and wolfed down some of the cooked mushrooms. All the next day he was seen out in the village, sitting under cars, howling and growling to himself and getting spooked by shadows – poor thing was

53

obviously hallucinating. I think that's where all the rumours of witchcraft started. The poor cat was never the same again, damaged and paranoid for evermore.'

'Magic mushrooms then.'

'Exactly, but what I'm trying to say is that it's only years later you can make sense of things. I always thought he was a witch-cat too and for months I wouldn't eat mushrooms because we'd been so firmly told not to that day! I suppose any memories I can give you are likely to be tainted by grown-up knowledge. All that naivety has long gone.'

'Well it's an autobiography so they're Joss's words,' Aidan said, raising his fingers in the air to indicate quote marks. 'I get the feeling she's still living in wonderland.'

'That's why she called me Alice. Disappointing for her though – I turned out to feel far more at home with reality.'

Up on the cliff path, Grace hauled the wheeled cart along behind her and wondered if it had been such a good idea. The path was narrow and stony and the poor rabbit was huddled at the back of his carrier looking as if he was feeling severely sick. Theo was being no use at all. He was skulking along yards behind her with his hands shoved deep into the pockets of his floor-trailing jeans, as if he didn't want to be seen to be part of this plan.

'We should have left it till the evening,' she called back to him. 'It wouldn't be so hot.'

'Well you can change your mind if you want but I'm not coming back up here.'

'What? Cos it's a bit steep? Wassup you wuss, too much for you is it?' she taunted him. It was true, it was a steep and rocky climb, but at the top was one of her favourite places in the whole of Tremorwell – a grassy headland with a small glade of gale-bent trees that sheltered a bench overlooking the sea, the village and across to Penmorrow up the hill on the far side of the bay. Ever since she was little she'd found it a good place to run off to when she felt torn between Jocelyn's more extreme notions of free living and Alice's counterbalancing sensible ones.

Joss would say, 'If you rig up a long rope to the walnut tree, you can swing right down the cliff to the east beach.' At which Grace would be straight out to the sheds plaiting old bailer twine.

Then Alice would get her on her own and it would be, 'Don't even think of doing it – half the cliff has crumbled away since Joss last swung on a rope. One slip and it's fifty foot onto rocks.'

At the top of the cliff Grace stopped to catch her breath and wait for Theo. The old bench was still there and the surrounding thick patches of thrift showed that not many people had spent long sitting on it, scuffing the ground. That was good. It meant that Grace could still claim it as her own refuge. Chas and Sam wouldn't be up there either, or Harry in pursuit of her rabbit with his shotgun. With luck the animal would be OK – there were plenty of rabbit droppings around so he'd have a chance to make his own free-range rabbit family.

'OK? Let him out yet?' Theo staggered up the last of the path and slumped down beside her. He pulled a pack of cigarettes out of his jeans and lit one, cupping his lighter carefully against the sea breeze.

'Good view,' he commented, looking out towards the sea and across to Penmorrow's perch on the opposite hillside.

'Glad you like it,' Grace said, wishing that hadn't

come out sounding so sharp and sarky. She really *was* glad he liked it. Sometimes they got on well, sometimes not. She enjoyed the good days – then he was like a real brother. She wanted him to like Cornwall too though, not just ordinary home things like lying around on the sitting-room floor and watching *Malcolm in the Middle* together.

Grace got up to scatter some rabbit food under the trees, then pulled the plastic pet-box off the truck and sat it on the bench beside her.

'Here we go bunny, freedom for you.' She opened the door and took out the bemused creature who sat for a moment on her lap, stretching his cramped legs.

'Have a lovely life, rabbit. Off you go.' She put him gently on the ground. The white rabbit looked around, choosing his direction, then, after a few tentative hops, gave a big kicking leap and bolted off into the bushes.

'He should be all right. Safe from Chas and Sam and Harry anyway,' Grace said, putting the empty box back on the wheeled truck.

'Shit! What was that?' Theo put his hand to his face and then looked at it, his fingers covered with blood. 'I've been shot or stung or something! That hurt!'

'Let's look.' Grace inspected his face. There was a small cut just below his eye. 'I don't think there's a bullet in there somehow,' she told him. There was a distant whooping below them. Chas and Sam were doing a mad dance down on the beach, waving some kind of weapon over their heads.

'It was them! They're watching us up here! What've they got? Can you see Theo?'

'Er . . . catapults, big fuck-off state of the art ones. Some nutters at school have got them to pick off the pigeons on the gym roof. Wait till I get back down

56

there . . .' Theo set off, running and sliding on the downward path.

Grace thought about Joss and about Alice and how differently they'd react. Joss would congratulate the boys on being crack shots. Alice would tell them they could have had someone's eye out.

Four

Alice stuffed the stained old kitchen curtains into the binbag. As she'd taken them down from the window the fabric had given way in her fingers and threads had parted and frayed away into holes. You didn't need curtains here, she thought as she looked out through the newly cleaned window into what should have been Gosling's garden. There was no-one living close enough to peer in and enough overgrown spiky shrubbery had spread across the paths to deter any casual passers-by. Maybe for winter some blinds might help to keep out the worst of the easterly winds – rough sailcloth in a deep oatmeal colour would look good, especially if the walls were painted. A quick brush round with some pale blue (Designers Guild Aqua came to mind) would lighten the whole mood – all that dull yellow ochre looked like a mustard-factory explosion.

Now that Alice had made a start on the cleaning of the cottage, its many good points and the possibility of simple but effective improvements were beginning to suggest themselves. If Gosling could be pulled back up to a more twenty-first century level of comfort, it could only be good for Penmorrow's holiday rental business. People who'd booked it once might actually want to come again another year, instead of racing home to tell their friends (in a tone of hugely amused incredulity) about the holiday cottage from hell. Perhaps that would make the dour-faced Mo smile a bit for a change.

Mo had seemed distinctly underwhelmed by Alice's efforts in the kitchen at Penmorrow itself, sensing criticism as Alice heaped out-of-date tins and jars into rubbish bags. Many of them had to be prised from where they'd welded themselves to the sticky marble larder shelves, and some of the tins had swollen with age and looked dangerously close to exploding.

'It'll take more than a bit of Mr Muscle and bleach to turn this place round,' Mo had grunted. 'Folks don't want to come staying where there's no power showers or Sky telly.'

'Well a freshen-up and a clear-out will give us a chance to see what's left that's most needed to be done, won't it?' Alice had cringed at her own overbright tone. She was doing the kids' presenter voice again and sounded as if she was jollying along a cross toddler. Mo had never much liked her, she knew that. Whenever she visited Penmorrow Mo would be sniffy about her clothes with comments like 'You won't want to wear those shoes down the muddy cliff path,' or 'Real silk is it, that shirt? Won't keep the draughts out here.' And if she asked about Alice's work she'd say, 'How're those kiddy books of yours going?' as if she refused to believe anyone in their right mind could make any kind of living writing about children at a boarding school. Alice tried not to take it personally – she guessed Mo would be just as scornful towards J.K. Rowling. Noel had claimed Mo was simply envious, but Alice knew it was about more than coveting material goods.

Mo had joined the Penmorrow commune as an infatuated teenager with romantic notions about art, having met Jocelyn when she'd given a talk on the life and work of Arthur Gillings to Mo's art A-level class at a north coast school. Joss had chain-smoked pungent, skinny roll-ups throughout and told her audience that underwear was unhealthy ('let your genitals *breathe* or they'll wither and *die*!'). With her long grey-blonde hair in a hundred beaded plaits (thanks to a Grenadan potter spending a few months at the house) and uninhibited revelations about the late Arthur's bed prowess, she had completely enchanted Mo.

Mo had then turned up at Penmorrow after her exams, bringing with her little more than her painting materials and total trust that the Penmorrow magic would conjure up for her a definitive and mould-breaking artistic style. But the decline of the commune had already begun. Several rooms were empty and their gaudily painted furnishings were collecting a dull coat of dust. Joss was moody and fretting, trying and failing to write a long-overdue follow-up to *Angel's Choice* and to get back into the public limelight and credit at the bank. Mo found it hard to decide in which direction her talent should take her – for surely, with a grade A at A level, she *had* talent? She first opted for washed-out watercolours that everyone, encouragingly, agreed could well be landscapes, and later angry bright acrylic still lives with paint applied so thickly they tended to chip and look clumsy.

As for lovers, Mo found no equivalent of the eminent Arthur, only Harry who served pasties in his café in the daytime and took Mo out to drink cider among the tourists in the Blue Cockle at night. If the mood took him, on the way home he'd grab her hand and pull her down the sea wall and they'd have fumbled, fully clothed sex on the damp sand beneath a beached dinghy, which she rather enjoyed. Paul, Alice's glamorous new American husband at the time, told Alice that Mo was a 'disappointed star-fucker who'd had to downgrade to the roadie'. Mo could have left Penmorrow but she'd exhausted her reserves of rebellion when she'd walked out on her bewildered parents and her comfortable Padstow home. After a few years she no longer had the energy to move on and settled, as helplessly as a wheel-less car abandoned in a swamp, into her role as Penmorrow's housekeeper and later as mother of Sam and Chas.

Recently, in the early half-waking moments, Mo had hatched a new dream. She looked forward to the day when she and Harry could flog the lot and move to a modern executive Truro townhouse. She dreamed of commonplace urban facilities that Penmorrow – and even Tremorwell – didn't possess: of gas-fired central heating and mains sewerage and street lights. She wanted an en suite bathroom with his and hers basins set in a peach Corian vanity unit, a kitchen with a stainless steel self-cleaning Teflon-lined oven and a small fenced-in garden with manageable bedding plants that assured her they were 'dwarf' varieties on their labels. She never wanted to see an Aga again, or single-glazed windows or a set of drain rods. But none of this could happen if Jocelyn took too long over the slow business of giving up her steely grip on Penmorrow, and if interferring bloody Alice intended to spruce it all back up to the standards of a going concern.

Out in Gosling's garden Alice could see that only gangly clumps of evening primrose, some ragged lavender and a single woody rock rose remained of the flower bed that faced the window, though its brick outlines were still just visible beneath a matted spread of speedwell and wild campanula. Gorse and wild montbretia had sneaked up the hillside from the sea edge and taken over from the agapanthus and day lilies that used to be flowering in July when Arthur Gillings had lived in the cottage. Alice remembered pulling petals off ox-eye daisies to chant, 'He loves me, he loves me not' out in the scorching sunlight on the front step while Arthur worked away inside. Now, scrubbing a J-cloth round the sink, she could almost smell the moist earthy scent of his clay, could almost hear him softly whistling as he worked.

As soon as she'd found out that other children tended to have people called 'fathers' in their lives, Alice had wondered if Arthur had been hers. Her friend Sally in the village lived in a house with only two other grown-ups whom she called Mummy and Daddy. Alice, at five, thought these were their names and hadn't understood why everyone had laughed when she'd shouted 'Daddy, look at the blue butterfly!' while she'd been playing in Sally's garden.

Alice had rushed home full of curiosity, telling Joss, 'Sally's got a mummy and daddy. Have I?' Joss had been in the garden at the time, tying up bean plants to their wigwam.

'I suppose this was bound to happen sooner or later,' she had commented wryly. She'd taken Alice's hand and sat down with her on the swing seat on the Penmorrow porch and explained, 'I am your mummy, it's just that you call me by my name. You call me Jocelyn the same way I call you Alice and not "Daughter", do you see?'

Alice only sort-of-saw. Sally's mummy didn't call

Sally 'Daughter'. Nobody she'd ever met was called that, not so far.

'And what about my daddy? Who is my daddy?'

'Oh not everybody has a daddy! You don't need one of those!' Jocelyn had told her.

'Sally's mummy Brenda says everyone has a daddy otherwise you can't be made.' Further than that, faced with a wide-eyed five year-old, Brenda hadn't been willing to explain and had copped out with 'You just ask Jocelyn, she'll tell you.'

'Well you were,' Joss had told her, laughing. 'You were knitted out of scraps of wool and stuffed with old socks.'

'Old socks?' Alice had been horrified. She'd seen plenty of old socks in Penmorrow. Old socks went smelly and had holes in them. People threw them away in the rubbish. She'd seen Milly put some of Arthur's on the compost heap.

'And what about Harry? Is he knitted too?' Harry was only a year old then. Alice was more willing to believe that he was a soft toy – he looked round and soft and squashy like her favourite teddy.

'Oh he's patchwork!' Joss had said breezily. And then Alice had known for sure none of this was true. She knew about patchwork. In Penmorrow there was a woman called Kelpie who was always doing it. Everywhere she went tiny bits of material fell around her. She sat by the hexagon window and sewed all day, putting together tiny flower prints and making star shapes that her friend Morgan quilted on a big frame and sent to London to be sold.

Alice knew about knitting too because Cathy and Mike who lived in the room across the landing from where she and the other young children slept, and who played music really loudly, had shown her how they made balls of wool by spinning hunks of fleece. They dyed long strings of it in a rusty old boiler that was rigged up in one of the sheds where she wasn't ever allowed to go by herself. They made huge hairy coats out of squares of wool, in diamond patterns with bobbles hanging off them and heavy mats of fringing round the collars. The colours were dark and smudgy, like being outside in the woods on a wet day.

None of these people made babies when they worked. Joss had made a mistake that day, she'd relied quite wrongly on the supreme credulousness of small children. Alice recognized then that Joss and•other grown-ups didn't always tell the truth. She had been told she *always* had to tell the truth. But was *that* true?

Jocelyn sat smoking in her peacock chair in the hexagon and prepared her mind for the afternoon session with Aidan. She was enjoying having her life documented like this, it gave her a boost to be reminded just what an icon she'd once been – Aidan was flatteringly reverent – and it was just as well to do it now while she still could. Every single episode from her crowded past was as clear as ever, but sometimes she felt that the present days were blurring into one another in a mushy, undefined way, as if there was so little difference between them that her memory was no longer bothering to register them properly.

Sixty-eight, she thought, was not for her a good age to be, not when she was feeling suddenly weakened like this. It was a pity that it had turned out to be true, this thing about cigarettes and alcohol causing more than a bit of wear and tear round the edges. She'd been certain she was different, that she'd got away with it and would become one of those fit, lithe centenarians who confound the medics by putting her healthy longevity down to a lifelong indulgence in wine and tobacco. Even so, even given her current frailty, she wouldn't go back and change anything – she'd had too good a time. But all the same, sixty-eight was a sad time to find her vitality petering out. It had neither the grandeur of wise old age nor the ripe-fruit quality of the middle years. *Nineteen* sixty-eight on the other hand had been a very good year. This afternoon she would tell Aidan all about it.

'So. How's it going? When are you coming back?' Noel's voice sounded very crisp and businesslike. He was in the office with a lot to do. He wasn't going to waste time asking Alice how she was or telling her he missed her. Alice was outside the Truro Homebase loading paint cans and various bits of essential hardware into the back of the car. She quickly rechecked her list as, one-handed because of the phone, she put them in – chrome handles to brighten up the kitchen cupboards, two screwdrivers, white eggshell paint for the woodwork, soft greeny-blue matt vinyl for the kitchen walls, three brushes, a bottle of white spirit, small paint buckets, a pack of drop cloths to protect the worktops and floor. She'd assumed there'd be old sheets at Penmorrow to use but as Mo had said grouchily, 'What do you think are on the bloody beds?'

At the other end of the phone she could hear Noel tapping his fingers on his desk – a sure sign that he expected a fast and decisive reply.

'Back? I can't come back just now, there's too much to do here. Why? Are you lonely without us? Are you missing me?'

'Yes of course I am.' Still brisk, she noted, still in time-is-money mode. 'It's just that usually when you go to Cornwall you leave a definite return date in the house diary and this time you haven't. And what about the children? Is Theo behaving?'

'Theo is fine. I hardly see him or Grace – they've taken to hanging around on the beach by the surf shack.' She laughed. 'They're starting to look a bit less smooth and London-ish. By the end of the summer . . .'

'*End* of the *summer*? Is that how long you're . . .'

'I don't know.' Alice slammed the boot shut, quickly climbed into the driving seat and started the car. 'I haven't made any coming-back plans. I just thought I'd stay for a bit longer and see what I can do to try and get the house in some kind of order. You should see it Noel, it's really got rundown and . . .'

'I think I can imagine.'

Alice smiled to herself, feeling Noel's shudder from almost three hundred miles away. 'Why don't you come down for a while? Maybe a long weekend?' she asked.

'Er . . . well I don't think I'd better take any more time off, not with Italy at the end of August.'

'Oh yes. Italy . . .' Alice checked her mirror and drove fast towards the exit, where, as she knew it would, the phone signal gave out and Noel was consigned mid-sentence back to his London desk and his profitable divorces. She felt as if she'd rudely slammed a door in his face, but there wasn't anything else she wanted to say to him. He'd been right of course, it was completely unlike her not to have already made carved-in-stone arrangements for returning home. It was how she was. She washed her hair every Monday and Friday, went to the Holmes Place gym three times a week, worked on her current book from ten till two thirty from Monday to Thursday and on Fridays had lunch with her friends Mags and Rebecca in Pasta Mama in Richmond. On Saturday evenings (whether they were socially out or not) she slinked around wearing stockings and suspenders beneath a shortish skirt for the later delight of Noel, plus on Wednesday evenings he favoured a sexy session that was genuinely steamy, in their capacious walk-in shower. Even her mild bouts of premenstrual tension were regular.

Alice stopped at the double roundabout and waited for an Asda truck to lumber past on its way to Falmouth. The villa in Italy – close to Siena – had been booked months ago. Alice liked to get the summer holiday organized as soon as New Year was over and the children had gone back to school. She and Noel took a short break in late February to somewhere warm (Dubai that year, Portugal the one before), which she fixed up each September when the school year started. Alice had never in her grown-up life made an arrangement that she'd later cancelled. The thought that she might even remotely be considering not going to Italy made her hands tremble on the steering wheel and she almost ran into the back of a Volvo that had slowed to take the left turn towards Mylor.

Of course they would go, as arranged, she told herself as she made an effort to concentrate. Why would they not? But there was so much to do here at Penmorrow. When Harry had asked her for help he surely hadn't just meant with Joss, who, although she wasn't quite her usual bossy and energetic self, certainly didn't require round-the-clock nursing. He meant the house. Each room needed to be gone through, cleaned thoroughly, redundant junk ruthlessly chucked out. Only when she and Mo and Harry had stripped the house back to its bare walls and furnishings would they be able to see if it would be possible simply to patch things up and rearrange, or if the whole dilapidation process had got so far out of hand that they would be forced to sell up.

'I only asked you down here to help sort out Joss, not to take the place apart,' Harry had grumbled to her over toast and coffee in the Penmorrow kitchen that morning. 'I know what needs to be done – I've lived with it, remember. There just isn't the cash to do it with, that's the bottom line.'

'I don't have any spare either,' Alice told him.

'Don't you?' Harry looked genuinely surprised. 'We were all under the impression . . .'

'Two teenagers in private schools. Noel's obsession with pension funds, house maintenance, two cars, these are serious outgoings,' Alice told him.

'Private schools!' Harry almost spat the words. 'What's wrong with the regular sort? Kids don't go anyway, wherever you send them. Sam and Chas hardly ever do. We didn't.'

'We didn't go because Joss got away with claiming she'd set up some kind of alternative school and that we were being home-taught.'

'Well we were. We had lessons most mornings. Usually.'

'We learned to read and write and do some basic sums. And that was down to Arthur and Milly, not Joss. We learned how to grow alfalfa, how to gut fish and how to make a more or less edible stew out of any given vegetables and half a hen. Anything else we had to pick up for ourselves. Keeping us isolated out here was practically child abuse.'

'Joss didn't believe in formal education. Inhibited minds, she said we'd end up with, if we went to school.'

'Couldn't be arsed to get out of bed and take us there, you mean. It was all right for her, she'd had her own education. It wasn't right not to let us have ours.'

And which bed was it she couldn't be arsed to get out of? Alice remembered, after Arthur had died, Jocelyn had made a point of sleeping in every room in Penmorrow and with whoever was in it. She said that grief made her restless, unsettled, that she needed the comfort of warm skin against hers and the exhilaration of the procreative force. Alice had been fourteen – an age of acute curiosity and observation, of keeping close tabs on what your surrounding adults get up to, having realized for the first time that they are flesh and blood and as unruly of thought and deed as sly teenagers could be. She'd been reading D.H. Lawrence at the time, *Lady Chatterley's Lover*, and was completely absorbed in the notion that sex could be thrilling for being kept secret. Sex wasn't any kind of secret at Penmorrow. Joss had always maintained that monogamy was drearily provincial and creatively stifling and had no place in her household. Several of the residents during Alice's childhood had arrived as couples but always one or the other of the pair would find themselves drifting into another's bed. Looking back, Alice suspected that much of the nocturnal visiting had been more to do with maintaining a credible Bohemian stance than with any real urge for sexual experiment. It must have been the cause of a lot of secret grief, one way or another. And all done to impress the commanding iconic presence of Jocelyn.

Grace was sitting high up in an oak tree in the woods behind Penmorrow, keeping watch on Chas and Sam. She was delighted they had no idea she was there as it showed they didn't know everything about woodcraft.

They should have heard her creeping through the brambles, heard twigs snapping in spite of her being so careful to avoid them. They thought they knew it all, but they didn't know enough to imagine anyone might want to be spying on them.

The two boys were wearing dark green tee shirts and their boxer shorts and had daubed mud all over their arms and faces. There were leafy twigs stuck in their hair. They should have been at school. Grace knew this because she'd seen Mo send them off in their grey and blue uniforms with lunch boxes early that morning. They'd run down the track past Gosling and when they got to the road, instead of making for the school bus stop outside the shop, she'd seen them dart back along the coast path round the hillside and out of sight of Penmorrow. Harry had said they hardly ever went to school, she'd heard him. He didn't seem to think it was a big problem, just something else to grumble about like the state of the drains or the birds pulling up his onion plants.

No-one skived off at Grace's school, which might have been partly down to having to wear a bright purple jacket. She could just imagine herself and her friends getting caught, a small posse of purple bodies, coming across an unexpected mother shopping in Warehouse. Mothers in these circumstances made you feel so guilty – it was their speciality, less crassly confrontational than simply shouting and getting cross. They'd say they were 'disappointed'. Posh London parents were always saying that, as if they'd been looking forward to some wonderful event but had been really badly let down. Alice had been 'disappointed' a few months earlier when Grace had been brought home early from Sophy's fourteenth birthday party because she'd drunk half a bottle of

Sophy's mum's sherry and been sick on their stairs. It wasn't just her, she'd told Alice (who'd claimed she was also 'mortified', a whole league up from 'disappointed'), they'd all had a go at the drinks cupboard. Sophy had keeled over in the garden and her brother Olly, who'd kept all the vodka to himself, had thrown a chair through the conservatory window. Sophy's mother had been 'disappointed' as well. Very.

The two boys had folded their school sweatshirts and trousers and hung them over a low branch. Their empty lunch boxes were lying open on the grass, displaying screwed up crisp packets and crumpled drinks cartons and abandoned bits of thick sandwich crust. They'd got a small fire going in a clearing in a copse of young oak saplings, and a thin wisp of smoke drifted up through the trees. That was how easy it had been for Grace to trace them. She wanted to know what they did with their days. There wasn't much point in asking them straight out as they didn't say much at Penmorrow, just grunted now and then and stared in a dazed sort of way if anyone asked them a question, which made Theo smirk and mutter 'Neanderthal' under his breath.

Grace could see a book open on the ground – Sam seemed to be reading it, running a finger along the page, mouthing the words and concentrating hard. Chas was doing something with a length of thin wire and she leaned down, hardly breathing as she gently parted the branches to get a closer look.

'How wide, Sam?' Chas turned to his brother, holding the wire bent in his hand.

'It says about a fist-width.' Sam looked up and frowned. 'This stuff doesn't look thick enough to me.'

'It is. Any thicker and they'd see it. They're not stupid.'

71

'They are. Especially the cross-breeds. No wild cunning.'

The two boys laughed softly, sharing a joke Grace didn't get.

Chas was pulling the wire into place and Grace could see that he'd made a loop like a noose. Sam, consulting a diagram in the book, bent one of the saplings over so that Chas could attach the wire to it with a piece of webbing, then together they secured their contraption into place using forked sticks.

'Dangle,' Chas said, standing back to admire his work.

'Strangle.' Sam joined his brother beneath Grace's tree, looking down at the tense wire.

She watched, amazed and just a bit frightened, as the two boys started circling their fire, chanting, 'Dangle, mangle, tangle, strangle,' at first moving slowly, chanting with a slow rhythm, then speeding up, faster and faster till they stopped on one extra fierce fast, 'Dangle-mangle-tangle-STRANGLE!' and collapsed on the ground laughing manically.

'Woss time?' Sam asked, sitting up and brushing grass and burrs off his tee shirt.

'Bus time, just about. Better go. Check this out tomorrow.' Grace watched as the two boys scooped up loose earth and moss with their hands and piled it onto the fire, treading it down so that it was compressed and smothered. Then they changed back into their school clothes, stowing their tee shirts in a brown canvas bag which Sam stuffed into a narrow hollow at shoulder-height up a tree. Looking as close as these two could get to resembling normal school-boys, they collected their lunch boxes, looked around one last time and set off back along through the woods towards the path and Penmorrow.

Grace gave them five minutes to get well ahead of her, then, feeling stiff and cold, clambered down her tree. Warily, she moved close to the wire thing they'd been making. She took hold of a long stick and prodded the forked twigs away from it. The bent-over sapling sprang upright, taking the wire noose with it. A trap, she realized. The boys had set a trap for a smallish animal, a rabbit or a fox. Or, it occurred to her with horror, a cat. Monty could come up here hunting. She imagined him, wriggling and terrified, thrashing about to escape and only making the noose fatally tighter. To the scene in her head she added heavy rain and a hungry fox. The imagined Monty was now soaked to sad feline skinniness and being chewed to certain death. Now she also knew what Chas and Sam had meant about 'cross-breeds' – they'd been laughing about her rescued rabbits, sure they'd easily catch one.

Grace shivered, then turned to the tree where the canvas bag was hidden. She pulled it out, removed the pair of tee shirts and placed them carefully in the noose, propping it up on the sapling so that its cloth prey hung down and drifted eerily in the breeze. 'Dangle, mangle, tangle, *strangle*!' she sang as she stuffed the bag back in the tree and picked her way out of the clearing and back to the path.

Five

It wasn't as if Mo hadn't been invited. There was no need for her to sulk. All morning she'd been like a child who'd said no to a bag of sweets out of stubborn pique and then regretted it. But Mo wasn't a child and Alice wasn't going to play coaxing games with her. As she drove Jocelyn and Aidan away from Penmorrow's purple paint-flaked front porch she waved goodbye to Mo and told herself she had no need to feel guilty. All the same, as she steered carefully down the deeply rutted track she could feel Mo staring after them, a scowl like a deep curse etched on her face, her hands gripped white-tight round a soggy tea towel. A casual passer-by would speculate that she might be about to strangle someone with it.

'I'm taking Joss and Aidan out for lunch at the Tresanton in St Mawes to talk about the book,' Alice had said after breakfast that morning. 'Would you and Harry like to join us?'

Mo had glared at her from across a plate of bacon, eggs and tomatoes which was on its way to the solitary bed and breakfast guest in the little morning room off the far side of the kitchen.

'I don't have time to go gadding off out for fancy

74

lunches,' had been Mo's speedy answer. Harry came in from the garden carrying a bunch of well-grown onions in time to hear her saying quickly, 'And neither has Harry. He's got the chickens and the veg to deal with.' She'd then added, with grudging grace, 'Thanks all the same.' Harry had raised his eyebrows at Alice but hadn't questioned Mo's decision. Alice knew better than to push him – he'd be panic-stricken at the possibility of defying Mo.

On the King Harry chain ferry, crossing the river Fal, Alice stepped out of the car to lean on the front rail and breathe in the steamy air of the deep valley. The day was wonderfully warm and she was thankful to be here where the air was scented by foliage and fields, and not in London with the stale smells of traffic fumes and aircraft fuel. If she was at home now, she'd be up at the top of the house in her little study, making notes for the next Gulliver School adventure. The girls she'd created eight years ago as nervous new junior boarders were now teenagers with more on their minds than inter-school tennis tournaments and the drama club auditions. They were moving on to sex and secrets and choices about life after Gulliver's. The powers-that-be at Pericles Productions, who turned the books into TV programmes and sold them so profitably to the networks, were close to dribbling with glee at this prospect. If she took the storylines in the direction they were now suggesting, the series would turn into a kind of boarding-school version of *Sex in the City*. She just knew that the next time she finished a book they would be positively salivating, thinking along the lines of Britney-in-a-gymslip. It was all a long way from her first stories, scribbled down at twelve and a mixture of Malory Towers, the Chalet School and her own lonely imaginative longings in her school-free anarchic existence at Penmorrow.

She looked back to the car where Jocelyn and Aidan sat close together on the back seat, talking intently and ignoring the scenery. Joss was looking at Aidan as if he was a delightful new pet. It was a look she'd seen many, many times before: Joss didn't really 'do' friendships with males but instead needed to captivate them, to have them admire and preferably adore her. That sparky need to attract was still there in spite of the ageing and the illness and Aidan looked as if he was all right with this, that he was playing along just far enough with the flirting game, rather in the manner, Alice thought, of a gay 'walker' attending a beautiful celebrity.

Both Joss and Aidan were wearing cream linen – Joss in a long wrap-around skirt and bell-sleeved tunic top, Aidan in a floppy unlined jacket. Ignoring the obvious difference in age, they reminded Alice of a pair of eccentric adult twins who had never shaken off their mother's habit of dressing them alike. Joss was wearing her plum lipstick and a lot of deep grey eyeshadow which accentuated the slightly sleepy look her face had acquired since her recent illness. Her long pale tapering plait lay between her left shoulder and Aidan's right, giving the bizarre impression that it could belong to either one of them. Noel had said he was sure her unchallengeable autocracy over Penmorrow was somehow contained in her hair, and had once amused himself for a day or two making elaborate plans to chop off the plait in the dead of night.

'Did you bring a hat? It gets hot on the hotel terrace,' Alice said as she switched on the car's engine and took her turn to be directed off the ferry.

'Don't *fuss*, sweetie,' Joss replied, treating Alice's reflection to a tight-jawed smile, 'I do know how to

76

live with the sun, you know. I find it highly energizing to absorb a few extra rays. It's like a dose of solar power for me.'

All the same, Alice was glad that, after she'd parked the car at the top of the hill and joined her mother and Aidan at the table overlooking the estuary at St Mawes, the attentive young waiter had made sure Joss's head was protected by a large canvas sunshade. Aidan put on a pair of mirrored Oakley sunglasses, then immediately took them off again as Joss gave him one of her pursed-mouth looks of amusement.

'Sorry – you can't see who I'm talking to with these on,' he said.

'Oh I'd know who you're talking to, my dear young man, there's only a choice of two of us. I can't see what you're thinking, that is the important thing.'

'Eyes being the windows of the soul?' he smiled.

'I hope this book you're putting together isn't full of clichés like *that*.' Jocelyn, frosty-faced, turned away from Aidan to study the wine list. He hid behind the menu and pulled a face at Alice, looking exactly like a thoroughly told-off school boy, which made her want to giggle.

'Some decent clarets anyway,' Jocelyn commented, then her mood instantly switched and her voice became loud and cheery. 'Now! Who's for a mad cocktail?' She called to a nearby waiter, 'A Margarita for me please.' Alice wondered if this was a good idea and Joss spotted the wondering look on her face, adding immediately, 'A very large one.'

'You always were a contrary old bat.' Alice grinned at her, knowing better than to start cooing concerns such as, 'Do you think you should?' Joss, as always, would do exactly as she chose.

'No, you're wrong you know, Alice. I'm not at all

contrary. If I was I'd have ordered something ghastly like a Diet Cola. You could have bet serious folding money on me ordering something strongly alcoholic.' She hesitated a moment, catching her breath and putting her hand to her chest. 'Besides, it's terribly good for the blood.' She was panting slightly.

'Are you all right?' Alice reached out and touched Joss's arm. The skin felt warm and soft. An unwelcome imaginative flash came into her mind of touching the same skin after death. How cold do we go? How hard and inflexible would it feel then?

'Of course I'm all right, darling.' Joss patted her daughter's hand, then returned it firmly to Alice's lap. 'Rather an excess of stairs up from the road, that's all.'

She took a deep restoring breath and declared, 'Now! Let's order! Sea bass for me, I think. It reminds me . . .' and here she leaned forward towards her biographer. 'You'll need this, Aidan. Aren't you going to make notes?' Obediently, Aidan took out his electronic recorder and Joss spoke up as loud and clear as an actress. 'Sea bass always reminds me of darling Arthur. We used to take his boat, wonderful it was, a classic Cornish crabber a bit like . . .' She scanned the many sailboats out in St Mawes harbour, then pointed. 'That one! Just like that one there with the orange sail! Oh look, Alice!' Jocelyn scraped back her chair and went to stand by the balcony rail and gaze out towards the estuary. 'Do you remember? We used to go round the Lizard to the Manacles and fish for mackerel. Or we'd anchor just off the Prussia Cove beach and cast for bass. We'd be up at five and out of Tremorwell bay before the fishermen. And lobster pots too, we had a good dozen of them. Sold any spare catch to the trippers, straight off the boat. They liked that sort of thing of course, made them feel "local". And often,' she returned to the table but kept her voice pitched high, fully intent on entertaining the entire terrace, 'very often actually, Arthur would buy them in cheap from a lovely boy in Chapel Creek, sail into Tremorwell and flog them off as newly caught. It made good trading sense.'

He hadn't just sold fish, Alice suddenly remembered. The little boat had often been loaded with rough wooden boxes. She used to sit on top of them, on a green and white checked blanket. The boxes had chinked as they moved and were kept under the ropes and spare rigging. 'Just a spot of brandy, to help keep the hotels stocked,' Arthur had told her, tapping the side of his nose and winking. He'd made quite a few sea trips at night, leaving Penmorrow after supper, wrapped up against the night chill in his holey old guernsey and a black felt hat with fringed ear flaps that Kelpie had made for him. He couldn't have gone all the way over to France, she realized now, but presumably just far enough to transfer cargo from another boat without exciting the interest of the coast-guard. She looked at Joss, waiting for her to tell all this to Aidan, but Joss was now gazing out to sea again, rapt in some secret memories that she wasn't prepared to share.

'The *Sunday Times* sent someone to photograph us on the boat just before Arthur's Tate retrospective,' she then went on. 'We took him up to Newlyn. I was to lean out from the prow like a ship's figurehead, wearing a sort of toga thing and with my hair flowing out loose. Sick as a pig, that photographer was. Absolutely sodding useless.'

After the bass and before the chocolate and lavender ice-cream, Alice went off to the loo and came back to find an unknown man sitting at their table, his chair

79

pulled up close to Jocelyn. She glanced at Aidan as she returned to her seat but he shrugged and shook his head vaguely.

'Alice! This is . . . tell me your name again?'

'Patrice Hillyard.' He held out a long-fingered, tanned hand for Alice to shake. Huge, big-toothed smile, a glint of gold filling. 'Here for a couple of days' break from the heaving city. And this is such a wondrous coincidence! I'm a lifelong admirer of Mrs Lewis. *Angel's Choice* was a pivotal 1950s work, up there with Sagan and John Braine. A work of genius.' He turned a full beam of a smile towards Joss, who was looking utterly delighted by the attention. Aidan seemed to have been instantly replaced in the captivation game. It crossed Alice's mind that Patrice sounded as though he'd been rehearsing that little speech, and had possibly uttered exactly those words only moments ago to her mother. Whether this was a repetition or not, Jocelyn was looking serenely pleased, beaming at her admirer.

'Please, Patrice, do call me Jocelyn,' she said, lightly touching his arm. Her silver and amethyst rings glinted against his tanned skin. To Alice, her long lilac-painted nails looked somehow predatory. She'd seen all this before. Poor Patrice. 'And I never held with marriage and all that "Mrs" business. You should know that if you know anything about me.' Patrice held up his hands and bowed his head in apology.

Jocelyn was little short of purring. Alice exchanged glances with Aidan, each of them expressing 'smarmy git'. Patrice was an unmistakable media man of some sort, shinily bald, tall, dressed in low-slung jeans plus a tee shirt that proclaimed 'Home is Where the Art Is' on the front. His right wrist sported a grubby pink and blue plaited friendship bracelet which Alice guessed, with no evidence at all, was a handmade gift from a pre-teen daughter to whom he had weekend access.

'The amazing thing is, I had written to you, some months ago, but as you never replied I thought, well, obviously you're not interested.' He smiled around the table at them all, inviting them to marvel at this serendipitous meeting. Alice watched her mother for an enlightening clue, but Joss showed no sign of recalling a letter.

'It's just a small series, in pre-production right now,' Patrice went on. 'Working title is *Whatever Happened To . . .*' He leaned conspiratorially close to Jocelyn and murmured, 'Not the greatest title, you'll agree, rather implies the past-it brigade, which of course in your case is far from . . .'

'Oh but it's true,' Joss demurred. 'Just a long ago one-hit wonder, that was me.'

'Ah but what a hit!' Patrice parried. 'Which is why I was wondering, though no, I'm sure you wouldn't consider changing your mind . . . would you?'

'Consider? What exactly?' Alice could see her mother's hands trembling slightly. The pearly nail varnish was twinkling in the sunlight and the fingers of her right hand went up to push a stray hair back from her face. Joss had her neck stretched taut, showing her still-slender jawline and once-famous cheek-bones to their best advantage. Opposite Alice, Aidan sighed gently. His knee started to jog up and down with suppressed impatience. She smiled across at him, sympathizing.

'A documentary, subject entirely yourself of course – about forty minutes.' Patrice's hands were expressive, fingers spread as if he was already framing shots. 'The here and now, the in between, the way-back-then for those, so few I'm sure, who didn't know . . .'

'Maybe you should give her a bit of time to consider,' Alice interrupted. Patrice's smile faded for a moment, then quickly reignited. 'Oh absolutely!' he agreed. 'No need for an instant decision, none at all. Though you must agree, this meeting today is so, oh how can I put it, surely so *serendipitous*, so cosmically, perfectly timed.'

He was using all the right words. As they left the restaurant a lazy hour later Alice realized her mother had agreed to allow an entire film crew the run of Penmorrow for at least a week at the height of the summer season. Well, she thought as she steered the car round the headland past St Mawes castle, Jocelyn would have to be the one who told Mo.

Oh God, she was a dull woman. At the Caprice, Noel paid the bill for lunch and wondered how he could quickly offload Paula without making her feel like handing in her notice. She was a terrific asset on reception at the office. She'd also been there just long enough to know his clients and was exactly enough of a phone-chatterer to get them to do plenty of useful confiding. They didn't always tell the truth to him. Truth, where high-profile divorce was concerned, could often cost a vast amount of money. If the wife in search of several millions in alimony was popping down to Cannes with a new love, she wasn't necessarily going to inform her lawyer. On the other hand her lawyer might need to know: if push came to shove in court it could be as well to have a cover story handy. He still shuddered at the memory of a cabinet minister he'd represented a few years previously, pleading immense cash-flow difficulties that would preclude decent alimony to his soon-to-be-ex wife. If he'd only *said* about the offshore moolah, Noel could

have helped him avoid all that tabloid press speculation, still sorted out a more than fair payout for his
wife, and the chap would have kept his personal
savings more or less intact.

Paula had gone down the far staircase to the loo
many minutes ago. She was probably looking at the
display of classic David Bailey celebrity mugshots
on the wall on the way back. Alice had said there
was a particularly stunning Marianne Faithfull. Noel
looked at his watch, wondering if he should simply
give Paula the afternoon off and tell her to go and
do some shopping. She'd like that – women did. He
hoped she'd think it was because she deserved the
time, that it was a reward for being such charming
company. She'd had that keen look though, right from
the moment she'd accepted a glass of champagne ('Ooh
I shouldn't!' Had she really said that? He almost
grimaced at the memory) and more than once he'd
caught her doing that thing she must have read somewhere was sexy – picking up long bits of food in her
fingers and practically fellating it. There was nothing
sexy about watching a woman sucking a thin chip.

Was it possible she hoped they'd leap into a taxi,
whizz back to Richmond and hurl themselves on his
hyper-chic chrome bed and rumple Alice's pink/purple
shot-silk throw, skidding around on it in the throes
of passion? Surely not. He certainly hoped not. He
couldn't bear the thought of even one more minute
hearing about her dog Beasley's tricks with the
boomerang or her weekly charity visits to Battersea
Dogs' Home to cheer up the terminally homeless
mutts. Nor did he want to hear the bizarre details
of Her Kevin's PhD thesis on Internet advertising
valuation. She probably hadn't been overenthralled by
his 'amusing' tales of Alice's mother's hippy home life

either. In fact she'd probably heard them all before, but had applied the simple good manners that kicked in when your meal was being paid for.

What he really wanted, Noel thought as Paula at last shimmied across the restaurant (and oh no, oh God, big swivel of the head and she'd stopped to gawp at Ringo Starr. Surely she knew you just Didn't Do That?), what he really wanted was to be with Alice and Theo and Grace. He wanted them to be there as usual when he came home from work. He missed the silly tick-tick-tick noise of Grace and Theo texting all their unseen mates, missed Alice in her Saturday night suspenders. He missed the smell of her clean hair and the way, when she was in her study working on a book, her fingers flew over the Mac keyboard as she raced to get the story out of her head and into the world. It was a bit like a birth, she'd told him, and stupidly he'd laughed, been dismissive. He wished he hadn't now. He wished he'd thought for more than a millisecond about what she was saying and made an effort to understand what she was getting at. After all, if she'd said it, it was because she'd thought it through carefully and chosen the words she really needed. You didn't get mindless flannel with Alice.

Paula, as expected, was delighted to take the rest of the afternoon off. Noel sent her off in a taxi in the direction of Knightsbridge and prayed she wouldn't spend a fortune in Harvey Nicks underwear department on something she guessed he'd enjoy. If she was hoping for an enthusiastic licking she'd do better to get the Beasley dog a new collar.

Noel walked down past the Ritz and decided he too would abandon the office for the day and take the tube straight home to Richmond. There was time for a spot of golf. At the thought of it, at the idea of deep-breathing fresh air on the edge of Richmond Park, he very nearly stopped walking and took a practice air-swing right there on Piccadilly. But Green Park station was closed. Thwarted travellers milled about on the pavement and the transport official, who looked bored at having to keep repeating the same explanations, sighed, 'Suspect package,' in the tone that Noel remembered from his prep school that suggested that this hurt him more than it hurt anyone else. Noel looked at his watch. Three o'clock – not really much point in going back to work anyway – he wouldn't get much done and wine at lunchtime always left him at less than full mental strength. He hailed a taxi and slumped comfortably in the corner with a former passenger's abandoned *Evening Standard*.

There was the usual depressing summer reading: strikes at airports, a row about a Wimbledon umpire, rain predicted to disrupt the next Test series and a flurry in suburban house sales. 'That's good news anyway,' Noel found himself commenting aloud, and then immediately wondered *why* it was of any relevance to him at all. He and Alice weren't planning to move, hadn't considered it. They'd had the house renovated to an incredible level of personal comfort exactly to suit their needs and tastes. And yet . . . as Noel entered the hallway of his silent immaculate home, he felt for a moment as if it belonged to some-one he'd never met before. He ran quickly upstairs, flung off his clothes and walked into the shower to try to wash in a more familiar mood.

'I'm getting old,' he thought as he wrapped a towel round his waist and stared at himself in the long mirror on the inside of his wardrobe door. He must be getting old, he thought, for he was feeling a new need to rush into some kind of change in his life before it was all too late. It wasn't going to be other women, not if the dull lunch with Paula had been anything to go by. Retirement could be less than five years away if he so wanted. Whatever was he going to fill his life with? Plenty of golf, for sure, but what else? Not gardening. Not pottering about on the Thames pretending he was A Sailor as so many in the district did, and definitely not self-improving cruising in the Med, being lectured to about the Treasures of Venice.

Noel wandered around the bedroom mussing up the cushions on the sofa (Mrs Pusey always stood them to strict triangular attention) and then sat on the bed. He flicked on the TV and half-heartedly watched a tennis match in which a pair of staggeringly muscular women battled it out with frightening intensity. Female players no longer, it crossed his mind, wore even slightly attractive knickers. The thick taut thighs held no interest for him any more. He remembered when he was a young teenager, gawping through the fence at the local tennis club tournaments just to catch a glimpse of underwear frills and a broad, stretched gusset. He couldn't imagine Theo, self-contained, surly Theo, sneaking glimpses of sporty knickers. He probably didn't need to, Noel thought, he probably had girls queueing up to peel off their low-cut thongs for him. He felt the absence of his son suddenly like a harsh chest pain. He reached for the phone, dialled the number for railway information and made a list of the train times to Truro.

Harry sat on a lopsided stool at the end of the poly-tunnel furthest from the path, smoking a fat spliff. It was left over from last year's crop (Passion No. 1) and had held its potency well. This variety gave quite a tranquillizing effect and he felt that the late afternoon, when Joss and the others came back from their swanky lunch, would be better faced if he was mellow and calm. He didn't like Joss when she'd been drinking at lunchtime. She'd be all over Aidan, giving him little fond touches and smiles full of memories of old seductions. She could be very caustic too, very above herself and grand. Harry had never been able to stand up to her – she had a way of making you feel that you'd barely lived and so hadn't any opinion worth considering. It was all a long way from when he was little and adored, and she'd called him 'my cherub Ariel' and hugged him tight. Alice had wriggled away and been the one for escaping into the village with her friend Sally and anyone of her age who happened to be staying at the house. She rounded up all the children who were old enough and led them to the beach where she had them writing little stories and making up bits of 'news' that she put together into a weekly magazine. He was too young for wandering – a plump toddler left behind with Jocelyn, who gathered him to her whenever she needed comfort and tickled the back of his neck till he squealed.

It was all right for Jocelyn: by the time she was thirty she'd travelled the world, talking to literary gatherings at festivals everywhere about her one book. Painters adopted her as their muse, smart journals snapped up her opinions, clothes designers had her in mind when their thoughts turned to 'Bohemian'. Nothing scared her, she had the complete perfect faith in herself that whatever she did, whatever she said, someone would be looking, listening and admiring. He should have broken away years ago and made his own way, but had been unnerved by his lack of any kind of education. People who could give you a job asked you questions about that sort of thing. Just lately though he'd started wondering about moving on, thinking that maybe he could get work on a farm or in a nursery. You didn't need certificates for that and he'd got all the experience and skill they'd be needing. But then there was Penmorrow. What would happen to it? Would his mother hang on like a sailor set adrift in a rickety old boat, waiting for it all to collapse around her?

There was a scuffling sound outside and Harry held the spliff behind his back and stubbed it out on the edge of the stool. Sam and Chas pushed open the flap of the tunnel and came in, bringing with them the fishy scent of the beach. That was depressing. There hadn't been time for them to go to the shore if they'd come home on the school bus. And they'd definitely got on it that morning – he'd taken them down to the village stop himself to make sure. He knew their tricks – one of them would have said, halfway up the hill, that he felt a bit sick. The driver would have stopped and almost thrown them out, keen to preserve a clean, odourless bus.

'Good day at school, boys?' he asked, certain he should at least make the effort to pretend he thought they'd been there.

'S'all right.' Sam sniffed.

'Just usual,' Chas agreed. The two boys looked solemn, standing in front of him in their crazy combination of tidy school clothes and manically wild hair, unsure what to say next and kicking their feet on the ground like impatient ponies.

'What are you doing in here?' he asked. 'Were you looking for me?'

The pair of them shrugged, grinning. 'Not specially, just, you know, looking round for stuff to do.'

Harry sighed, even more depressed. They knew, these canny, sly lads of his, they knew exactly what he was growing. He'd be lucky this year if by the time it came to harvest this little lot, they hadn't been in already, stripped the plants and had the potent buds up to dry, ready for a schoolful of eager, paying customers.

Six

Alice was lying stretched flat out on her front on a dusty wooden floor, clearing a heap of long-discarded cardboard picture mounts from under a bed in one of the biggest upstairs bedrooms. She moved carefully, wary of splinters and the possible presence of desiccated mouse bodies. The contrast between the under-bed conditions here and at her own home could hardly have been more extreme. Beneath the Richmond bed no dust lurked, no ancient hair clips (fourteen picked up so far, where had they come from?), no matty clumps of spider nest, only a large white storage box on wheels (mail order, from the Holding Company). This stored Alice's out-of-season clothes and currently contained a collection of dry-cleaned, moth-zapped, tissue-folded cashmere sweaters, each one in its own air-drained polythene casing. Grace, whose idea of being careful with her clothes was to heap them on the bed rather than the floor, accused her mother of near-fetishism over her biannual storage rituals. But, as Alice pointed out, if you'd been brought up dressed in purple crochet (unravelling) and folksy recycled patchwork, you tended to treasure everything pattably delicate, costly and above all brand new.

Jocelyn had decreed that this was the room Patrice was to have when he and his crew came to film her. It hadn't been part of the bed and breakfast set-up for, although it overlooked the beach and was in relatively good condition, it was the room next to Jocelyn's own and, as she put it, she didn't want to wake at night and hear strangers indulging in noisy sex.

'I've had years and years of erotic sound effects,' she'd declared over supper, adding, 'a very good many of them my own,' which made Theo and Grace and the twins giggle and splutter into their fish pie. 'And besides,' she added, 'that bed won't take much more activity. We must consider it retired.'

'Are you going to tell Patrice that?' Aidan had asked her, looking cheeky.

'Certainly not, Aidan my sweet.' Joss had reached across and patted his cheek like a fond grandma with a treasured infant. 'You are.'

The crumpled cardboard that Alice was retrieving must have belonged to miserable Milly, way, way back when this had been her room. She'd both slept in here and used it as her studio. Perhaps that accounted for her sorrow, Alice guessed as she burrowed about among the dust. Perhaps it was all that breathing in of oily fumes and pungent solvent thinners – it couldn't do anyone any good. Milly had preferred to drape material from her walls rather than to paint them, so there were no gaudy exuberant splodges here, simply a still-delicate washed-out dirty pink like the colour of a plaster that's stayed too long on a cut. There also remained hooks all round the walls at ceiling height, from where the lengths of soft silky sari fabrics had been hung to look like long slim flags, using garden canes as curtain poles.

The fabrics had been collected from Milly's

wandering days in India and Afghanistan. They were multicoloured, hung randomly so that some clashed, some blended. Alice remembered them clearly: purple with gold thread, pinks with navy and silver embroidery, sharp cool green with lemon stars, tiny chips of icy beads stitched with scarlet thread onto sky-coloured silk, borders of swirling gold and orange. The hangings had drifted gently, wafted continuously by the permanent draughts in the house. Alice remembered thinking the effect was as if the walls were swaying all the time, and had loved it in the shadowy half-light when Milly lit candles around her easel in the centre of the room. There'd been a row about that, she recalled now as she dragged the last piece of distorted cardboard out from beneath the saggy mahogany bed. It had been the only time Jocelyn had been furious about candle-burning.

There were plenty of candles in the house, kept for various seasonal festivities. Candles were on the go every evening on the long dining-room table, burning in tall intricately twisted ceramic holders abandoned by a resident who'd left in a hurry, fleeing a paternity order. They were often sickly scented with patchouli which Harry had grumbled about, complaining that they stank and put him off his food.

Joss had told Milly she wasn't allowed candles in her room because of all the fabrics and because of her oil paints. For some unknown reason she wasn't even allowed to smoke in the house (though others were) and used to sit out by herself on the front porch at night, puffing guiltily like a schoolgirl. Jocelyn had stormed into her room one evening and found Milly on her green velvet floor cushion, reading Alice and Sally and a pair of visiting American children a ghost story by candlelight. They had reached the scariest point in

92

the story. The effect of Jocelyn flinging open the door, silhouetted against the landing light with her cascade of wild yellow hair and her flowing purple kaftan decorated with tiny glinting mirrors, had pitched the children – and Milly too – into shrieking hysterics.

After that for a while there'd been an atmosphere of disappointed anger – Alice remembered it could be felt all over the house. Thinking back, it was hard to tell if that feeling filtered through from all the residents, or if it was just that Joss's own moods dominated and affected everyone. Milly had been punished – at a special House Meeting the residents had voted that she should clean out the chicken shed, repaint it and mend the broken catch on the door. She'd chosen to do it on a chill and windy day, with vicious rain ripping into her hair and clothes, making her look even more bedraggled and tragic than ever.

So there had been some rules, Alice thought as she emerged from beneath the bed and sat up, her head spinning slightly. She could feel cobwebs in her hair, sticky with long-dead insect carcasses. Harry was at the doorway, rock-still, arms folded, just watching. She wondered how long he'd been there and why he hadn't said anything.

'Harry, do you remember if there were any house rules actually written down for this place? About who could do what and about housework and food shopping and stuff? I've always thought of it as being completely anarchic but it can't really have been. And do you remember Milly being punished for lighting candles? It seems strange that she couldn't be trusted to decide for herself what was safe and what wasn't.'

Harry came in and started collecting up the card mounts, piling them tidily in size order on top of the mattress. He took his time thinking before saying, 'There were all those meetings where anyone who wanted to speak had to wait their turn to sit on that huge squashy suede bag thing. There was a special name for it, but I can't quite . . .' He closed his eyes and rubbed his forehead hard with his thumb knuckle, looking as if he was trying to knead out the memory.

'The beef bag! That was it!' Harry, pleased with his technique, grinned at his upturned thumb as if it was solely responsible for the recalled memory.

'Oh yes, that was it. If you had a complaint or wanted to change how the domestic set-up worked, you had to line up to take your turn on it at one of the house meetings.' Alice laughed. 'When I was little I used to think it was called that because it was actually stuffed with old meat. And it was a sort of dirty maroony red colour which I thought was from blood. It scared me a lot.'

'A lot of things scared me.' Harry was looking pensive now, wary even.

'What sort of things?' Alice asked him quietly. He shrugged and the thumb went back up to his head.

'People coming and going all the time, I suppose. That feeling that you weren't really very safe.'

'What did you not feel safe about?'

Harry sat down on the mattress, which creaked grumpily at being disturbed. He picked up a piece of torn cardboard and started tearing tiny, evenly spaced rips into it. 'Dunno. Nothing particular, just a feeling. Like . . .' he hesitated, scrabbling for the right words. 'You didn't know who to get close to because then they'd just go. Especially if Joss had a row with them. There was that music bloke, the American rock star she took up with for a bit. All velvet and leather. I liked him, we played beach cricket for hours. We had a laugh. Then one day he'd just gone. No goodbye, no nothing.'

Alice remembered. 'Ah yes, Jamie. Sat in the poly-tunnel playing his guitar and singing to the chickens. I wonder what happened to him.'

'See, that's what I mean. Once people went beyond the far gate and out of the village it was like they'd died or something.'

'Perhaps he had. We could ask Joss.'

Harry laughed. 'Yeah and you know what she'll say? It'll be, "Oh darlings, so many people, such a long time, you can't expect me to remember every waif and stray who fetched up here." '

'Or she'll do that looking-into-the-distance thing and say, "Best forgotten sweetie, best forgotten." Still,' Alice said, 'I suppose she thinks of them as *her* collection of memories, not really anything to do with us. That's probably why she hadn't bothered to tell me about this autobiography. Probably didn't want to think we'd have anything relevant to add.'

'But we were here. So of course it was to do with us,' Harry pointed out as he gathered up the unwieldy heap of cardboard and stuffed it in Alice's binbag. 'And that's what pisses me off about her bloody book. These should be our memories too, well everything after we were born, anyway. Perhaps they *would* have been if her bloody ego hadn't swooped them all up and claimed them for Jocelyn's Corner.' He picked up the bulging bag and stamped out through the door, calling back to Alice, 'I'll take this lot down by the sheds and burn it. Best to be rid.'

Grace was lying on her raffia mat on the beach, about to start reading the first chapter of Jocelyn's sole oeuvre, *Angel's Choice*. She'd found a drawerful of the books in the big chest in Joss's bedroom when she'd been looking for scissors to trim her fringe. She hadn't been snooping around, she'd asked Joss about the scissors and been told to help herself, to look wherever she thought that scissors might possibly be. There hadn't been any in the bathroom. She'd searched the damp cupboards beneath the basin where the shelves had been crammed with little brown bottles of dried-up ancient herbal remedies, fat glass jars of aspirin which must have pre-dated all kinds of modern packaging regulations, and rolls and rolls of grubby crêpe bandages with their ends neatly secured in place with curved nappy pins. Grace couldn't help thinking, as she tried to read the faded labels, that her own mother would have had a fit: all medicines in the Richmond house were locked away in a sparkling chrome and glass cupboard high out of reach of any visiting human under five feet tall. Alice even bought paracetamol in packs of no more than twelve, as if she anticipated Theo and Grace pulling such a terminal sulk after a minor spat that they'd be sure to wolf the lot.

In the drawer in Joss's giant oak chest, there must have been well over thirty copies of the book, all carefully piled up and covered with tissue paper. Grace had looked through them, interested to see that there were several different covers. The dates of publication varied and the latest ones just had the words: 'First published in 1959'.

She knew about the book of course; she'd always known that Jocelyn had written something years before that had been hugely famous. There'd been a film of the book too, but although she knew that, she hadn't thought to check whether they'd got it down at Blockbusters, any more than she'd thought of looking in Waterstones to see if *Angel's Choice* was on the shelves. Once, at school, the morning after her mother had been to an open evening, Mrs MacDonald who taught English had been weird in a class and kept looking at her. At the end of the lesson Old MacDonald had kept her behind and been creepy, saying things like 'your eminent grandmother' and 'seminal classic'. It had all been a bit unintelligible for a twelve-year-old and had made Grace and Sophy giggle because they were pretty sure 'seminal' was a rude word.

From Joss's collection in the drawer, Grace had taken what looked like the latest copy of the book, a paperback dated only a few years ago and with a cover that had a blurry oil painting of a mostly blue girl looking at herself in a bedroom mirror, her hands together as if she was praying, though with the fingers splayed out. The painting, it said, in tiny letters on the back cover, was by Melissa Thorpe-Appleby. The room the painted girl was standing in looked dismal and cramped, as if she'd grown too big for it but couldn't escape. Reflected in the mirror was a bare light bulb hanging from the ceiling and books, like strewn home-work, lying on a bed that was a saggy brass one, a lot like Jocelyn's own. Also on the back of the book it said:

'A timeless rite-of-passage tale of the hazards of honesty, of painful decisions and family strife. The accomplished artistry and the enduring relevance of *Angel's Choice* effortlessly survive the passing decades.'

Grace wondered now why she hadn't read it before. It hadn't even been offered to her, which was a surprise, as her mother was always on at her to read more. There wasn't a copy of *Angel's Choice* in the Richmond house, that was for sure. Alice's Gulliver

School books were lined up proudly in order on the bookshelves in the sitting room where Noel thought they looked a bit silly – like toys among antiques, he'd said. Grace had read all those – Alice gave her the manuscripts as soon as she'd finished them so that Grace could check them over for dated vocabulary and unlikely clothes. She was pretty good though, her mum, and hardly ever got anything much wrong. Which was worrying. It meant she kept a close ear and eye on Grace and her friends, listened perhaps a bit too hard in the car on the school run when Grace thought she was well into some dull thing about money or education on Radio Four. But as for this book, Grace had always known Joss had written one (she knew that was how Penmorrow had been bought), but had assumed it was some dull old thing about really old grown-up people. But it wasn't. It was about a girl of fifteen. Her age. Well, her age soon enough, anyway.

Grace rolled onto her side and groped into her bag for the sunscreen. If she was in for a long afternoon's read she wanted to get a gorgeous even tan doing it, not a seared-meat look. A few yards away, across at the beach café, she could see some of the surfer boys looking in her direction. Theo was probably there – he'd taken to hanging out with them and was putting in lots of practice on a borrowed surfboard. She hoped he'd tell her if she looked minging in her red bikini. He hadn't commented at all. Either he just didn't bother to look, or he thought she wasn't worth looking at. Or he was being stepbrotherly and kind and just avoiding saying that her tummy hung out over the front in a really, like, offputting way, or that she needed a bit more up top to carry off a halter neck. Grace quickly smeared factor six over her legs and the bits of her back that she could reach and lay down on her front.

She shoved her old and fraying straw hat on and pulled it down low so that the shadow of its brim fell across the pages, and started to read.

Jocelyn wasn't supposed to react like this. What was there about this refurbished kitchen that was not likeable? Alice just didn't get it. All that work, from scrubbing out murky corners that no rubber-gloved hand had approached with a J-cloth for years, to painting a wash of pale aqua paint all over the walls and ceiling. What had been the bloody point?

'You just don't understand, do you Alice?' Joss looked at her daughter with an expression of resigned despair. 'You never have. You can't just leave things alone, let them lie, let them rot away if their time has come.'

Jocelyn considered that Alice was looking very pleased with herself. In fact she was annoyingly bouncy, like a puppy who's just so cleverly retrieved a thrown ball. What she didn't realize was that in this case, to Jocelyn, it was as if she'd returned carrying a trophy that was shocking and foul – a severed hand came to mind.

'I thought that was what I was here for – to help stop things rotting away.' Alice was smiling, still sure of herself, showing off her efforts. Joss ran her fingers along the scrubbed wooden worktop, then along the smooth, newly painted window ledge. It felt too clean, too silky, too not-hers.

'Where did it come from, Alice, this urge to organize and meddle, to list things, to polish things up, make them into the shiny gleamy things that they simply weren't and were never meant to be?'

She gazed at the sleek blue walls and breathed in the acrid scent of new paint and dedicated cleaning activity. Alice could scrub a place down till its very soul was beaten into submission and drowned in Flash. She was standing there, slender and urban – quite the Smart Lady, looking as trim and tidy as this kitchen, her hair all glossy and her cream linen trousers so damn clean. She wasn't saying anything now. That was wise. Right now that was the only thing Joss was pleased about, that her daughter still knew better than to attempt to resort to reason in the face of her mother's fury, to leap in trying to justify, 'But Joss . . .'

'You were just the same as a child,' Jocelyn continued, grim-faced, picking at a tiny bubble of paint just on the edge of the door frame. 'You were always wanting your room organized, putting your dolly tidily to bed each night in a nasty plastic toy cot that Sally's mother – what was her name? Beryl . . . no . . . Brenda – had given you on your birthday.' Alice started a slow smile, remembering. Jocelyn glared. Alice mustn't mistake this moment for one of cosy reminiscence.

' "She's my baby. And babies sleep in cots." ' Joss mimicked the child-Alice being pretend-mummy. 'When had you ever seen a baby in a cot? Cots are baby-prisons complete with bars.'

All Penmorrow babies slept in their parents' beds and when they grew too big, they curled up with other toddlers on the big mattress in the playroom. They looked like kittens, sprawled and snuggled together, milky, warm and soft.

'And where are my daisy curtains?' Joss demanded, banging the rubbish bin (New, gaudy chrome. Why? From where?) open and poking about with her hand.

'I binned them, of course. Last week. When I took them down they just fell apart. Do you know, I'm surprised that people who've rented this place haven't reported you to the trading standards office. It was barely habitable. People are used to . . .'

'I *know* what people are used to . . .' Jocelyn waved her hand, dismissing Alice's opinion. 'They come here for something different.'

'Well they sure as hell get that here,' Alice snapped. 'And I don't think you *do* know what people are used to – Penmorrow is a mad time warp. What people like on holiday is fresh, clean accommodation that isn't like some *slum* compared to their own homes. They want drawers that open easily and aren't stuck shut by years of grease. They want shelves that aren't skid-marked with rusty metal stains from the bottoms of damp pans.' She turned back to the sink, in which for the first time she could see a reflective shine.

'Now do you want some tea? And the chance to inspect the mugs, note that all the stains have been bleached out from the bottoms of them?' Alice ran the water for the kettle (another shiny new chrome item), banging it down hard on the worktop.

Joss looked at the stark, bare kitchen window and felt tears salting up and threatening to overflow. She'd made those curtains herself, stitching their hems by hand as she and Arthur sat by the cottage fire (smoky and unreliable even then), listening to the winter wind hurtling round the trees. Arthur had just started on his remote phase, heading for death, though neither of them knew it. He'd moved out of the main house and shut himself away down here in Gosling which had, till then, been his studio. He no longer wanted to be part of the shifting Penmorrow population and rejected communal living as wholeheartedly as he'd once welcomed it. He wanted only to see Joss, no-one else. He didn't want to work any more, didn't want her to tell him if galleries had called, if commissions came in. He'd come to the end, he'd said. Life's work done. He would live from now as a rich retiree, as entitled to call a halt to production as if he'd been an assembly-line factory worker.

Joss brought food down from the house, cooked rice and steaks for him and spent the nights curling her younger, stronger body round his, whispering reassurance about the sounds and sights outside. They were shadows of trees, not giant goblins, she'd tell him when he woke in the dark and the moon cast eerie shapes on the sloping ceiling. It was for his fears that she'd made the curtains, so that as the darkness of winter afternoons came on and he wanted a cup of tea, he wouldn't stand for hours trembling at the door between the kitchen and sitting room, trying to make out whether the shapes on the walls were devils' dancing limbs or simply waving birch twigs.

Arthur had built the kitchen cupboards. He'd said it was what men did when they were cast away from real life and had to fashion their own dwellings. Had he been mad at this point? She couldn't really remember. Jocelyn wandered into the sitting room and sat heavily on the tired old sofa. Alice followed, offering a mug of tea. Joss waved it away, bracelets jangling. Arthur had said he was a man content to be adrift, no longer part of life's mainstream. If he was *mad*, it didn't show in his handiwork. She'd watched him planing the wood, expertly cutting the joints for the drawers. At least bloody Alice hadn't taken her paintbrush to all that. Jocelyn could see she'd tightened up the hinges, made the doors hang straight, lined up the edges. It wasn't drastic, perhaps it was even practical, but Jocelyn found herself resenting even that, as if Alice had dared to smarten up the memory of Arthur himself. The cupboard handles had gone, though. Joss tried to tell herself they'd just been scrappy bits of wood, but she'd watched Arthur chiselling their shapes by hand from bits of oak chopped out of the firewood that had come from the basket by the hearth.

'You've thrown away the kitchen handles. Arthur's handles.'

'They were falling to bits, Joss,' Alice told her in an irritating, 'let's-be-practical' way. 'Half of them were missing anyway and the others were ingrained with filth. You can't expect the renters to put up with that. I wouldn't, no-one would.'

'But they're getting *art*,' Joss snapped. 'Or they were.' In their place were now silvery things shaped like starfish. Not even sensible either – the sharp ends would catch on jacket pockets, pull holes in loose shirts. Joss looked at them with disdain. 'I suppose you think *those* are "contemporary". Amusing even. Well you're wrong.' She hauled herself out of the sofa, leaning on her stick for support. 'What have you done upstairs? I'd better look. If you've painted over the mural in the bathroom . . .'

'I haven't done anything up there. I haven't had time,' Alice said, adding, not quite far enough under her breath, 'yet.'

Jocelyn walked slowly up the stairs, holding tight to the rail and feeling depressed at the lack of her former easy balance. She glanced into Alice's room on the left of the small landing. It was so tidy you'd hardly know it was in use. How, Joss wondered, had she managed to produce such a prissy, neat housewife of a daughter? Grace's room, opposite, was far more cheering. The bed was a messy nest of duvet, strewn-about clothes and magazines with Monty the cat sprawled sleeping across the rumpled pillows. That was more like it.

                    *   *   *

Bloody sodding hell, Alice muttered to herself as she strode down the path to the village, snapping twigs off branches as she went. Bloody fucking sodding lousy hell. What was the point?

She was in need of a drink and the anonymity of being alone in a crowded pub surrounded by the convivial conversations of people she didn't know. It would be busy, the car park was packed and families with crisps and cans of drink overflowed from the garden into the street and across to the beach.

'You're talking to yourself, Alice.' Aidan was at a table by the pub wall, looking through a pile of manuscript. So the book was coming along then.

'Oh hi Aidan. Sorry, I was miles away. I just fancied a drink – what are you having? I'll get you one.'

The bar was crowded with holidaymakers. Conscious of her rudeness but feeling that her need was greater, Alice shimmied her way to the bar, past groups in sailing gear who were being indecisive about what they wanted to drink. On an impulse she ordered a bottle of chilled cava and carried it with a pair of glasses back to Aidan.

'Hmm. Sparkly stuff – what are we celebrating?'

'Bugger all. I'm doing compensating. Just had a run-in with my mother. I can't get anything right. I mean what's the point of Harry dragging me all the way down here to help out and then complaining when I try to improve things a bit?' Alice wrenched the top off the bottle, anger giving her a burst of extra strength.

'Maybe that's the point: it was Harry doing the dragging, not Jocelyn. Perhaps she doesn't want anything changed.'

'She wants the rest of her life to be comfortable though, doesn't she? So how's that going to work if

Penmorrow collapses around her ears? What will they all live on? The way it's going, the council will be round one day, digging through the binbags and clutter to find her dead under a mountain of memorabilia, surrounded by empty bottles and gnawing rats.'

Aidan laughed. 'Harry and Mo won't let it come to that.'

'Harry and Mo want out. Well Mo does, you can just tell. I mean, who'd want to live all their grown-up life under the thumb of a demanding mother-in-law anyway? I think Mo's been a saint to put up with Joss all these years as it is, but . . .'

'But?'

'Mo's different this time. She's got a resentful look about her, all the time.' Alice stopped and took a deep sip of her drink. She could feel its coolness trickling down inside her, soothing. 'Hey, you don't want to hear about this. I feel like a silly teenager who's grumbling that their mother's a cow and doesn't understand.'

Aidan topped up their glasses. 'Was it like that when you *were* a teenager?'

'What's this, research? Aren't you off duty?'

'No, not really. If it's relevant, don't expect me to leave it out. But I'm interested, whether or not.'

'My teen rebellion took the form of reading geography books, doing maths and English O level by secret postal tuition and climbing out of my window to spend nights on the beach with a bunch of French exchange students.'

Aidan laughed. 'What, you mean you wouldn't have been allowed to? Like a normal kid?'

'Huh, no such luck. Jocelyn would probably have set up a womb blessing or something to speed me on my merry sexual way. It wasn't the climbing out that was rebellious, it was the keeping my love life to myself!'

It was getting late and the clientele in the pub garden had altered – families with children had been replaced by older teenagers and holidaymakers in search of pub food. Alice realized then that she hadn't eaten since her lunchtime tuna sandwich and the drink had gone to her head. She hoped Grace and Theo had had the sense to forage for supper in the Penmorrow larder. Neither of them lacked basic cooking skills. The Richmond kitchen was often heaped with evidence of late-night feasting, with stuck-on pasta in saucepans and cheese carelessly grated onto the floor and into the cat.

Alice noticed a curvaceous blonde girl looking slightly lost in the garden, glancing round as if for someone she'd mislaid. Eventually, the girl caught sight of Aidan and made her way to them. She placed both hands on the table and leaned forward, showing a cavernous cleavage and the edges of a frilled pink bra. 'Do you have an escort?' she asked Aidan, her voice barely more than a sexy whisper.

Aidan smiled politely, looking unsure. 'Er, well I'm with this lady actually, but thanks for the offer.'

The girl looked blank for a moment, then stood up and laughed, 'God no! I meant in the car park! The blue Escort – it's blocking me in!'

'Oh. Sorry, a bit confused there. Um, no. No car here at all, sorry!'

Alice could barely stop giggling. 'Escort! Imagine if she'd been really offering a service, here in Tremorwell!'

'She'd hardly have picked me for the ideal paying companion anyway.' Aidan put on a mock-glum expression.

106

'Oh I don't know, you're not so bad,' she said before she thought about it. Now that she *did* think about it, she wondered if he'd misinterpret. But it wouldn't matter if he did, would it. She must be, what, at least seventeen years older than him? And she was firmly, solidly, very committedly married to Noel. Wryly, she thought how irrelevant these details would have seemed to her own mother. How very different she was from Jocelyn.

Seven

Noel didn't usually go in for surprises. They were so hard to get right. Alice had never liked them, not even in the form of presents, although he was pretty sure even she wouldn't turn her nose up at an unexpected diamond necklace. She had hated it when he'd tried to whisk her away for a mystery weekend. There he'd been, dancing round the bedroom, triumphantly brandishing air tickets that he wouldn't let her see and feeling slightly foolish, but, instead of swooning with appropriate delight, she'd gone into an immediate panic-flap.

'But I *have* to know where we're going!' she'd wailed. 'How will anyone know where to get hold of us in an emergency? What do I take? Hot place or cold? City, country, coast?' All the spontaneity of the gesture had fizzled away like bubbles from stale champagne, so that in the end he'd simply given in and shouted, frustrated and thwarted, 'OK then, it's bloody Venice. Happy now?'

And she had been. Perfectly. Easy as that. And they'd had a wonderful time. He should have known better really; Alice was simply one of those people who need to feel they have complete control over everything they're doing. And, as she'd pointed out when they'd explored just about every last alleyway in the entire city, the whole trip could have been ruined by taking the wrong shoes.

Noel sipped bitter coffee in his first-class seat on the train and wondered what Alice would say when he turned up at Penmorrow. She probably wouldn't appreciate his impulsiveness. She might accuse him of trying to catch her out, though at what Noel couldn't begin to imagine. If Alice was going to have a torrid affair she'd be certain to jot down a note of her plans for passionate trysts in the kitchen diary. And Tremorwell village was hardly the adultery centre of England – who would dare try to keep an extramarital dalliance secret from those all-seeing demon keepers of the post office? On the other hand Alice might simply be delighted to see him. Surely after weeks in the company of her demanding mother, crabby sister-in-law and spookily silent brother she was just about certain to be.

The train was running more than an hour late. In a world-weary voice, the conductor announced over the PA that the train ahead had run into some cows that had strayed onto the line. Noel couldn't decide whether his tone of mild amusement was down to the train being one that belonged to a rival company, or whether he just thought it laughable that cows were daft enough to stroll under a train and get themselves killed.

Long stops at remote stations had smokers leaving their seats to light up together on the platforms by open doors and make amiable grumbling conversation. Hot, dusty, country air wafted in, bringing the scent of nearby slurry and the sleepy cooing of wood pigeons. The barely populated stations reminded Noel of posters from the 1950s advertising days out by rail. But where there would have been lovingly tended flower beds and busy, chuffing engines, now there were only abandoned sidings filled with plumes of purple loosestrife, spindly but thriving in the parched ground.

As they dawdled through central Cornwall, Noel entertained himself watching a lone female passenger trying to look as if she was above being interested in the macabre sight of the dead cows, but taking frequent furtive glances out of the window on the north side of the train, waiting to glimpse the gory trackside clean-up operation. She was two rows along, facing Noel across the aisle, and he found himself fascinated by the sight of her bare legs beneath the table as she flexed her ankles. He watched the long calf muscles tense and untense. Was she fending off DVT, he wondered? She had kicked off her high-heeled strappy shoes, which looked far too narrow to accommodate her splayed toes and made her feet look like miniature diver's flippers. Up and down and round and round went the slim ankles, and the gold nail polish on her toes flashed up and down with them.

She was in her late twenties, Noel guessed, and she had long loose thick dark hair and skin tanned to an almost unfashionable depth, giving her limbs the kind of swarthy look that might, he thought, also be due to an excess of hair. He liked that – there was something feral and heated and rude about it. Alice, lovely as she was, was very fair and only sparsely fuzzed and far too zealous (for his tastes), in the depilation department. It had been one of the things he'd liked (now firmly past tense) about Paula – when looking in her mirror she clearly turned a blind eye to a faint but definable moustache. He found himself wondering if the girl's naked toes were furry too (for surely there weren't (yet) women in the nation who waxed their toes? Were there?) and he tried to focus on them as she exercised her legs.

He couldn't decide if she was actually *that* attractive – it would be easy enough to put his feelings of comfortable randiness down to the movement of the train. It reminded him of school-bound bus journeys years ago on which he could rely on having constant erections. He'd got one now that his schoolboy self would have called a real boner. He'd have to start thinking about something else soon or he'd have to tote his bag in front of him when he stood up to get off at Redruth. Eventually the girl caught him staring. He lifted his gaze from floor level and found himself looking into long green slanted eyes. She was laughing at him and he could tell that she could tell what was going on in his trousers.

'You going all the way?' she asked, almost suppressing a giggle. The voice was Australian, or possibly New Zealand. Noel wasn't going to make the mistake of guessing.

'All the way . . . ? Oh, to Penzance. No, Redruth. You?'

'Me too. We could share a cab maybe?'

Oh God, thought Noel, what was this? A proposition. For the second time in a fortnight was this a chance for extra-curricular nookie? Unlikely, there was too much of a knowing tease in her voice.

'Possibly. Are you heading south from there, to the coast?'

'Some back-end place called Tremorwell,' she said. 'I've got to go to a defunct old hippy commune to make a feature. Television.'

'Aha, Penmorrow . . .'

111

' . . . Penmorrow, you're only a day away. And a bloody long one it's been so far, I'd say.'

If Aidan wasn't going to mention it, then the grown-up thing to do was to forget it and carry on as if nothing had happened. Alice, driving him, Grace, Theo and the twins towards St Ives, decided he'd probably only kissed her because he felt sorry for her. And he was drunk at the time as well. They both were, come to that. She and Aidan had stayed at the pub till closing time and eaten only a bag of smoky bacon crisps and two packs of dry roasted peanuts to soak up the drink. Alice was pretty much astounded at herself, being the kind of woman who hardly ever had more than a couple of white wine spritzers and could always be counted on to be capable of driving home legally from a party.

It had been one of those nights where the moon and stars hadn't turned up at all, and the glow from Tremorwell's solitary street lamp petered out long before the path up through the trees to Penmorrow. It had felt like walking in a black vacuum and Alice and Aidan had giggled and stumbled, holding onto each other tight for fear of being gobbled up by an invisible bottomless ravine. They'd been in sight of Gosling (and possibly of Grace at her window, a thought which made Alice's insides flicker) when they'd tripped awkwardly over some tangled tendrils and fallen against an oak tree, still clutched together. That was when Aidan had kissed her, pressing her body hard between himself and the tree. He'd tasted salty from the peanuts, and the unexpected spontaneity of it all had given her a searingly fierce sexual rush.

Sex with Noel, which she would have ticked on a customer-survey card as 'very good' (between

112

'excellent' and 'satisfactory') suddenly seemed almost coldly regular and formulaic, prebooked and reduced to the level of twice-weekly games of tennis with a comfortable friend. Last night she hadn't been the one who'd pulled away, she remembered now, and she imagined, blushmakingly, what might have happened if Aidan hadn't shifted his foot onto a dry branch which had broken with such a loud snap that it had sounded like a sharp telling-off.

It wasn't *entirely* my fault, Alice thought as she turned onto the main road at Lelant and headed for St Ives town centre. It was just one of those silly moments and she should be way past having them. She trusted that Aidan didn't get any juvenile notions that she was likely to want to repeat the experience. Not that *he'd* want to, she reasoned to herself. Not that he was likely to find her particularly stunning in the bright light of day, not in anything but the deepest pitch dark and through an extra blur of alcohol, not a woman so many years older than him. If they'd been back in London, say in a crowded after-work bar, he'd have been spoilt for choice among the glossy twenty-something girls. He'd surely have ignored Alice, would have dismissed her as a middle-aged, middle-class, off-duty mum boringly likely to start talking house prices and school reports. Still, nagging at the back of her brain was an article she'd read in one of the Sunday papers, about how unattached men around the age of thirty or so prefer to have flings with older women because they're not desperate to find a partner for reproduction purposes but can be unashamedly casual in sexual matters. Not that this was a sexual matter. Not at all. Chill, as Grace would say, it was only a snog. Nothing to get rattled about.

'You want Porthmeor. By the Tate?' Chas volunteered

from the far back of the car as Alice drove down the hill towards the town centre. She could see him scowling at her in the rear-view mirror. It was the first thing he'd said to her all day. Sam hadn't spoken either, though both had clambered into the car eagerly enough after helping Theo tie the surfboards onto the roof rack. What a cheery day out this was going to be. It was Saturday – a comparatively quiet day with so many holidaymakers jammed bonnet to bumper either on their way home or on their way down to Cornwall, leaving more space on the beach for local residents.

It had seemed the best thing all round – to take all the children and disappear for the day, get well out of Jocelyn's way and give her some quiet time to herself. She didn't imagine Joss would spend any of it mulling over the disagreement they'd had. Her mother didn't go in for self-doubt – once she'd declared a thing to be so, then so it was. Instead she'd probably harass Mo, make her sort through all the pillows in the house to find the ones with the plumpest feather content for the grand arrival of Patrice. She would follow her into his room, checking that she'd gone right into the corners with the floor polisher and that the freshly washed curtains had been ironed so they hung without creases. She would make Mo hang a big feathered and beaded dream-catcher at the window and get Harry to bring in the Pan statue from her own room. If she was only half as fussy for the B. & B. visitors who paid cash, some of them might be tempted to make return visits and recommend the place to friends. In fact if she'd only send the Pan statue to Christies, she wouldn't need to take in paying guests for several years to come.

'Sloping off?' Harry had asked Alice when she'd arrived to collect the twins in the middle of the morning. He was busy stringing together bulbs of garlic to sell in the village shop. She was tempted to suggest they hang them in the kitchen doorway to ward off the worst aspects of their mother.

'Most useful thing I can do. I've been told in no uncertain terms that I'm interfering and superfluous,' Alice had replied.

'But you're not,' he'd protested.

'Well you're the only one who thinks that way,' Alice said. 'I'm thinking about going back home. I'll wait till Monday when the roads are quiet.'

'But you can't! What about all these film people? They're coming this afternoon. Mo's tearing her hair out as it is.'

'Look – I can't stay for ever – for one thing we're off to Italy in a few weeks. And after what Joss said yesterday, I might as well go sooner than later. She likes things exactly the rotting and mouldering way they are. You and I and Mo think things should be spruced up a bit. But guess who wins? Guess who always bloody wins? So there you go. As Grace would put it, I'm outa here.'

'*She* doesn't know how much it takes for things to be "the way they are". It's a losing battle.' Harry lit a skinny roll-up and inhaled hard. From the smell of it he was smoking a blend of something more than pure tobacco.

'Then give in. Stop fighting. Tell her if she wants to afford to keep Penmorrow, even the way it is, she'll have to sell some of Arthur's work. There's enough of his stuff here to keep her in gin and fags for the rest of her days. And you and Mo as well.'

'There might not *be* that many days.' Harry looked mournful and what was left of Alice's patience completely evaporated.

'Well that would mean problems were over all round then, wouldn't it?' she snapped, feeling bad immediately after. She crossed her fingers quickly to ward off the evil spirits her outburst must have called up.

'Sorry – I shouldn't have said that. Still, just mention it, Harry. The statues. I know they represent her memories but they're also solid lumps of hugely useful cash. And you know, if they're seen in the background of this TV programme, it would only take one enterprising thief to work out that we've zilch here in the way of proper security. One big hire van and a few strong blokes and they could be gone overnight.'

'Couldn't you tell her?' Harry sat down on the old rocking chair and picked at the tobacco falling from the end of his cigarette.

'Yes Harry, I could. But I've told her most of it before. I think it's time it came from you. Perhaps the surprise element might shock her into action.'

Miraculously there was a vacant space in the car park above Porthmeor. The beach wasn't as overpopulated as Alice had expected, with just a few families and bunches of teenagers at well-mannered distances from each other. 'Out of sniping range' Noel would say, convinced that it was one of life's laws that any family group on a British beach would become a miniature war zone before the first hour is up, with squabbles about sand in sandwiches, unfairness about ice creams and anxious nagging over hats and sunblock. Alice trusted that her little gathering would manage to get through the hours without bickering – on the day's form so far they'd be lucky if any of the kids actually spoke.

The two families nearest to where Alice's group had settled didn't look like the loud, arguing types either:

each consisted of tidy two-parents, two-infants set-ups with full-scale backpacked picnic equipment, sensible bags of various sunscreens and a selection of new sand toys for the children. One patient father tried fending off the many fat, greedy seagulls that worked the beach in search of scraps and soft-touch humans, and were sneaking up on a toddler's sausage roll. Alice watched, amused, as he politely suggested to the birds that they go away, as if they were importunate buskers on the London underground. He had a gentle, hyper-posh voice of the sort that is hardly ever heard any more and reminded her of Nigel Pargetter from *The Archers*. The gulls gazed at him, as possibly many humans did, as if he was an obsolete old fossil.

Padding at the sand like a cat, Grace selected a patch that pleased her and quickly peeled her dress off down to her pink bikini. She unrolled her mat, lay down on her tummy, squirmed into a comfortable sandy dent and unpacked Jocelyn's book from her bag. Aidan and Alice settled themselves onto Alice's plastic-backed tartan Marks & Spencers picnic rug. Alice sat primly at the far edge, fingers laced together around the front of her legs. The rug was double-bed sized, but not king-size. She felt suddenly shy of stripping to her swimsuit and lying down beside Aidan. Ridiculous, she reasoned to herself. It would be nothing to do with any intimacy, for what else were you supposed to do on a beach?

Several surfers were in the water, stretched like big sleek otters on their boards and paddling gently out towards the line-up point where the best waves could be picked up. On the far side of Grace, Chas and Sam and Theo silently clambered into wetsuits, grabbed their bodyboards and tramped off to the section of the sea that seemed to be reserved for their particular skill.

'Is it segregation for practical reasons, do you think, or is it a status thing?' Aidan asked, shading his eyes with his hand as he stared out to sea.

'What? Sorry, I was miles away,' Alice replied, processing his question quickly. 'It's practical. The bodyboarders are closer to shore and there's lots more of them. Mostly they're just holiday kids fooling about. The surfers would come ploughing through the middle and half-kill them.'

'If they're any good. Most of them seem to fall off after a couple of yards.'

'Well they all have to learn. Theo told me that all the best ones are up at Newquay this weekend at the Rip Curl contest. Perhaps you should have gone there.' Alice bit her lip, she'd sounded so rude. The second time today too. This wasn't like her.

'Mum! That was a bit full-on.' Grace looked up from her book and glared at her.

'Sorry, I didn't mean . . . What I meant was it might have been more entertaining.' This didn't sound much better.

'Oh I don't know . . .' Aidan grinned at her and she felt herself going pink and confused. She glanced across at Grace to see if she was watching them but Grace was now deep in concentration with her mobile phone, muttering and cursing quietly.

'Mingin'. There's no signal down here. I'm going up to the road – need to text Sophy. Anyone want anything from the caff? I'm getting hungry.'

Alice delved into her bag and found her purse. 'You could get some pasties for you and the boys,' she said. 'They must be famished by now. Aidan? Want one?'

'Mmm. Sounds good. Anything but vegetarian for me. They always overdo the swede. Want me to come up and give you a hand?'

Grace looked at him with that lip-curled, over-puzzled incredulity that Alice recognized as a teen specialty.

'Er, no?' Grace said. 'Like I can't carry six pasties?'

'Fine, no worries.' Aidan shrugged and grinned at her, just as Alice was about to retaliate for Grace's comment about her own rudeness.

Grace stalked off across the sand, her lower half wrapped in a scarlet translucent sarong dotted with starfish and her long fair hair flicking around her head in the breeze. She had lost her London pallor and much of the skinny tonelessness that had been the result of so little activity. Here, she swam in the sea every morning, taking up a Penmorrow tradition that Jocelyn had only recently relinquished. Groups of boys stared after her as she passed. Alice felt as if one more strand of the plaited threads that bound her daughter to her had loosened and come adrift. Nearly fifteen. She'd be going soon, just a few more fast years and then all the remaining threads would unravel at once and drop free onto open ground between them.

'Beautiful girl,' Aidan commented. 'You don't mind me saying that, do you?'

'No, it's fine.' Alice couldn't look at him, didn't want him to notice her brimming eyes.

'Because it's just an observation. I'm not into perving after teenagers. I bet you looked just like that at her age. Which reminds me, has Joss said anything to you about photos for the book? Are you the keeper of the family albums or is she in charge of that too?'

Alice laughed. 'What do you think? Have a guess? Actually I'm not sure what she's done with photos. Joss tended to be photographed by people who wanted to keep the shots for their own uses, magazine articles and that. I don't really know how much she's kept for herself. I don't remember ever seeing her with a camera when Harry and I were kids. Arthur used to take some of all of us together sometimes, on the beach and round the garden and things.' Alice thought for a moment, then added, 'Besides, is she likely to want to put in any that aren't just of her? Sorry. That sounded catty.'

'Yes it did rather. I'll put it down to you still feeling a bit hard-done-by from yesterday, shall I?'

'Yeah, I know. And as Grace would say, "Get over it".'

'That would be the grown-up thing to do.'

It was possible he wasn't just referring to Joss, but Alice chose to assume he was. She pushed her hand into the warm sand and let it trickle through her fingers. Only inches beneath the dry heat the grains were damp and cold. She wondered if female turtles, clambering up the Caribbean beaches, understood their eggs would be cooked and killed if they didn't lay them deep enough. How brilliant it must be to be a creature that came complete with such inborn wisdom and why did humans, who assumed they were so clever, seem to be born with none at all?

'Grown-up isn't the thing I do best when I'm with Jocelyn,' she told Aidan. 'She brings out the stroppy kid in me.'

'I wouldn't have thought she'd have minded you being a stroppy kid. I thought she was well into rebellion.'

Alice laughed. 'But mine took such a contrary form: lying on the beach for hours reading books about boarding school and normal families, worrying about whether Harry and the other kids had properly balanced meals or were all going to perish from lentil overdose. All those secret exams.'

'So when other kids your age were sneaking out to all-night parties and smoking spliffs out of their bedroom windows, you were swotting up on quadratic equations?'

'Hmm,' Alice agreed. 'That's about the size of it. She wouldn't have minded at all about the other stuff but maths and history, that was what any old ordinary child did. We were supposed to be "different".'

'Arty sort of different?'

'Oh yes, absolutely. The minute we were big enough to hold a brush we were practically drowned in vats of poster paints. That little room by the back door where Harry keeps the potato sacks and racks of vegetables, that must have been a boot room or something originally, well that was full of kit – enough to stock a decent-sized art supply shop. We had all sorts of paper, every size of brush, oil paints, watercolours, tubes and tubes of gouache, lino-cutting stuff, screen-printing equipment, anything we could need. I think Jocelyn must have been given a Winsor and Newton catalogue to choose from and simply said, "OK, get me the lot." And Milly taught us all to draw, you know, properly. Those were the only really formal lessons I remember. At one time there were six of us kids in Gosling every afternoon, all silent with easels and a life model, for hours and hours.'

'Were you any good?' Aidan asked.

Alice considered for a moment. 'Absolutely useless when it came to drawing, but I loved playing with colour. I'm the same now. Give me a rack full of Sanderson shade cards and I'm as happy as . . .'

'. . . Cheese and onion, a couple of steaks, two chicken and leek and a mushroom one.' Grace flumped down onto the sand with her bag of hot pasties. Alice, startled and with her mind still on colour wheels,

121

imagined a row of mushrooms lying with their undersides showing, all in delectable shades of pinky fawns like the tummies of piglets.

The boys were coming out of the water, running up the sand yelling and laughing and playing some game that involved jabbing their bodyboards at each other's feet. All the earlier sullen silence had vanished. Alice peered down the beach, checking that it wasn't just the twins making all the noise, but they seemed to be including Theo quite cheerily in their joshing about. It was the first time she'd seen Sam and Chas behaving like ordinary, relaxed kids. As they approached they became quiet, moving close together, glancing covertly at the adults and obviously talking plans and secrets that she and Aidan weren't intended to hear.

The beach-browsing seagulls, attracted by the scent of the pasties, collected close to Alice's picnic rug. Theo hurled bits of pasty far beyond them to make them move away but they were soon back, squawking and jostling and seeming to dare each other to grab food from human hands.

'Don't feed them Theo, you're only encouraging them,' Alice warned him, but he exchanged glances with Sam and Chas and the three of them spluttered into crumb-strewn giggles which had the big fearless birds pecking right around their feet.

'Here, use this.' Chas put his hand into his bag and pulled out his catapult.

'I don't think that's . . .' Alice began, then stopped as Theo fired a pastry missile far out towards the sea. Amazingly a couple of the birds flew after it.

'Too far,' Sam muttered.

'Yeah! I'll go for halfway,' Theo said, reloading.

'Down to where they're flying,' Chas pointed to gulls

wheeling over the holidaymakers, selecting the ones with food. 'And aim it high.'

Theo fired again and a bird caught the morsel of pastry in its mouth, then dived down to the sea. Sam and Chas cheered loudly.

'Let me!' Chas grabbed the weapon and loaded it with something from a small plastic box that he'd taken from his bag. Alice couldn't see what was in it, but was suspicious that he'd carefully put it on the side of him that was hidden from her. Whatever he was firing, the gulls seemed to like it and swallowed piece after piece whole.

'What are they up to?' Aidan murmured to Alice. 'They've got a devil look about them.'

Alice thought so too, but all she could make out was that they were simply enjoying firing the catapult to feed the gulls.

'Theo, you're not using . . .' Grace began, looking worried.

'Using what?' Alice chipped in. 'You're not using poison of any sort, are you?'

Sam looked at her in a pitying way. 'Poison? Where would we get poison?'

'Slug bait, rat poison. I bet Harry's got both those in one of the sheds.'

'There wouldn't be slug stuff, he's or-gan-ic.' Sam's expression could hardly have been more condescending. As Alice was still looking at him, wondering what great entertainment these boys were finding in supplying food to greedy gulls, there was a minor but distinct explosion further down the beach. Small children started screaming. Alice heard shouts and swearing from a party of sunbathers. A girl stood up, her pale blue swimsuit splattered with what looked like blood.

'Result!' Sam chuckled, grabbing pellets of what looked like bread from the box beside Chas and quickly firing them into the air.

Another explosion, closer this time, sent a gull hurtling down onto the family closest to them. The Nigel Pargetter man turned and stared at Alice, puzzled and suspicious, before emptying a box of tissues to wipe down his wailing children.

'Jesus, what the fuck . . . ?' Aidan said, leaping up to see what had happened. 'That poor gull plummeted down like a bomb!'

Sam, Chas and Theo were now rolling about on the sand, helpless with laughter.

'It works! It works!' Sam spluttered joyously.

'Oh you are *sooo* juvenile,' Grace told them, gathering her clothes, towel, book and bag together.

Two more gulls crashed dead to the sand and the three boys cheered each one loudly. A third bird blew up in mid-air, falling to the ground, at the same time scattering its remains across a barbecue of nearly cooked sausages.

'Best yet!' Sam yelled, dancing triumphantly up and down on the sand.

'Sit down, you evil child!' Alice hissed at him, aware that the boys' antics were drawing attention to their party. Whatever had they done to those poor birds? All heads on the beach seemed to be turning their way to where Chas stood waving his catapult for everyone to see and bowing as if to acknowledge his achievements.

'OK, that's it. Get your stuff, we're going. Now.' Alice had her rug folded and clipped neatly into place within seconds and she shepherded the still-laughing boys up the steps to the road. Aidan and Grace followed.

'You vicious little brats, all of you,' she said as she

bundled the boys, sandy wet bodyboards and all, into the car. 'We'll be lucky if no-one's followed us to get the car number and report you to the RSPCA. What in hell do you think you're playing at? And what did you kill those birds with?'

'Sodium bicarb and stuff from their school lab.' Theo managed to get the words out through his giggles.

'Only wrapped a ton of it in bread didn't we?' Sam bragged. Alice was appalled – the boy was delighted with himself and had no concept of the cruelty of his acts. Was the child a psychopath in the making? Were all three of them?

'When they go in the sea and get water,' Chas was now explaining calmly, as if narrating a valid experiment, 'the stuff swells up in their gullet and goes bang. Simple.'

'Not simple, wicked. Downright wicked.' Alice glared at them by way of the rear-view mirror as she drove fast out of the town.

'Wicked's right,' Theo chuckled.

'Not your meaning of wicked. I mean evil, sinful, vicious, immoral, mean, foul, atrocious . . .'

'You know a lot of words, Alice.' Sam looked quite awe-struck.

'It's her job. She writes,' Grace told him.

Fuming, Alice sped through Hayle and hurtled as fast as she could back to Tremorwell, convinced every time she looked in the mirror and saw a pale car following that the police were on her tail. Grace slumped into a corner staring out at the fields, and the boys and Aidan lapsed into silence. Thank God, she thought, as she turned up the Penmorrow driveway and could see that no car was in pursuit. On Monday she would take Theo and Grace back to London, away from these lawless, wild brothers.

Hardly able to see for fury, Alice slewed the Galaxy into the turning place at the front of the house, setting the wind chimes clanging. A taxi was just pulling away. The sainted Patrice, she assumed, but then in the front doorway there, unexpected, unannounced and, she realized with shocked disloyalty, unwelcome, was Noel.

'Alice. Darling, hello!' he greeted her, opening the car door and helping her out. 'Have you all had a lovely day?'

Eight

Jocelyn lit the four purple candles that she had lined up on her window ledge in small plain silver holders. The scent of lavender drifted onto the air, which Jocelyn wasn't too keen on. It was a scent which from childhood she'd associated with old ladies and she certainly didn't intend to count herself among their number, not for a long time yet. And if the day did arrive when she was ready to concede she had achieved glorious ancientness, she wasn't going to be a cardiganed bundle with cauliflower hair, tartan slippers and that sickly decay-masking scent. Still, it was the colour that was important here and she'd been lucky to find these candles in the cupboard under the stairs where, among the dusters, floor mops and brooms, boxes of plain household candles were stored for the frequent times of winter power failure.

Many years ago she'd kept a special shelf crammed with fat, waxy church candles, multicoloured candles with spicy scents, short chubby black and red ones for celebrating the autumn and spring festivals of Samhain and Imbolg, along with the slender gold ones that were lit for Yule. She missed having a houseful of people for these seasonal celebration times. Lammastide had just passed with no ceremony to mark it. Perhaps, while the family were there, she'd do something about that. There would be Patrice and his crew as well – it would be good to lay on something special for them. The spirit of the passing season wouldn't mind too much about a bit of mistiming.

Next, she rolled back the oval plaited rug that lay between her bed and the window. Kelpie had made this, thirty, probably closer to forty, years before, braiding together long swathes of silky fabrics in night-shade purple and applemint green and acorn brown. There'd been an argument, she remembered, when Milly had accused Kelpie of stealing some of the lengths of material that hung from her wall in order to finish the project. Small, skinny Milly had slapped Kelpie's face and Kelpie, a solidly built tall woman, had swatted Milly aside like a cat flicking away a wasp and sent her flying against a door frame, where she'd cut her head open right across her eyebrow.

Jocelyn sat on the bed, puffed from rolling the heavy rug. She remembered Kelpie offering to stitch the cut herself using her finest patchwork needle, and Milly locking herself in the downstairs cloakroom, shrieking, bleeding and terrified that she'd be held down and forcibly sewn up. In the end Arthur and a visiting playwright from New Zealand had driven her to the nearest Casualty department, and after her treatment calmed her down with enough cider at a Falmouth pub to knock her into a coma for the night.

The floorboards beneath the rug were darker than those that surrounded it, not being bleached out by the morning sun streaming in through the window. The colours of the rug too were drained away to flat tones of murky swamp shades, reminding Jocelyn of moss on a damp stone wall. Grave colours, she thought. Sombre and earthy and dank. She didn't want a grave, she'd decided. They reverted to scrubby neglect too quickly and she didn't agree with making a fetish of the dead, mawkishly tending nasty, marble chipped plots with gaudy flowers in jars that became slimy with algae and spattered muddy rain. She would be cremated and then her ashes would be scattered on Arthur's grave. She'd told Mo where her funeral instructions were, though she wasn't sure she trusted her to carry them out – she might think her request to have the Rolling Stones 'Sympathy for the Devil' played as her coffin was committed to the flames was merely a joke. It wasn't – she was fond of the memory of their poor dear doomed guitarist Brian Jones sitting on the Penmorrow porch in late afternoon sun, gently playing his sitar, his blond hair gleaming like the last of the day's rays.

Ideally she'd be burned high on a blazing driftwood pyre at sunset on Tremorwell's beach and the entire village would turn out for a good send-off party with mead and marijuana all round, but this was a more legally cowed age than in her youth and she'd have to make do with the crematorium over at Truro. How many people would come, she wondered. Would her obituary be gratifyingly prominent in the newspapers? She had composed four versions (one for each of the broadsheets) and she kept them updated when there was anything significant to add. These days there rarely was, but with her biography and Patrice's programme, she – or Aidan, for surely this could be delegated to him – should be able to add a few more relevant lines.

Jocelyn clutched the side of the bed as she bent to draw a circle on the floor with blue chalk. She stretched her arm out as far as she could and hoped it wouldn't be a problem that some of the circle extended under the bed. Her joints and muscles still felt lithe and pliable, thanks to years of daily yoga, but her balance was no longer to be trusted and she was conscious that her frame was weak and her breath was short. She felt her bones being dried out and becoming brittle, like old wood that's been too long in the wind and sun. When she looked down at the floor, things took a while to focus, as if her eyesight was having trouble keeping up to speed with her head. It was like being drunk. In fact that was exactly what it was like, she thought as she dusted the blue chalk from her fingertips, it was the same as being mildly and unpleasantly drunk but with no chance of recovery, and none of the lovely anything-possible recklessness about it. She would happily endure the worst-ever hangover just to get her old strong sense of self back again.

Perhaps this would do it. This charm to nourish the wits and renew the powers was well worth a shot. Jocelyn put a small dish containing sprigs of lavender soaked in oil in the centre of her blue circle. Alongside she placed stalks of blue vervain collected that morning from the herb garden outside the kitchen, and a long length of black silk cord that had once been threaded through the hood of Arthur's black velvet cloak. Then she stepped into the circle, sat cross-legged on the floor and with the chalk wrote around the circle's circumference while murmuring the words:

Verbena hastata, Quattuor elementa, Quattuor loco, Hasta verbena, Viam monstra.

She tied the vervain stalks together, using the cord, and dipped the ends into the oil. With this wand she retraced the chalk circle. From downstairs she could hear people arriving, people talking in loud urban voices. Patrice? Already? She tried hard not to be distracted as she gently covered the oiled, inscribed floor with the rug again. No-one must know what she'd done. If they found the circle, Mo and Alice knew enough of spellcraft to recognize from this that she'd felt vulnerable, had needed help from the powers to top up her vital wisdom. Slowly and with great care, clutching the door frame tight as she stepped onto a firm wooden chair, she climbed up and hung the vervain wand high above her door, on the inside where no-one could see it to speculate on what it meant. It was a shame, she thought, as she stepped back down to the floor, that Alice hadn't passed a working knowledge of these natural arts on to Grace. The girl should have spent more time at Penmorrow. She should have been educated in more useful skills than any so-called education system could give her. At least, she hoped they were useful: she would see over the next weeks if her health and energy were restored.

'Aren't you pleased to see me?' Noel was saying it in that teasing way that was confident of getting an exuberant 'Of course, darling!' by way of a reply. He was unpacking his bag and trying to find space for shirts in the tiny wardrobe in the Gosling bedroom. Alice was slamming about with the chest of drawers, moving her clothes around so he'd have room for his. He seemed to have brought quite a lot, though whether that was because he'd moved in for the summer's duration or because in the west side of England you could need to cater for at least three seasons'-worth of weather per weekend, she couldn't work out. She didn't want to ask him. She was already ashamedly conscious that her fury with the boys had made her

131

grumpy and unwelcoming – she'd barely said hallo to the over-jolly, large-scale young woman in the short slinky dress and strappy high shoes who'd arrived with Noel. If she now asked, 'How long are you staying?' in her current mood, he could only interpret it as, 'How soon are you going?'

The drawers in the chest had swollen from years of damp air and were sticking. Noel thought privately that Alice was being unnecessarily violent with them – surely she only needed to manipulate them gently to get them to budge. Shoving hard wasn't the way to results.

'Here, let me,' he said, taking hold of her hands and moving her aside. She snatched her arms away from him.

'Noel, I can do this. I'm quite capable.'

He backed off, hands raised. 'OK, OK, look, I know. And I know you hate surprises so would you rather I just went back to London? Only it was a bit of a slow service today and if you don't mind I'd rather get a night's sleep before I get back on the train again.'

Alice sat down heavily on the bed and ran her hands through her hair, pushing it back off her face. Her nose and the skin above her cheekbones were a livid sun-scorched pink and her hair was overbleached and looked unusually coarse. This wasn't, Noel noted, the usual sleek London Alice. Her skin was slick with the heat. She smelled of seashore and had damp sand on her toes and the absence of her normal sheeny, clean 'finish' was affecting him in the same rather smutty loin-stirring way that the girl on the train (Kathy? Katie?) did. In fact, if Alice hadn't been in such a spiky mood he'd have had a go at a fast and furious roll-around on the bed. Given the 'by

132

appointment' nature of their sex life, that would be taking her by surprise in two senses.

'You've caught the sun,' he commented, reaching out a finger to stroke the tip of her nose. She pulled her head back, but calmly now, without anger. And at last she smiled, showing a pale fan of lines at the outer edges of her eyes.

'I know. It takes seconds. Factor fifteen moisturizer just can't cope.' She was relaxing at last. 'Look Noel . . .' she began, standing up and going to the window.

'What's wrong? Is it Jocelyn? Is she being difficult?' When wasn't she, he wondered silently.

'No, well, partly. Sorry, I'm just a bit stressed. You won't believe what the boys did today on the beach. Theo as well, I'm afraid. You'll have to talk to him.'

But she could tell, as soon as she'd related the day's events, that he wouldn't. She could see his mouth twitching at the corners in a hopeless attempt to make sure she didn't catch him laughing. He was more likely to clasp Theo to him in 'that's ma boy' style. What was so funny about killing small wild creatures? Was this a man-thing? A hunting-instinct thing? Or did it come under Applied Science? She'd never, she realized, understand the male psyche.

Supper was a simple chicken-leg and lamb-chop barbecue out on the side terrace, just off the kitchen. Alice had marinaded the meat in oil, lemon and herbs but as she carried the big wooden bowl containing a rocket and Parmesan salad out to the old sun-bleached table she wondered if Noel's train companion, Australian Katie (or 'Kay-dee?' as she'd uttered it in an Antipodean upward lilt) would think their English cook-out efforts paltry compared with the barbies of her home nation. Katie was a strong-looking girl with chunkily muscled arms that made her spaghetti-strapped, flounce-hemmed little cotton dress seem oddly incongruous. In spite of teetering around on pink jewelled mules that a hundred yards of Cornish cliff-path walking would completely demolish, she looked like someone who could single-handedly spear a speeding kangaroo, skin it and have the thing turning on an outback spit with no trouble at all. Alice imagined her perched on a fallen tree trunk under the vast Queensland sky, perfecting a French manicure while the beast sizzled over the flame. Alice laid out the cutlery and watched Katie opening a bottle of wine, hauling out the cork with no more effort than if she was pulling a thread from a needle. Noel was also watching her a lot, Alice noticed. He was hanging around, getting in Mo's way, poking at the barbecue's flames and pretending to be useful, scraping bits of ancient rust from the old Weber's frame while Mo flicked him impatiently away with a spatula as she turned the meat.

Patrice was going to be late, by twenty-four hours. Katie explained that she'd been sent on ahead to check out the venue, as she put it, and report back about what they'd need for the shoot.

'Just lights and stuff?' she told them all as they sat at the wooden garden table where Theo was obsessively chipping off bits of lichen and piling it into a row of little heaps, exactly parallel to his knife. 'I mean it's whether he'll need his full rig or just the essentials.' She grinned around at them all, assuming they'd have some idea what she was talking about. Joss nodded solemnly as if she did. It was some years since she'd been in the media spotlight and the last occasion had involved a truckload of technicians, a small van dedicated entirely to sound production and most of the village finding an urgent reason why they needed to pop into Penmorrow for a good gawp.

'Nah, it's not like that now. Then it was union rules, you had to have a stack of folks for every little job. All that's gone,' Katie said, dismissing Harry's anxious murmur about parking arrangements and a high-season village shortage of B. & B. accomodation. 'Be just me and Patrice I guess, oh and the camera guy.'

'No make-up artist? No stylist?' Grace looked disappointed. She knew about this: these were jobs that some of her friends' parents did – including Sophy's supremely glamorous mum who, Alice recalled, had sported neon-pink Prada trainers in the mothers' race back in Grace's prep-school days.

'No sorry guys, it's a budget-aware era, this.'

Alice watched Noel watching Katie pick up a chop bone and gnaw at it, head slightly on one side like a cat chewing a mouse. She was surprised she felt so detached about seeing him so obviously attracted. Somehow, confusingly, she felt she'd mind more if Katie was getting the same attention from Aidan. Aidan, on the other hand, wasn't showing any interest in the girl at all. He was further along the table and had bravely placed himself between Chas and Sam, possibly intending to keep them from getting up to any mealtime mischief. Alice felt grateful, recognizing that it was Jocelyn he was concerned for. If these two juvenile demons (plus of course Theo, who was old enough to know far better) were tempted to try to add to their murderous tally here on the premises, Joss would not be at all amused. Or at least Alice assumed she wouldn't be – as always you could never tell with Jocelyn. She could go either way – compliment the boys on a cleverly learnt survival skill or be as angry

135

as a transatlantic sailor whose crew has proudly shot an albatross.

'So you Brits haven't caught up with proper barbies?' Katie asked Mo, who was handing round a bowl of fragrant lemon rice. They all turned to look at the rusty, crusty old Weber that had a broom handle where the third of its leg tripod should be, and which leaked copious thick smoke from beneath its warped lid.

'It does for us,' Mo said frostily. 'It's not as if we use it very often.'

Katie laughed. 'Yeah I can see that!' Jocelyn raised her eyebrows, alert to the girl's unrestrained lack of tact.

Alice thought again of the image of Katie beside a roaring pit of fire with her kill suspended over it.

'We all have huge gas-powered things, with built-in spits and separately controlled grill areas. Nice to see a more primitive spirit lives on in this crazy old place though.' She gave a small trill of laughter and then added, 'God, listen to me. The stuff I come out with! Take no notice folks, I've got no mental editing facility. I just come out with everything I'm thinking!'

'Nothing wrong with that, my dear.' Joss reached across and took hold of Katie's wrist. 'I'm just the same. You and I will get on terrifically.'

Katie, her attention now on a meaty chicken thigh, did not notice the sharp glint in Jocelyn's eye. But Alice did and recognized that her mother had said exactly the opposite of what she truly meant.

Grace walked down the hill to the beach by herself after supper. She'd asked Theo to come with her: they often went down to the shore together in the early evenings to skim stones into the flat sea and then have

136

a drink (Coke for her, illicit Stella for him) on the sea wall across the road from the pub. Tonight she'd particularly wanted to get him back to herself again, away from Chas and Sam. He wasn't really like them, they were too young and wild and silly for him, but, having heard a programme in her mum's car about alpha males and bonding rituals, she could understand why he wanted them to let him join in with the stupid things they did. She realized he'd keep doing stupid stuff till he was better at something than them, then he'd have proved himself to be top dog and stop. Tonight, Theo had said he thought he should hang out with his dad, seeing as he'd come all that way to surprise them. Grace's personal opinion on this was that she didn't see why Noel should expect them all to stop doing things they usually did just to enjoy his sainted presence.

Grace had Jocelyn's binoculars slung round her neck and she was heading for the lower slopes of the far cliff to see if she could spot the rabbit that she'd set free. It shouldn't be difficult, the creature was big and white and should be pretty easy to pick out grazing in the twilight. Her cat Monty trotted along beside her, his head pert and his ears flickering constantly at the faintest rustling sounds in the undergrowth. Where the path met the village road he'd stop, miaow after her for a few worried moments, then head back for Gosling and his own hunting ground.

She didn't feel at all nervous being alone in the dusk, but revelled in the freedom to walk where she chose. She didn't go out by herself in the evenings back at home. She didn't know any other girls who did, either. If they went out to a party or to see a film they were delivered and collected by car, as if the busy suburban streets were full of pervy murderers or pre-teen mobile-phone muggers lying in wait for defenceless girls. It was brilliant here. Her mother seemed to think bad stuff like that wouldn't happen and Grace felt as if she had, like the cat, a personal territory with no real boundaries other than the distance she could cover on foot.

The village shop was just closing up. Mrs Rice was picking up a box of courgettes from the vegetable selection outside the store. 'Your uncle Harry should grow these,' she called out to Grace as she approached. 'We could soon shift them here.' Grace doubted it, the box Mrs Rice was carrying looked full and heavy.

'He does grow them,' she said. 'He sells them to the organic shop down at Chapel Creek.'

'Oh well, *organic*.' Mrs Rice sniffed. 'That's a bit of a fancy thing. An excuse for fancy prices too. It'll just be a fad, you know, what folks round here want is *value*.'

Grace smiled politely, feeling unqualified to argue any kind of case, and went to walk on past the shop. Mrs Rice hadn't finished with her. 'So what else does Uncle Harry grow up there in his plastic tunnels?' A note of sly inquisitiveness in her voice made Grace wary. Theo had said he was growing a load of dope but had also told her that Chas and Sam had dried some of the leaves and smoked it but it wasn't any good.

'Tomatoes, aubergines, peppers, that sort of thing,' Grace said, thinking quickly and listing the contents of her mother's luscious ratatouille recipe. 'And garlic and shallots and onions and all sorts of stuff really.'

Mrs Rice stood square in front of the shop doorway, resting the box of courgettes on her hips and looking as if she was expecting additional information. 'I wouldn't mind coming up and taking a look myself,' she said. 'See if I can get my Bill interested. After all if there's a profit in *organic*, it might be worth looking into.' She gave Grace a smile that didn't quite hide suspicion and disappeared into the shop.

'You don't have to do that.' Mo took the pile of dirty plates from Katie and clattered them down hard on the draining board.

'No? Oh, but I like to do my bit, join in, you know?' Katie made a move towards the tea towel that hung on the Aga rail but Mo was too quick for her.

'Alice and I can manage. It's a fine starry night. Why don't you go and sit outside on the porch?' Katie looked doubtful.

'Take the rest of the wine,' Alice suggested. 'Noel's out there.'

'OK, no worries.' Katie's dainty shoes tripped across the rough flag floor as she went out. Jocelyn had gone to bed early, to be fresh, she'd told Alice privately, for Patrice's arrival the next day. Aidan had gone to his room to sort out notes for a complicated chapter about Jocelyn's time in New York with Andy Warhol, and the boys had gone to watch something lurid and violent on the TV in the twins' room. Alice could smell cigarettes: this was one house that Noel felt free to smoke in and she could hear the swing seat on the verandah creaking gently. There were tiny lights out there, little star-shaped silvery things strung along the length of the porch which gave an almost glamorous feel to the old place, casting wispy angular shadows over the flaking purple paintwork and splintery wood. The wind chimes by the doorway jangled softly.

'What do you think of her?' Mo whispered, jerking

her head in the direction of the doorway as soon as Katie was out of sight.

'Katie? She's all right, why?'

Mo frowned and shoved a pair of plates into the last available slot in the dishwasher.

'She's not all right, she's trouble.'

Alice laughed, then wished she hadn't. Mo straightened up and scowled ferociously at her. It just wasn't possible to explain to Mo that she wasn't laughing *at* her, only at her instant decision that Katie was 'trouble'. Was this what happened if you never travelled beyond the county boundary?

Mo shook her shaggy head at her as if in despair that Alice couldn't see what she could see. The kitchen light shone through her cloud of parched wiry hair strands and through the thin cheesecloth fibres of her white smock top, making Mo look as if her entire self was a loosely woven being. It was an odd illusion: she usually gave an impression of utter solidity, plodding around the place in her splay-footed plum-coloured single-strapped shoes, broad, flat and roomy as a baby's first sandal. And she seemed weighed down by layers of clothes, the smock tops over voluminous crushed velvet skirts over ancient broderie anglaise petticoats that she'd found in a chest in the attic. Now, charged with some demonic feeling of premonition, Alice had the impression that she was close to levitating.

'She's after your Noel, that one,' Mo went on, flinging knives into their slots in the machine with frightening accuracy. Chillingly, Alice had a vision of herself standing barefoot on the damp dewy grass while Mo aimed daggers at her toes. She smiled at Mo, trying to erase the image. 'Oh I don't suppose she is, I expect she's just a friendly sort,' she said, then added, before she could stop herself, 'and anyway, if you really think that's true, why did you insist she go out there?'

Mo turned from the dishes and smiled at her. 'To see what would happen,' she told her. 'We simple country folk take our entertainment where we can get it. And anyway, you were the one who told her to take the wine and go and sit with Noel.'

Mo left the room before Alice could think of a retort. Alice filled the sink and started washing the salad bowls and sharp knives, splashing them about crossly. There were no sounds from the verandah other than the slight creaking of the seat. It was rhythmic, insistent, as if a couple were having leisurely sex on a squeaky bed. The thought of sex brought Aidan to her mind, not Noel, and she tried to banish the picture that was taking shape in her head, of herself and Aidan continuing what had started up against the old oak tree. Light footsteps sounded behind her and she looked round, half-expecting him to have guessed at her reverie and turned up to drag her out to get on with it. Instead, Noel was there with two empty glasses.

'Another bottle, I think,' he said, putting the glasses on the table, then pulling her towards him and squeezing her tight against him. 'Unless . . .' he went on, nuzzling her hair, 'unless we make a dash for the cottage and get a passion session in before Grace gets back. What do you say?'

Alice pushed him away gently. 'And what about Theo? He sleeps on the sofa bed just below our room. Every creak and squeak . . .'

'Ah but he's watching telly with the primitive cousins. Ah come on Alice, it's been ages.' He closed in on her again and put a hand behind her back, pulling her against him. 'And feel for yourself.' He took her hand – oblivious to it being wet and sudsy from the sink – and held it against the taut front of his chinos. 'See? I'm feeling very pleased to see you!'

He sounded a bit drunk and smelled of too many cigarettes. Alice considered for a moment. Years ago she'd been an avid reader of agony columns in women's magazines. If she was now asking, 'Shall I, shan't I?' she knew the answer had to be, 'Yes you should.' Instead she disentangled her hand from his and smiled at him. 'Better save it for another time, Noel. When it'll be a bit less risky.'

'Ah, "risky",' he said, his leer turning to a sneer. 'Well you wouldn't want to do anything "risky", now would you Alice? Shall we book an hour in for Thursday week then? Got your diary?'

'Ssh! Do you want the whole house to hear you?' she hissed at him. 'I only meant what's the point of starting something that will have to be stopped the minute the kids walk into the house? You can hear every whisper in Gosling. When I'm trying to get to sleep I can even hear the bloody cat purring downstairs!' But he'd gone. Grabbing another bottle, the glasses and the corkscrew all in a swift manoeuvre, he'd swung out of the door. Alice turned back to her dishes, feeling like a foolish Cinderella, and out on the verandah the swing seat creaked on.

There were loads of rabbits up on the top of the hill but from where she was, only halfway up, Grace couldn't see her white one. A couple of times she thought he was there, but it was always one of the cross-breeds, a wild ordinary taupe one with a flash of white across its back or a black one with white patches. She climbed further up the cliff, slightly nervous now that it was almost properly dark. The layout of the shrubs and undergrowth was less familiar to her than on the Penmorrow side. Here, she couldn't immediately tell which places she should race past in case a crazed murderer was lurking in the hope of finding a lone wandering female. Far more likely, and almost worse because it was so possible, was that round any dense shrub there could be a couple having torrid sex. Theo had once told her that Sam had said he'd seen someone doing exactly that up on this cliffside. Of course that probably wasn't true. It was the sort of thing Sam and Chas would invent to impress Theo and make him think they knew stuff that he didn't. Hardly likely – Theo had more girls from her school with his number stored in their phones than any other boy in his year. Even Sophy's mum (a *mum*!) when she came to pick up Sophy from their house, did that silly smiley thing and flicked her hair about if he was there.

Grace was almost at the top of the hill now, creeping slowly and carefully so as not to frighten any rabbits. Just ahead she could see some by the old bench, grazing in the gloom and not seeming to care that she was there. She wondered if that was because some of them were crossed with pet-shop ones and were half tame. Surely then, they'd have been easy prey for foxes? Missing her step on the path, she kicked a big stone which clattered down towards the beach. The rabbits scattered, racing off in different directions among the trees. Grace caught a glimpse of a big flash of white as they ran. So he was safe, the latest rabbit, so far.

Grace sat on the bench and looked out across the bay. The lights on the Penmorrow porch made the

143

place look a bit like a ship's deck with its rigging all festively lit. The Big Shepherd statue on the grass in front of the house was a looming silhouette, surely enough to frighten off anyone who thought they'd go burgling at the house. She could see someone moving about so she raised her binoculars to view what was happening over there. The Australian woman, Katie, was sitting on the swing seat, one long leg crossed over the other. The binoculars were good ones – Joss used them for bird-watching up at the Hayle estuary and had told her that through them she could make out the brands of shampoo on bathroom window ledges half a mile away. Katie had her shoe hanging off, dangling from her foot. Grace had liked the shoes. They were London ones, high and long and pointy, the sort her mother wore for parties and Sophy's mum wore any old time. Noel came into view just then and sat next to Katie on the swing seat. Grace watched him hand her a glass of wine. Then, mystified, she watched him take hold of Katie's foot, place it on his lap and start massaging it.

Katie didn't look very comfortable, Grace thought, with her leg crossed high up and hauled across to Noel. *She* didn't feel completely comfortable now either, as she realized that this was something she maybe shouldn't be watching. Then Noel released the foot and ran his hand slowly up Katie's leg. What the hell did he think he was doing, Grace wondered, and where was her mum? The hand didn't stop when it got to the edge of Katie's skirt either, but disappeared beneath. Katie was lying back in the seat, her long hair draped over the back of it. Instead of clamping her knees together and brushing Noel's hand away, she was sprawled out like a relaxed cat, enjoying herself, enjoying him.

Quickly Grace moved the binoculars to another part of the house. She focused on the sitting-room window, the hexagonal one with the all-round view. Jocelyn was there, standing like one of Arthur's statues, watching Noel and Katie. Grace knew she'd never tell what she saw; Jocelyn wouldn't either, but she'd make sure Noel knew what she knew.

Nine

Alice was down in the kitchen early, making herself a pot of tea really quietly so that she didn't disturb Theo. Noel was all right, he was so deeply asleep that only a screaming Harrier jet from the nearby naval base would stir him. Grace too was comatose, stretched across her bed with one foot poking out from beneath the duvet and the plump tabby body of her cat sprawled on top of her. The white patch of fur under Monty's chin had a pinkish tinge to it. Blood from a recently devoured mouse, Alice guessed, seeing as he hadn't leapt up and raced down the stairs ahead of her in crazed anticipation of a tin being opened.

In the sitting room Alice could see Theo snuggled deep into his pillows with his mobile phone, like a comfort toy, propped up on the arm of the sofa bed. For a teenager he was a relatively light sleeper, and Alice tiptoed around the kitchen hoping he wouldn't wake up and decide that this was a good time to do some talking. Knowing that she'd been so furious with him over the seagulls, his way of getting back into favour would be to sit with her and chat, on the basis that few adults can resist a teenager who is making an effort to connect. He'd noisily munch toast and marmalade (having picked out any bits of peel and heaped them up like kindling for a miniature fire) and chatter away about almost anything that came into his head, rambling on about football or music, about his exams and which universities he should apply to, all to make her feel that he needed her and cared about her opinions. He might be a moody teenager, he'd be telling her, but as a special concession he could do the thing called 'conversation' when necessary.

Normally she would – as intended – find this flattering as well as enlightening, but today, less than an hour after waking, she was already feeling exhausted at the thought of the week ahead, of Jocelyn swanning around glorying in the flattering attentions of Patrice, and of Mo feeling even more harassed and hard-done-by but stubbornly hanging onto her martyr's role as chief overworked domestic dogsbody. Harry had admitted that it had been bad enough when Aidan (whom he'd at least stopped calling The Ghost) had arrived. Joss had gone supremely grand, he'd grumbled, barely deigning to light her own cigarettes, and had, at mealtimes, sat haughtily at the head of the table waiting like an empress for her food to be served, scorning to carry so much as a single dish.

'She ordered Mo to go and mix her another gin and tonic once, exactly as if she was some useless servant,' he told Alice. 'She'd poured the first one straight onto the floor in disgust, all over the rug can you believe, and complained the ice was "off". How can ice go off? It's always fresh – God knows she gets through enough of it.'

'What did Mo do? Didn't she tell her to get lost?'

'She was so amazed, she just went and did what Joss said.'

'Well I suppose Joss wasn't quite herself then, don't

forget. Perhaps feeling ill affected her taste buds,' Alice reminded him. 'I'm sure Mo was just being kind.' Privately, Alice considered it had been a bad move on Mo's part. Jocelyn had always been rather imperious but now that she was heading fast into being less robust, it would be a mistake to give in to any foot-stamping episodes. They'd only get worse. On the other hand, Alice calculated, Mo, in her current mood, might enjoy having plenty to grouch about.

'Huh. I might have known you'd see it from her side,' Harry said. 'You always did take the opposite view.'

'Sorry. Only trying to keep a balance.'

And was it always such a good thing, this effort to see everything from both sides, Alice asked herself as she poured a virtuous non-fattening cereal and some semi-skimmed milk into a bowl. She'd tried doing that in her first marriage, only finding out too late that being constantly placatory and reasonable was one of the things that drove Paul, Grace's father, absolutely crazy, to the point of violence and beyond. Now she was in danger of doing it again with Noel. When she'd noticed him eyeing Katie in a blatantly lusting way, she'd put it down to a few weeks' lack of sex, as if it was all her own fault that he'd got a heightened libido level. On the other hand (there she went again . . .) she hadn't exactly gone out of her way to divert his sexual attention back to herself. That, and in her imagination the agony aunts of her teen years wagged their massed fingers, was probably a big marital mistake. What nagged her was that she'd done for once what suited only her, not the sensible thing, not what pleased somebody else. It was something at which she wasn't too practised.

Alice took her cereal and tea out through the kitchen

door and sat in the sun at the old marble table in the scrubby little neglected garden. Fat-flowered hydrangeas fought for air and space with dense camellias. Lemon balm had taken over what used to be a herb patch. Plant-wise, it was a true example of the fittest surviving. She reached down and pushed back some of the stems, delighted to reveal a row of stones set into the ground on which Arthur had carved a series of mouse families to amuse her and Harry many years before. He'd made up funny little stories about them as he worked, she remembered. Around and among these, fronds of chervil had colonized the cracks in the paving and where tough perennials used to flourish, bindweed had twined itself around the ferns and the wild geraniums and strangled most of the vitality out of them.

It wouldn't actually take much, Alice calculated as she looked around, to make this garden a stunning little gem. Worn-out city holidaymakers (*paying* holidaymakers) would surely love to sit here and relax in the sun, just as she did. Hacking back much of the shrubbery and the gloomy laurels would reveal a wonderful view out towards the sea. Clearing back the weeds would give struggling plants a chance to breathe and bloom again. The problem for Mo and Harry was that this 'not much' that it would 'take' was only one more item on the long, long list.

Alice went back into the kitchen and brought out her notebook and pen and started to make a list of her own. She would get Noel and Theo started on clearing this small patch of garden this morning, and they could mend the broken bench that was slumped lopsided like a collapsed drunk against the kitchen wall. Theo, after yesterday's debacle, wouldn't dare refuse and Noel would want to spend time with his son. She could use that little wheeled cart that Grace had rediscovered and fetch some of the big old pots that were abandoned near the chicken sheds and plant thick clumps of agapanthus in them. If Jocelyn objected to this just as she had with the painted kitchen, well it could all be abandoned to grow back to chaos in its own good time. For now though, Alice tipped the last third of her cereal down into the drain. She was pretty sure that the cardboard box it came in couldn't have tasted more dreary. She would go out later, find a proper supermarket and shop for food she really liked, starting with a big fat pack of butter-stuffed chocolate croissants.

Grace had finished *Angels' Choice* before she went to sleep and it had made her feel quite strange and emotionally bruised. The book had left her with a lot of questions, but one which *didn't* spring to mind was why hadn't her mother encouraged her to read it before now. Grace would have been surprised if she had – this wasn't at all a comfortable read. Grace couldn't have even begun to understand it a couple of years before, not like she had with *Tess of the D'Urbervilles* and *Wuthering Heights*.

The basic story was simple enough: Angel is fifteen and lives with her parents not far from her much more affluent uncle and aunt. Uncle Gordon is a top-level high court judge with an important career – her father is a struggling electrician. Angel babysits for her relatives' children and afterwards Uncle Gordon drives her home and rapes her in the back of his car. When she'd reached this point in the book Grace had felt like hurling it across the room, furious with Angel for not making enough effort to stop him. For God's sake, Grace wanted to shout at her, you don't get meekly into the back of a car in a dark alley (which also happened to be terrifyingly miles off the home-bound route) just because your uncle tells you to. *And* you fight him off! Angel didn't even try; she just lay there on the cold leather seat in her ripped clothes, mentally disconnected but physically almost compliant, passively waiting for it to be over. Jocelyn had gone full out with an almost sick-making sex scene here, all pig-like snorts and smells and greasy, heavy, pushing flesh. The uncle had blunt, stubby fingers, sweaty and waxy like fat crayons. Grace could almost feel them denting her own tender skin as she read. She had had to read these bits twice, make sure she was feeling revolted because that was how it was meant to be, not just because it was her own grandmother who'd written it. And then stupid dumb Angel had kept quiet about what had happened. So of course it all happened again. Big surprise, you stupid girl, Grace had thought. You just want to shake people like that, for being so wet and cowardly.

It was only when she read further that she started to understand how back then there were things too shameful to talk about. Social disgrace was a seriously fearful prospect. These days, it occurred to Grace, Angel would have not only dragged Uncle Gordon through the courts but also through the tabloid press and probably 'fessed up on something like *Kilroy* as well. When Angel realized she was pregnant and at last told who did this to her, she was simply not believed and was beaten by her father for incriminating his sainted, successful brother and accused of being a whore. Grace's fury at Angel turned then to outrage at her parents. Why would they think she was lying? Hers wouldn't. And then Angel was *ordered* to lie, to keep Uncle Gordon's career from being publicly wrecked and the comfortable family from being destroyed. That was Angel's ultimate choice – to bring shame and ruin to his (and her own) family, or to let herself be condemned and shunned as the local slut.

Some things astonished Grace about what it must have been like for a girl in Angel's position back in those days, especially the fact that in rape trials everyone got to know the victim's name as well as that of the person accused. She was also amazed by the stigma of unmarried pregnancy and the emotional price people were expected to pay to maintain even the most fragile, dishonest respectability. For her, it was like reading a social history book. And then there was the incest thing. Grace, brought up when child abuse was the bogeyman buzz-phrase of every newspaper and an early-evening storyline on *EastEnders*, found herself having to imagine a time when it was the last thing anyone would even think of daring to mention. No wonder, she thought, that the book was such a sensation in its day.

The problem with having read the book was that Grace now saw Jocelyn in a different light. From being a lovably eccentric woman with a wacky, star-studded and occasionally notorious past, Jocelyn had overnight turned into a person with issues and complications that Grace really didn't want to dwell on. Suppose Jocelyn *was* Angel? Suppose this had really all happened to her and she'd only been able to get her anger out by writing it down as fiction? Was that why she only wrote the one book? Some stuff you really didn't want to know, even though you were dying to ask. You weren't meant to know, not one generation to another. That morning when she pushed Monty off her legs and climbed out of bed, Grace needed a bit of time to think before she faced Jocelyn again. She wouldn't be able to help looking at her in an uncomfortably questioning way. There was also the horrible thing she'd seen Noel getting up to as well, with his hand snaking up Katie's skirt and Katie lying back enjoying it. She had no wish to see him either, in case something about his attitude made her want to tell her mother what she'd seen. Angel wasn't the only one with tricky decisions.

Grace crept to the stairs, peeking into her mother's room. Only Noel was there in the bed, breathing slowly and heavily, just short of snoring. He hadn't been a bad stepfather, she conceded, or at least she'd thought he hadn't. Suppose he did hands-up-the-skirt stuff with women all the time? And what a sodding pain that she had to think about this.

Grace found Alice out on the scruffy, overgrown little terrace. 'Hi Mum, is anything happening today? What time's that film man coming?' She almost whispered her question, afraid that the cottage would spring into life behind her with Noel bounding down the stairs eager to get on with the day. He might suggest (oh grim) they all go out and do something together As A Family. No way, no thanks, she thought.

'I hadn't got anything planned, just a bit of garden stuff,' Alice said, smiling up at her daughter. 'There's a couple of things I'd like Noel and Theo to do here but you and I could go out on our own if you like, though I want to get back in time to be here for when Patrice arrives and I told Mo I'd do supper, even though she was a bit sulky about the idea. Why, what do you fancy doing?'

Grace grinned at her. 'You never say that. Not at home.'

'Never say what?'

'You never say, "I haven't got anything planned."'

153

Stuff you do is *always* planned. All your days are written down. Now that you're here you're going all different.'

Alice pushed her hair back, twisted it up and secured it with a camellia twig. 'Just chillin', as you kids say. Anyway you haven't answered the question. What shall we do? Are you too old for the Seal Sanctuary?'

Grace wrinkled her nose up. 'Well, yeah, I suppose.' She was fidgety, jumping about on the chervil stems. 'Let's just go out, OK? Decide where once we're on the road.' She glanced inside the cottage, where all was still quiet. 'Let's go now, quick.'

'Well let me finish my cup of tea, and you must have some breakfast too.'

'I'll grab some on the way. Come on, Mum, please.' Grace hauled Alice out of her chair and sent her up the stairs to dress. Grace flung on her favourite Quiksilver baggies and a tee shirt, snatched a hooded fleece top and raced back down the stairs and out to the car. She hadn't even cleaned her teeth so she reached into the Galaxy's glove compartment to find chewing gum. Just for once, that would have to do.

Harry and Mo sat silent and peaceful on rickety cane chairs in the polytunnel with mugs of mint tea and the luxury of a spliff each for once, not a shared one. Harry was very pleased with his plants this year. There'd been plenty of sun and they were growing tall and bushy. The buds were forming well and were already sticky with resin, and the big fan leaves were just starting to fade to yellow. Soon it would be time for the harvest. The stems were sturdy and deeply ridged all the way up their length, like fat stalks of angelica. In their room at the top of the house Harry had a foot-long length he'd kept from one of his

154

best-ever stems. At the broadest end it was nearly five inches in diameter, and its hollow dried-out inside flesh was a pale primrose colour. He'd thought of making a pipe from it, or an instrument of some kind like a recorder, but as with many things, he hadn't got round to it. The stem sat on the mantelpiece, alongside bits of strange-shaped pebbles from the beach, old shells that Mo kept saying she'd make into mobiles and the big box of chicken feathers that were used when she made dream-catchers. One day, he thought, he'd get a binbag and simply sweep the lot into it and chuck it out for the binmen to take. It was going to be the only way to sort things, in the end, just give up and let go. If only Jocelyn would do the same with the rest of the house. And maybe even with the house itself.

Mo, he thought, was looking tired and dejected. She didn't say much these days, not to him anyway, and when she did speak she was snappy. She seemed caught up in faraway thoughts of her own and he hadn't been invited to share them. He didn't know what to say to her that would please her. When she'd complained about the care of Penmorrow being too much for them he'd done his best, getting Alice down from London. In fact, now he took a deep toke on the spliff and recalled in a heady blur of smoke, that had been Mo's idea. 'Alice should do her bit' – those had been her very words. The mood she was in these days, she'd deny it for sure. She seemed to resent Alice's presence even more than she'd resented her absence. Who could know with anyone, even the person who was supposed to be closest to you, how to get it right?

Mo was looking glassy-eyed now. Harry glanced at her wiry, prematurely greying hair and wondered why, when she was a couple of years younger than Alice, she looked as if she was almost as old as Joss. That was what happened, he thought – considering this, by way of the dope's effects, to be a deep piece of philosophical insight – when you modelled yourself on someone from the wrong generation. Mo had arrived at Penmorrow so full of admiration for Jocelyn, eager to be a free spirit like her, and to please her. She'd made a lifetime habit of emulating her with even the smallest things, like all that rustly velvet clothing and the heavy amber beads and crystals and keeping her hair long. She should get it properly cut and coloured and conditioned back to youthful smooth-ness, Harry thought, surprising himself. She should decide that she was herself, not some second-hand faded old hippy. And she should do it fast, before she too became debilitated and started thinking about the approach of the end of her life, rather than the good-time middle bits that they were surely allowed to have sometime soon.

Alice turned the car out of the winding Tremorwell lane and joined the main road west, pulling into a long slow line of traffic heading for Penzance. It wasn't even ten yet but the Sunday motorists were out in force, and they all seemed to be making for the far tip of the county. At the side of the road, just past the garage, was a hitch-hiker. Alice, her car slowed to a crawl by the sheer traffic volume, thought of how she used to hitch everywhere when she was a young teenager. A night out in Truro would involve herself and Sally taking turns to hide in a ditch so that motorists would think the hitcher was all alone and either feel worried for their safety or hopeful that they were wanting more than a car ride.

'It's Aidan!' Grace interrupted Alice's thoughts.

'We'll have to stop, he'll see us.' Alice pulled over, reluctantly, sure that Grace would resent this unexpected companion on their trip.

'Course we will. Anyway, Aidan's cool.' Grace already had the window down, waving to him. Alice pulled into the layby where Aidan waited, and stopped the car.

'What happened to your own car?' she asked as he climbed in.

'Bit of starter-motor trouble,' he said, settling himself into the back of the Galaxy behind Grace. 'I don't think it likes the sea air. It's happier with pure North London fug.'

Alice looked back at him by way of her mirror.

'So where are you heading? Where do you want us to drop you?' She'd sounded abrupt without meaning to. It wasn't very fair of her but she'd prefer to spend the morning with just Grace. Or with just Aidan. She could see him smiling at her. He looked very boyish with his chic glasses and hair tweaked up in that slightly Tintin way that all youngish men seemed to like. Theo spent ages tweaking his into shape in front of anything with a slightly mirrored surface. In her opinion it made them all resemble birds with titchy crests, like soft little finches caught in a breeze.

'I've got a day off from Jocelyn's magnum opus,' he told her, 'so I'm going to see a film. They're showing *Blue Juice* as a one-off down in Penzance so I thought I'd see it, check out the surf scene. Or at least as it used to be.'

'Yeah right, and Catherine Zeta Jones,' Grace teased him.

'Yeah, well, OK, she's a babe. Back then anyway. She's looking too Hollywood for me these days.'

Alice wondered if that was polite-speak for 'older'

but decided against commenting. She'd only be inviting a flurry of embarrassing cover-ups, verbally.

The car slowed again as traffic joined the road from a junction, a steady crawl of a long line of cars.

'Why are there so many people on the road? Are they all going to Land's End?' Grace asked.

'Who knows? Perhaps they're all going to their various churches,' Alice said.

'Do you think so?' Aidan looked surprised. 'I had this down as pagan country.'

'That's spending too much time with Jocelyn,' Alice laughed. 'She's convinced you the whole county is a hotbed of spells and heathen festivals. You're forgetting all the Cornish Methodists.'

'She does that, your mother,' Aidan told her. 'She winds you in like a spider with silk so that you end up thinking her world is the only one that exists. It's good for the book but a bit much when you're back on planet Reality.'

'I like that,' Grace commented. 'I like her world.'

'Oh don't get me wrong.' Aidan leaned forward to reassure Grace. 'It's just that it's so far removed from my personal reality.'

'Which is?' Alice asked, signalling to a carful of holiday family to join the traffic queue in front of her.

'Oh you know, the usual.' He was smiling – looking as if he missed his home. 'Manky flat in Kentish Town, beer cans everywhere, pizza boxes under the bed, you know, usual sad-bloke-on-his-own stuff.'

'Sounds like Theo.' Grace was laughing at him. Alice thought so too – it sounded laddish, juvenile, non-responsible. All the things that she and Noel simply weren't. She pictured vividly the things Aidan left out: a zebra-print thong scrunched up at the far end of the duvet, cast off in sexual abandon by a lithe, taut-skinned girlfriend; an unsavoury heap of boy-smelling clothing desperate for someone to launder it; photos Blu-Tacked to the wall of drink-sodden party debris and girls in strappy little dresses, with sleek long hair, clutching each other lovingly and pulling daft expressions, cigarette in one hand, a sickly drink concoction in the other. Aidan's world, a pre-settled, youthful world.

'So you weren't a church-goer then?' Aidan asked Alice.

'What's this? More research?'

'I suppose so. Joss is very vague sometimes. I'm having to pull this book together from all sources. You don't get that with a footballer's memoirs.'

'Suppose not,' Alice conceded. Her mother was a woman much given to reinterpreting events of the past. Or, at least, to leaving out the bits that were more or less humdrum. If Alice had been a devout Christian and had insisted on being baptized and confirmed, Joss would probably have skipped over that and mentioned some Beltane extravaganza she'd hosted instead.

'Actually, when I was Grace's age I sometimes used to go to the Sunday morning service at the Tremorwell village church with my friend Sally.' Aidan had his electronic recorder out again and was pecking at its works, reminding her of Theo and his phone. Aidan even had the tip of his tongue out between his teeth as Theo did when he concentrated. What was I thinking of? Alice asked herself, feeling mildly mortified that she still found this young man so attractive. One day, she thought, not too far on from now, she'd turn into a caricature: she'd be accosting strangers like the two 'Oooh! Young man!' harridans on the Harry Enfield show.

'What did Jocelyn think of you taking up conventional religion?' Aidan asked. It was a professional question, she recognized. She could sense the deep lack of real interest.

'I didn't tell her,' Alice replied truthfully. 'She disapproved of all organized religions. She believed, still does, that they're systems by which the poor – and especially the female poor – were kept in guilt-ridden terror of eternal damnation.'

Behind her she heard the recorder being switched off. He simply didn't want to know any more and was now, she could see, staring out of the window, his knee jigging up and down impatiently, waiting like a child for the next thing. The film he wanted to see.

Alice remembered the church outings. She'd enjoyed having this secret from Jocelyn. She had loved the hymn-singing and had been enormously envious of Sally, who told her that they sang a hymn every morning at her school assembly. Alice had added this to her grievance list of things she minded missing out on from not going to school. She sang well – Sally said she'd have been a dead cert for the school choir. Sometimes, to annoy Jocelyn, she would belt out her favourites while she was doing jobs around Penmorrow, shelling peas in the kitchen or sweeping leaves from the verandah. 'Fight the Good Fight' went down particularly badly: Joss couldn't resist clucking over what she called the 'offensive paternalism' of the words, though contrarily even she was quite fond of 'Eternal Father Strong to Save' and in a good mood might be tempted to join in.

At the beginning of the summer season, Alice remembered, the vicar would greet unfamiliar faces in his holiday-swollen flock and would welcome this year's 'swallows', smiling graciously round at them and expressing the unctuous hope that they wouldn't fly away too soon. Everyone would laugh politely, the locals pretending they hadn't heard this annual analogy before. On the Sunday after the August bank holiday he would return to his metaphor, usually in his sermon, trusting the summer swallows would find spiritual sustenance in their winter quarters till their safe return the next year.

It was in the church when she was fifteen, Alice remembered, that she'd first thought about leaving Penmorrow. It had occurred to her that she too could be a swallow. At the end of the summer with Marcel, he'd asked her to go to France with him. She'd told him she couldn't and he'd simply shrugged and said, 'But you could,' setting free the whole of the rest of the world for her. She hadn't wanted to go then, because she hadn't wanted to stay with him, but from then onwards she had it in mind that one day she could leave the village and return in a new guise as a visitor, a whole-summer one or just for occasional weekends. It was a few years more before she actually left – but it was enough at the time to have absorbed the exhilarating notion that flight was possible.

Grace was now being silent – Alice assumed the burst of early-morning energy had been sapped away and that she was about to lay her head against the car window and doze off again. She turned off the main road and drove along by the sea through Marazion and past St Michael's Mount, purely for the pleasure of being so close to the water and seeing clutches of family visitors setting up their windbreaks and toddler tents, pitching in for a long, leisurely day in the sun. Aidan got out here, happy to walk along the seafront, as the tide was out, into Penzance.

'We missed out on all that, really, didn't we?' she

commented to Grace as they slowed to let a heavily equipped family haul their coolboxes and beach toys across the road.

'What? Missed out where?' Grace snapped back to life.

'Ordinary English seaside holidays, like all these people. Staying in rented cottages and hanging out on the beach all day. Sandwiches and flasks of tea.'

'God Mum, you sound like those people who go on about the good old days. Anyway, we always came to Penmorrow. Why would we need to rent somewhere?'

'Yes but . . . well to me it was a sort of home visit, not a holiday. We didn't often spend whole days going to the beach, because it was always just *there*, down the path. And then we've always gone to Greece or Florida or . . .'

'Italy like later. Mum?'

'Hmm?' Alice was negotiating the roundabout now and watching the Isles of Scilly helicopter taking off from the Penzance heliport.

'Do we *have* to go to Italy? Can't we just stay here?'

'Well it's all booked. And what about Theo and Noel?'

'What about them? They can still go if they want to.'

Alice gave her a sharp look. Grace had never done this before – split herself and her mother away from the other two. That hadn't been the idea when she and Noel married: living separately, each was a lone and lonely parent bringing up a solitary child. Together they formed a family – something so very much cosier. Or so she'd always thought.

'Why don't you want to go?'

Grace shrugged. 'Dunno. I'm just OK here. Actually, I don't even much want to go back to London.' She shuddered. 'Traffic, everyone going on about what

162

they're wearing all the time and all that homework just so the school can creep up the league table. Netball, ugh.'

'It probably isn't that different down here,' Alice said, smiling at her.

'But it might be. We should try it.' Grace was quiet for a moment, then she said, 'I read Jocelyn's book.'

'I know. I saw you with it at St Ives. What did you think of it?'

'Not sure. Brilliant I suppose but . . . was Angel actually Joss? Did all that stuff happen to her?'

'That's what everyone's been asking ever since she wrote it, especially as she never wrote another. No-one got any sense out of her about it. Sometimes she'd say it was someone she knew but mostly she said she'd just made it up. I never met any of her family so who knows? If it *was* her it would come out in Aidan's book, I'd expect.'

'But didn't *you* want to know? Didn't you ask her yourself years ago? And why didn't you see any grand-parents or aunts and uncles?' Grace sounded quite fierce, frustrated by Alice's apparent indifference.

'Of course I asked! But what can you do if she keeps changing her mind? One thing she did say, though, was that it was almost worse in her family to have made it all up. Her family were devout Christians and thought she was an irredeemable sinner for having so much as imagined it all. She did say she'd have got less grief if it had all been true, which is pretty damning, wouldn't you say? And she was an only child of quite old parents. I might have met them when I was tiny, but I think they're long dead.'

Alice steered the Galaxy into a space in the Safeway car park. Just beside the store was the railway, and she watched as a train hurtled past on the first stretch of

163

the journey to London. Penzance station was a small, pretty seaside terminus. She remembered the many times she'd got on the train there, wearing sand-filled flip-flops and old scruffy shorts and clutching a straw bag and a rucksack. Then the shock of arriving at Paddington where everyone raced about in neat city suits (Smart Lady attire) and high heels and carrying elegant little handbags. Almost two worlds, she thought as she approached the supermarket door, where a notice requested that customers make sure they were suitably attired and not enter the stores bare-footed and bare-chested. She somehow didn't imagine she'd be seeing Elvis in the cat-food aisle in here. But if she did, she'd smile at him and say a quick hello. A Cornish Elvis wouldn't stare through her as if she didn't exist or give her that look that Londoners did, as if you were the loony they dreaded sitting next to on the tube. Maybe Grace had a point, perhaps they should give it a try, living down here where no-one checked out your handbag to see if it was (oh the shame) last year's Prada, and you could get change out of £50 for a lobster supper.

As she wheeled her trolley towards the bakery section, she imagined herself and Noel living full-time in Tremorwell. This was the first time for many years that she'd really felt as if she was part of the place again and not a short-term guest. What would it be like for Noel if they stayed on? If they gave up on Richmond? Perhaps he'd be a happy retiree at first and would roam the county playing golf. But soon he'd be bored and would start thinking he could make an enthusiastic new-blood difference to the local parish council. Women would vote for him, certainly. Next thing you knew he'd be bigging it up in local politics and become a bar-room lecturer on boundaries and by-laws. As for living at Penmorrow, that would be hopeless – like putting two tigers in a box. Mentally, he and Jocelyn would rip each other to shreds along with everyone else's nerves. A terrible scenario, completely hopeless.

She hoped Aidan would enjoy his film. Somehow she felt she could be reasonably certain that he wouldn't be thinking of her as he watched Catherine Zeta Jones strutting about in her bikini.

Ten

You'd think God had turned up for a visit, Harry thought, as Patrice and Jocelyn hugged theatrically on the Penmorrow verandah and the wind chimes jangled like mad wedding bells from each side of the porch. There wasn't even a camera running yet, but Jocelyn was going full out for dramatic effect. She was wearing what she called her rainbow elf outfit: multicoloured hand-painted silk trousers beneath a matching long jagged-hemmed coat with dangling pointy sleeves like a medieval maiden. It had been made for her by Ossie Clark as a generous thank-you for hospitality many, many years ago, and was kept as a treasure in tissue paper and a dark wardrobe. Too surprised to refuse, Katie had been roped in after lunch to interweave a matching rainbow of slender braids into Joss's plait to perfect the co-ordinated look she wanted.

'It's really *now*!' Katie had exclaimed, admiring the delicate swirls of colour on the fabric. 'This old hippy gear's *sooo* this summer.' It was a comment that on any other occasion might have gone down less than well with Jocelyn (or indeed with anyone), but Jocelyn was too pleased with herself and too excited at the prospect of being centre stage to find fault or offence.

Harry met Mo's eye across the pathway and they exchanged a mutual lip-curl at the mwah-mwah kissing. Patrice was impressively surrounded by silver flight cases full of equipment which Katie, along with Nick the cameraman, had unloaded from Patrice's Discovery. Jocelyn was gazing at all this heaped-up kit, as enraptured as if they were lavish presents gift-wrapped especially for her. Harry, by contrast, distrusted all this flashy paraphernalia, associating it with the kind of show-off men who drove low-slung cars with personalized number plates.

Greetings and introductions over, Patrice took Joss's hand and jumped back down the verandah steps, pulling her with him, keen to inspect the Big Shepherd statue and the pair of angrily snarling bronze sheep that made up his depleted flock on the front meadow. Harry feared for her balance, but the attention of Patrice seemed to inject new vitality into her.

'Are these the only sheep left?' he asked. 'I heard there were at least six, including two of them,' and he lowered his voice only slightly to stage-whisper, '*in flagrante.*'

'Oh, given away, drifted away, wandered as sheep do,' Jocelyn told him airily. 'Larry Olivier had one, and poor Jimi had one in London to take back to the States with him. But then of course he died, poor love, as so many did . . .'

'Jimi? Heavens! We *must* have all this in shot at some point!' Excitedly, Patrice wheeled Jocelyn round and placed her beside Big Shepherd, alongside whose mottled greeny-brown bulk she looked extraordinarily delicate and slender in her floaty silks.

'*Isn't* this thrilling?' Patrice asked the assembled company. Harry trusted that he didn't expect an honest reply. It didn't seem thrilling at all to him or to

Mo; more disruptively unwelcome and likely to lead, when this motley entourage had left, to a long, tedious period of Joss being grumpily discontented. She'd be like a child after too many ice creams: bad-tempered, unmanageable and wanting more. And where was Alice? Where had she vanished to so early in the day, leaving Noel, when he'd come trailing up to the house in search of her, looking like a complete spoon. A complete abandoned spoon.

'So nobody's seen her?' Noel had asked rather bemusedly, accepting a slice of compensatory toast from Mo. There'd been a bit of an awkward silence in the kitchen then while each of them speculated on why Alice would have vanished without bothering to tell Noel, till Katie had proffered the suggestion that Alice might have popped out to get a newspaper.

'In the *car*?' Sam had added an extra lashing of scorn to his usual amount. 'Don't be *schtoopid*, the shop's only down the lane!' Mo had reached out and cuffed him across the head, like a mother lion. Joss had frowned and tutted, disapproving deeply of physical discipline, although, Harry reflected, it could probably sometimes be a lot less painful all round than the emotional sort.

'And of course you will show me absolutely everything? For the full Penmorrow flavour?' Harry heard Patrice saying, the level of enthusiasm rising ever higher in his voice. He hoped, sincerely, that Jocelyn *wouldn't* show him quite everything. If his special-project polytunnel got any kind of TV exposure Harry would be making his escape from Penmorrow faster than he'd anticipated, by courtesy of something custodial dished out by Truro Magistrates Court.

*   *   *

'So where did you go? And why didn't you wake me? We could have all gone out together somewhere.' Noel was on the Gosling terrace surrounded by discarded sections of newspaper when Alice and Grace came back. He had read every word of the *Sunday Times* and even had a shufti at the Appointments section, mainly to tut-tut at the mega salaries offered for jobs that didn't seem to have any real meaning, such as Transaction Valuation Analyst. What the buggery, he'd thought, was that when it was at home? Was it a jumped-up term that really meant 'Counting the money in the shop till'? Or was he getting old and out of touch?

'We just dashed out to Penzance – did a bit of supermarket stuff, you know. Sorry – we were a bit longer than we thought we'd be.' Alice sat beside him and opened a bottle of beer for each of them. She was looking pleased with life, quite radiant really in her new windblown sort of way. He should, Noel thought, have made more effort with her last night. She might have been more persuadable than she'd let on. He would have done if he hadn't drunk so much of Jocelyn's port after supper. The foray into that Oz girl's underwear had come to nothing when she'd laughed and swatted him away. Insulting really. She'd said, and her very words still stung, 'If I'd fancied a clumsy fumble I'd have gone for your schoolboy son, matey.' She'd taken her time saying it, though – he'd got his hand close to a nest of warm, damp pussy first. Decidedly *not* a girl who went in for the full Brazilian waxing, thank the Lord.

'We went to the shell shop and bought these,' Grace told him, holding out a Safeway bag to show him her booty. 'I'm going to make a shell mirror for my room here.'

169

'*Your* room? I thought Gosling was part of the great Penmorrow holiday rental empire.'

Alice gave him a sharp look as Grace went back into the house, which he felt mystified about interpreting other than to realize he'd said the wrong thing. When, here, he thought with irritation, did he ever manage to say the right thing?

'She just wants to do something creative, Noel. Who knows, it might fit in with one of her GCSE Art projects when the time comes.'

'Good, good, whatever she wants.' He raised his glass, conciliatory, then added, 'I see someone's been touching up that tatty old mural in the bathroom. The mermaid's got her tail fin back.'

Alice laughed. 'Don't tell Joss, for God's sake. She made me promise not to touch it. I interpreted that as "Don't paint over it" and just filled in bits that had faded or gone missing. At least now it doesn't look downright shabby. I brightened up the mackerels' stripes and the clownfish too, where the orange had chipped off, and I put some of the silvery flashes back on the seaweed. I'm pretty sure she painted it herself, though if she finds out what I've done she'll tell me it was Picasso, the day before he died or something.'

'Whole place needs gutting, if you ask me. Start again, get the builders in. There's really no point fannying about dabbling at bits and bobs and hoping it'll look like something anyone would actually pay serious money to take a holiday in.'

Alice frowned at him. 'Not everyone wants show-home standard when they get away. Some people who come here are looking for an atmosphere, a history.' Even as she spoke, Alice recognized that she'd thought along similar lines to Noel only a few weeks ago. She could hardly believe what she'd just said, she who kept her spice jars in alphabetical order and had been considering changing her fabulous blue glass worktop for charcoal granite purely because a few smeary fingerprints tended to show up on it. She who bought a new front doormat every March 1st (the same day that every curtain in the house went to the dry-cleaners) and reminded Mrs Pusey to dust the light bulbs. Even the lavender hedge lining her front garden path stood tidily to attention, there was never a stray crisp packet crackling about under the seats in her car and every one of the white Egyptian cotton sheets in the airing cupboard had a size label (S, D, K) for easy identification.

'We could go out now if you want, all four of us, drive somewhere by the sea and have an early supper somewhere?' Alice suggested to Noel. Where, she wondered, had the day gone? She wasn't really hungry – she and Grace had sat on the bench by the Penzance harbour car park eating chips out of a paper bag and licking ketchup off their fingers. Her Richmond persona didn't do that sort of thing, she'd told herself as she'd chucked a couple of lush, fatty morsels to a persistent gull, but then in Richmond you couldn't get chips as good as these.

'Mum said she wanted to cook fish for all these poncey people at the house. Something special, something they wouldn't get up country,' Sam was saying. He, Chas, Theo and Grace sauntered up the hill behind the village sucking ice lollies, catching the drips with their tongues as they melted fast in the late afternoon sun.

'So?' Theo said. 'Let her. Wossa problem?'

'Yeah but then she said trouble was, you could get anything anywhere. She said that cooking man from Padstow had told everyone on telly how to cook everything Cornwall's got,' Sam went on. 'So I got this idea. Carp. Most expensive fish in the world. *Exclusive*, is the word.'

Theo looked at him, puzzled. 'So what do we do, get a boat and go out and catch them or what?'

Chas sighed, despairing. 'It's a freshwater fish, right?' Theo scowled, feeling he was being pointed out as the idiot in the bunch. Sam joined in, pointing down towards the bay. 'And look, Theo, even you townies can see that the big wet stuff out there is seawater. Salt water is what's out there, not fresh.'

'Or not,' Sam said with a devilish grin. He jumped up onto a wall outside the square-fronted three-story city-dweller's dream of a four-square Georgian country house, and peered through the fuchsia hedge into a densely foliaged garden. Grace read the sign on the wall by the gate: 'Hamilton House. Gardens open Tuesday and Friday. It's closed, we can't go in.'

Sam gave her a pitying look. 'Course we can't go in. Not on those days, you have to pay and it's full of grockles. Some old bloke takes ancient trippers round in poncey groups and tells them what the plants are. Palms and stuff. It's really big, goes all the way down to the seafront, nearly. There's a great aerial runway in there too and ropes and stuff for little kids to play on.'

Theo looked at him blankly. 'So? Do you two wanna sneak in there and play?'

Chas jumped up on the wall next to Sam. 'They've got the carp in there, I've seen them. The pond's huge, practically a lake. The fish are big ones, massive even. It's deep though and carp are sly bastards.'

Grace looked mystified. 'So what's the big deal? Can't Mo just cook something else? What's wrong with cod or something? Plaice, sole, monkfish, jellied bloody eels? Why's it have to be carp? Are you sure she'd want them?'

Chas and Sam stared at her, silently and intently. Why wouldn't they say something, she wondered, they were so quiet and . . . twin-like.

'What? *What?*'

'Mum wants something *different*,' Chas said. 'She hardly ever gets her own way. Sometimes she should, that's all.'

'So you see, for us, carp isn't just *fish*,' Sam added. 'Carp is a *mission*.'

Grace looked at Theo, wondering if he actually got the point of this, if there was one. It would be helpful, she thought, if he'd enlighten her.

'Aha – like hunter-gatherers,' Theo said, a smile spreading slowly as he looked at Hamilton House's locked gates.

Oh, a boy thing, Grace thought, relieved. Well that let her off the hook, then. When *her* mum wanted some weird food that was a bit different she just went to a new deli or something. That was the point of living in a town. If Alice wanted Thai stuff she went to the oriental supermarket on the Kew Road. If she wanted authentic Asian spices she drove over to Southall. For an ace Chinese takeaway she just rang up The Good Earth and they delivered. Easy. That's what evolution was about, surely. In fact it wasn't only women who'd found these modern things called shops; even Noel sometimes came home with a bag from Harrods food hall with something gorgeous that someone else had concocted for an unfamiliar meal.

'So what we're going to do first is we're going to the beach.' Sam and Chas looked at each other in a way that Grace could tell meant they'd made a big decision. 'And we're going to give you two a lesson in your hunter-gatherer survival techniques. That's if you're up for it.'

Grace sighed. Survival techniques. Right. This sounded like the trek you had to do in the sixth form if you wanted to get the Duke of Edinburgh's silver award. Stuff about being careful you didn't prod the roof of your tent or the rain would get in. Instructions to wee downstream of where you want to drink the water (which sounded fine in theory, so long as there wasn't another D of E group camping two hundred yards *up* the hill), and to collect only bits of kindling that were dry and upright on the forest floor, not lying in soaking mud. And of course, as Sophy would say, always keep your vodka in a mineral-water bottle so no-one suspects.

Sam and Chas led the way to the beach and then up to the rocks at the far end, intent on carrying out the first stage of their 'mission'. Theo and Grace followed, trailing a bit and wondering what they were in for. Grace decided that on balance she was quite pleased to be included and it wasn't as if there was anything else to do. You could have a bit too much time alone for reading and lying in the sun, she thought, though she'd like to have been wearing shoes more suitable than flip-flops for climbing if they were going to be scrambling up the cliffside.

'You don't say anything, right? Not to anyone?' Sam warned at the foot of the rocky hillside, just past where a small headland jutted out to the sea's edge.

'OK,' Theo agreed.

'Sure, but what's the big mystery?' Sam ignored Grace's question and began to climb the rocks, which were damp and claggy with seaweed.

'Up there, in that cave. We've got the stuff ready. You got any matches?' Chas asked Theo.

174

Theo clambered across the rocks, his feet in their fat-soled trainers slipping awkwardly. 'I've got matches. Is that it? You kids come up here to smoke gear?'

'Er, like we'd need to?' Sam said, shaking his shaggy head at Theo in scorn. 'We can do all that at home.'

Grace skidded on the rocks and she was lagging behind, trying to find less precarious places to put her feet. She slid into a rock pool and slimy weed tangled itself round her ankles, but at last she reached the small ledge at the front of the murky, damp cave that Sam and Chas seemed to have made their headquarters. There was a mothy brown blanket hanging from a jutting rock, one of their school lunch boxes was lying open on the floor and a heap of soft-drinks cans glinted in the gloomy far corner next to an old rusty bucket that stank horribly of dead sea-life. There were two heaps of wood close to the cave's entrance, one of fairly thick branches and another of twigs and smaller sticks. There'd been a fire on the ledge before – she could see pale grey scuffings of ash on the rocks. She thought of the clearing in the woods where she'd watched the boys doing their bizarre ritual trap-setting. Did these two have dens all over the village? Were they turning into feral children?

'Doesn't the sea get up this far?' she asked. 'I mean, if you keep stuff in here . . .'

'Only at spring tides, most times not even then,' Chas told her. 'It's neaps just now.' Then he gave her a lordly grin. 'I don't suppose you know what that is, townie girl.'

'Course I do, stupid. I live by the Thames, we know about tides too.'

'Well good. Anyway, what we've got to do is this. First we light the fire. Matches, Theo.'

Chas and Sam built a small wigwam of dry twigs, scattered dried-out grasses pulled from the hilllside over it, and Theo tried unsuccessfully to light a match.

'They're damp,' he said, adding a third one to the kindling.

'Give us it here.' Chas took the box from him, removed a match and started rolling it in his hair.

'What are you doing? Are you mad?' Grace was amazed, almost expecting to see Chas's head burst into flames.

'Electricity in your hair, it dries it out.' He struck the match and it flared. 'Simple!'

Sam handed drinks round while they waited for the fire to glow hot and fierce, then, when it had burnt down to scorching embers, he brought the bucket from the back of the cave and tipped a mixture of seashells and snail shells over the coals.

'We'll give it a while. Come back after dark and collect them when they're ready and cooled down,' Sam said.

'Yeah but ready for *what*?' Theo asked. 'It looks like some kind of spell or something. The kind of thing Joss might do.' He sniggered and Grace glared at him. She didn't want him slagging off Jocelyn. However crazy her grandmother might be, she knew stuff. Useful stuff. Like how to get a boy to fancy you by doing things with herbs and oils. Half her class at school liked to think they were witches. Her mum said it was a craze, too much watching *Sabrina* and *Buffy*, a typical girls'-school thing, and she even put a bit of it in the books she wrote. They got together in cliquey groups, lighting candles and concocting spells and carrying bits of painted cloth to represent people they wanted to control or get revenge on. They were completely, stupidly ignorant of the Law of Threefold

176

Return, by which they were for sure going to get back three times the power that they'd hexed on others. Then they'd feel it where it hurt. Joss knew all this for real, not just for playing with, from way back. Grace wasn't going to diss her: she was sure she was going to need plenty of that kind of knowing to help her on her way to being a grown-up.

'Just think of this as fishfood.' Sam scuffed his foot over the coals so that they died down on the scorching shells. 'I'll say no more.'

'We should have brought the children,' Alice said to Noel as she drove down the quayside at Porthleven. 'It wasn't very fair just to leave a note, especially for Theo – he'll be wanting to spend time with you.'

'Well they should have been there,' Noel countered. 'We could have waited in all evening for them to turn up and ended up starving. They'll be all right; when they get back from wherever they've been they can get a bit of lentil pie or whatever else Mo is boiling up in her cauldron.'

Alice backed the Galaxy into a space alongside the harbour, carefully keeping a good safe distance from the sheer edge. If she was too close, Noel would be stepping down twenty feet, splatted into the muddy low-tide water. And how horrid am I, she asked herself as she switched off the engine, to wonder if that would be such a bad thing? 'You're very unfair to Mo,' she told him. 'She's a brilliant cook, especially given the vagaries of the Penmorrow people's various diet requirements that she's had to put up with over the years. She can do anything from all-out vegan to the Atkins all-protein by way of Raymond Blanc. Plus nearly all the veg is home-grown and organic.'

'I know, I know. It's just that it's hard to feel you're

getting the full gourmet experience from someone who looks like she's still cooking in a cave.'

Alice bit her lip to keep herself quiet. She was tempted to ask him why on earth he'd come to see them at all if he was going to be so bloody supercilious about absolutely bloody everything. She looked him over closely as she locked the car and crossed the road to the restaurant. Noel didn't 'do' casual clothes terribly successfully, just as he didn't 'do' Penmorrow in a terribly good mood. At this moment he reminded her of Tony Blair, having the same slightly gauche air about him and looking as if he wasn't quite sure what to do with his hands. He was wearing jeans but they were hyper-clean, fresh from Mrs Pusey's fearsome ironing. His dark blue polo shirt had good-boy creases on the sleeves and the cream cotton sweater was so symmetrically draped round his shoulders it looked as if he'd spent time in front of a mirror pinning it into place. He was no more comfortable in his surroundings than he was in his clothes, even though Alice had chosen the Smokehouse restaurant as being the closest to a contemporary urban eaterie for him. He stopped in the doorway and peered round suspiciously as if he expected it to be full of either hooray yachtsmen taking up too much space with their massive yellow Henri Lloyd jackets, or fishermen smelling of trawlers and smoking pipes stuffed with evil sour tobacco.

The Smokehouse was a bright modern fun place with pale wood-strip flooring, a big open bar area with chrome stools, plain wooden tables and lots of white and turquoise paint. The staff and customers were young, tanned and sun-bleached, as if they'd just come in from a hot day in the surf. A Beach Boys hits compilation was playing in the background to complete the ambience. The whole feel to the place was warm, casual and somewhat Antipodean, she thought – in which case Noel should like it, seeing as he'd shown so much interest in that Katie girl over dinner the night before. She watched him as he slid onto the restaurant's scarlet bench against the wall and looked around with amusement at their fellow diners.

'What do you fancy to eat?' she asked, accepting a menu from a pretty young waitress dressed in a tight pink skimpy tee shirt with 'Good Girl' picked out in rhinestones, and scuffed jeans so low-slung the words 'Calvin Klein' could be clearly read at the top of her pants.

'Hmm. Not sure,' he said, frowning at the list of choices but glancing not covertly enough at the waitress's bare, blonde-fuzzed tanned tummy. 'I definitely *don't* want a pizza.'

'Me neither,' Alice agreed abruptly. 'I'm going to have the mussels with the tomatoey stuff and chips.' More chips, she thought, stroking her own stomach. She'd put on pounds if she didn't watch it.

'Chips?' Noel's left eyebrow went up. Alice gave him a straight, unsmiling gaze back.

'Yes, chips,' she told him brightly. 'You get potatoes, see, cut them into long thin wedges and cook them in boiling fat. Preferably twice.'

He laughed, which annoyed her even further. 'I know what they *are*, my darling, it's just that I don't think I've ever seen you actually *eat* one. It must be something to do with the climate down here.'

Maybe it was, she thought. Or maybe, and a small regretful cloud passed over her conscience, maybe I don't at the moment much like the pettily snobbish man I married.

The moment passed, leaving her feeling cooled. It reminded her of Arthur Gillings. Towards the end of his life he'd had moments of sudden intense silence, staring into the distance as if there was something out there that he was trying hard to see. Sometimes he would shudder as if a chill had blown on him from somewhere. 'Just a goose on my grave,' he'd say if anyone commented. These moments were more and more frequent as his last inactive months went on, and soon no-one commented on the shudders and the silences. Although he stopped mentioning the geese, Alice, who was just fourteen, could sense their ominous presence and could somehow feel them gathering and stamping hard on some distant patch of ground.

'. . . the villa should be easily big enough if they want to.' Alice became aware that Noel was speaking and that she hadn't been listening.

'Sorry. I was miles away for a moment, what were you saying?' The waitress arrived at their table and opened a bottle of champagne that Alice hadn't noticed Noel ordering. The cork exploded noisily and hit the ceiling.

'Not really properly chilled,' Noel admonished the girl and reached out to touch the bottle. 'I suppose it'll do though.' The girl smiled broadly at him, showing a flash of a gold tongue stud. Looking pained, for Noel loathed body piercings, he turned back to Alice. 'I was just saying, if Grace and Theo want to bring a friend each, there'd be room. In Italy. At the villa?' Alice realized she must be looking crazily blank.

'Ah Italy. Sorry, I'd almost forgotten we were going.' She felt exhausted at the thought of venturing as far as Truro, let alone the great open world beyond Heathrow. She was beginning to understand how Mo and Harry managed to stay so resolutely untravelled. What, after all, was the point? Why leave such a beautiful place with its fabulous view just to go and look at another place with a fabulous view?

'I can see that.' Noel drank half his glass of champagne in one swift gulp. 'It was your idea in the first place to book it, remember. Don't you want to go now?'

Alice hesitated. Probably, she thought, she was just feeling lazy about packing up and moving off again. It was a feeling that was hard to shake off, as if an invisible spider with the finest invisible silk had started binding her up without her noticing.

'Why are we going?' she heard herself ask.

'*Why*? What sort of a question's that?' Noel topped up both their glasses. 'It's a holiday. For us, for the children. It's what people do in the summer.'

'Why?'

'Why holidays? Because . . . battery recharging, rekindling sparks, that sort of thing? Look,' Noel took hold of her hand, 'what's the matter with you? It's your bloody mother, isn't it. She's been having a go at you about me. I can tell.'

Alice slid her hand away and picked up her glass. 'No she hasn't. Actually she hasn't mentioned you at all. She's more concerned with herself at the moment.'

'Ah, the man from the telly. And of course she is concerned with herself, when isn't she?'

'No. I meant the fact that she's realized she's actually mortal.'

'Left it a bit late,' he spluttered into his drink. 'Most of us work that one out in our mid-teens!'

'Ah but do we? And *should* we? Isn't it better, or at least luckier, not to have any notions of anything more than perpetual vitality, especially when you *are* young?'

'Well when you *are* young, I suppose,' Noel conceded. 'But Jocelyn is pushing seventy. A nodding acquaintance with the Grim Reaper can't be that much of a surprise, surely.'

'But that's the thing. For her it is. And I think that's incredibly lucky. She's lived her life assuming that all that's available for the young, the curious, the optimistic is always going to be there for her. I envy her.' Alice was surprised to feel tearful suddenly. It didn't seem to be just because of the champagne.

'You didn't answer my question,' Noel persisted as the food arrived. 'Do you think Grace and Theo would like to bring anyone to Tuscany?'

'Oh, possibly.' Alice brightened as she poked a fork into the first tender mussel. 'I think we should suggest they invite Chas and Sam.'

Eleven

'I'll get some 3-in-1 for that creaky bed.' Noel came up behind Alice while she was honeying toast in the kitchen and squeezed himself against her. 'Half the village must have heard it.' He nuzzled her neck and chuckled. 'And heard you as well.'

He smelled of blokey shower gel, sharp and tangy. Alice felt guilty; she simply wanted to pull away, to go out to the terrace with her tea and toast and sit quietly by herself, like an animal that turns on its mate as soon as copulation is over. Noel, by contrast, was full of post-coital affection – something he didn't go in for a lot back home, especially on working-day mornings when he usually got up in a tearing hurry, showered and raced off to the office with little more than a shouted 'Bye, see you tonight.'

'Why don't you go and sit in the sun, Noel, and I'll bring some toast out for you,' she offered, wriggling out of his clutches.

'OK, sounds good. Are the kids back from their sleepover up at the house yet?' he asked.

'Not yet. Grace is probably swimming in the bay and Theo won't even be awake. That seems to be the pattern so far.'

'Strange how they've happily hooked up with the wild-boy cousins. You'd have thought the age gap would get in the way.' He laughed. 'That seagull thing though, just the sort of stunt to impress Theo.'

'Hmm, not Grace though,' Alice said. 'Can't see what she's found in common with them.'

Noel grinned at her. 'And yet you think she'd want them to come to Italy.'

'Well they've hardly seen anything of the world beyond the Tamar bridge.'

'Staying out like that perhaps Grace and Theo were being tactful,' Noel suggested. 'Maybe they thought we'd like a bit of teen-free time together. And how right they . . .'

'. . . Tea? Or do you fancy coffee this morning?' Alice interrupted quickly. She really didn't want to talk about it. She didn't even want to think about it. Sex with Noel, even on the most mechanically dutiful occasions, was usually pretty good. Sex with Noel while she was thinking about Aidan was phenomenal, quite blush-makingly so. Noel was right – it was just as well the children hadn't been anywhere near the place. He was looking very pleased with himself. Alice was glad. It made up in some way for the uncomfortable remoteness she felt towards him. It must be the Penmorrow premises, she decided as she took her first sweet, luxuriant bite of the toast. Everything would be all right, back to normal once they were back in London. And why, she wondered, did that thought seem so depressing?

The couple who'd been renting Cygnet had left three days early. It was like that sometimes and Mo resented it every time, taking the disgruntled premature departures as a personal slur on her standards as a housekeeper. Secretly, Harry thought this lot had a point. The couple, thirty-somethings from Potters Bar and apparently taking an experimental break from their usual fully catered Mediterranean holidays, stated in their list of complaints that they expected their holiday cottage to have a shower that did more than grudgingly trickle. They had chosen the property specifically for its relative remoteness – having a pair of giggling mud-smeared boys casually dropping in whenever they felt like it and demanding biscuits and crisps had made it impossible to relax. They preferred a sink that wasn't crazed with germ-ridden scratches and, if the bathroom floor really had to have carpet instead of hygienic tiles, could it please be one that wasn't mould-eaten all round the edges and smelled like a dead rat in a drain?

This last had made Harry (but definitely not Mo) chuckle. How innocent – and quite generous really – of these urban visitors not to conclude that if something smelled like a dead rat in a drain then in all likelihood it *was* a dead rat. He'd have to get the side panel off the bath (not difficult, one sharp punch in the right place on the painted plasterboard and it easily gave up and fell down) and see what was lurking in there. It was possible that big old cat of Grace's had taken some creature in and let it scuttle away to die in a dark corner. Or, and the suspicion was deeply uncomfortable, it was also possible that Chas and Sam had sneaked into the bathroom on one of their drop-ins and slid a bit of rotting wildlife down beneath the bath taps just for the hell of it. Little sods, he wouldn't put it past them. It would be their idea of revenge if Mr and Mrs Potters Bar didn't have a satisfactory supply of their favourite prawn cocktail Wotsits in the food cupboard.

'I suppose they think they'll be getting a refund. If they do they can think again. They stayed more than half the week,' Mo commented sourly as she surveyed the kitchen that looked as if it had been abandoned by panicked fugitives. The sink contained a tottering pile of dirty plates and saucepans. A blue and white striped jug on the draining board held just about the entire stock of the cottage cutlery soaking in murky, grease-slicked water. The fridge was humming at full pelt as it hadn't been shut properly, and the icebox at the top was quickly forming a lumpy berg where the opening flap's broken spring didn't quite meet the casing.

'That's another thing on their list,' Harry said, peering at the long, detailed note. 'They've complained there wasn't a dishwasher.'

Mo snorted, tipping the jug-water down the sink. Spoons and forks clattered after it to join the rest of the crockery. 'Dishwasher! They were never told there was one. There's only the two of them and they went out most nights! Some people don't know they're bloody born.'

Harry, though, had seen the inside of the Gosling kitchen now that Alice had given it a bit of a spruce-up. It was amazing how much more inviting it looked without all the surface clutter, with a set of shiny new door handles, the quarry-tiled floor scoured till it shone and the curtains chucked out. She'd even ordered (and paid for) a new cooker for it. It still wasn't exactly showroom standard, but Alice did have a knack of geting the best out of what there was.

'It is a bit run-down though, Mo, you must admit. Maybe we should ask Alice to . . .'

'Alice? What does she know about the holiday-rent trade? OK she's all right with a bit of paint, but once

186

we start on that track we'll be thousands of pounds down the line that we won't get back in profit.'

'Well we could charge a bit more, get it back off the punters. It makes good business sense.'

Mo stared at him. She looked quite sexily furious and formidable with her wet, soapy hands in challenge position on her hips and her eyes hard and angry. 'And say doing this place up costs, what? Five thousand? And we put the rent up from three hundred a week to maybe four hundred and fifty? And that's mid-season, there'd be a lot less margin outside that. How long would it be before we got back the outlay? Work it out, Harry; any cash we put into this place means we're stuck with it that much longer. *Years* longer. Is that what you want? Cos I don't.'

'What we'll do *is* . . .' Patrice stopped in mid-sentence and stared round the orchard, taking in the scene and, Alice presumed, working out the best film angle. The grass was long and sun-scorched, shot through with buttercups and wild cornflowers. The apple trees looked like something from a fairy tale, their low branches, bending to the ground, weighed down with masses of gleaming scarlet fruit. Plums were already ripening and attracting idly buzzing wasps. Chickens ran about squawking and pecking at the legs of the intruders to their home ground. Joss's ancient tortoise, speeded up by the hot sun, made frantic circuits of his territory, stopping only to snatch a dandelion leaf in his fierce jaws or crash frustratedly into the biggest stones that lay around, in the hope that one would miraculously prove mateable.

Alice and Joss, Noel and all the children were in the orchard along with Patrice, Katie, Nick and a skinny lad called Dez, who sniffed a lot and said, when Theo asked what he did, that he was 'Work Sperience'. Aidan had stayed in the house to make some progress with the book. Alice had assumed Joss would want to be alone with the crew – the programme was about *her*, after all, but she'd been almost insistent that they join in. 'You can come and make sure I don't have spinach on my teeth, and that my hair isn't unravelling, that sort of thing,' she'd said to Alice, who gathered she was supposed to feel honoured at being allotted a task. 'And you can remind me if I forget things.'

And here she addressed Patrice. 'One does, you know, when one's so very old.' Alice didn't contradict her. This must be Jocelyn's new ploy – having spent years insisting she was still ripe with youth's vitality, she was now going to fast-forward into majestic old age and insist instead that she was due the deference of extreme antiquity. She had taken to using a stick, more for wielding than for walking, a stout, lumpily carved glossy piece of wood that Alice remembered Arthur using to help him get around in the last weeks of his life. If Joss was a city woman, Alice thought, she'd be the kind who prodded everyone out of her way with the stick, shouting, 'Let me through, I'm eighty-six!', slyly reversing her true age figures.

Patrice didn't seem to have made any kind of cohesive plan for his programme. 'We'll just see how it's hanging,' he said, grinning at the assembled company and making Theo and Grace cringe at his choice of words. There wasn't much, Alice was reminded as she caught Grace's anguished expression, that could be more scathing than a teenager catching out a grown-up with dated terminology.

'What we'll do *is*,' Patrice said again, though now he seemed to have made his mind up, 'is you can talk us through where exactly we're at and tell us about the parts of Penmorrow that have the most significance to *you*. Dig?' Jocelyn nodded. Idly, Chas aimed his catapult and sent a stone clattering through the tallest plum tree. Sparrows whooshed up into the air, flapping angrily.

'Behave,' Noel warned him quietly.

'No! No, it's fine! All part of the ambience!' Patrice told Noel.

'He'll regret saying *that*,' Noel commented to Alice. 'I dread to think how far those two will push the *ambience* envelope.'

'OK we're running!' Katie called to Patrice.

'Just ignore the camera,' Patrice told Joss, squeezing her wrist. Jocelyn gave him a smile that Alice interpreted as suggesting the words 'grandmothers' and 'eggs' and the two of them trailed off among the trees, accompanied by Nick and Katie and with Dez shambling after them through the orchard, dragging flexes and complicated-looking gadgets. Chas and Sam ran ahead, kicking at fallen apples and grinning back over their shoulders towards the camera. Joss and Patrice drifted ahead out of hearing range, leaving the others to sit and relax on the ancient sun-greyed wicker chairs at the lichen-bloomed table.

'I wonder what she's telling them,' Noel said, perching himself carefully on a collapsing chair. 'I bet she's listing who had sex with whom out here under the stars.'

'I doubt it – for quite a few years no-one in their right mind would have had sex here; there used to be a couple of old pigs – Gloucester Old Spots – running loose. They had thoroughly evil tempers.'

'Did you eat them?' Grace asked.

'No – we'd had them so long they were more like

pets. In the end they went to a farm up the road in exchange for freezer packs of lamb, all pre-cut and looking clean like stuff from the supermarket.'

'Bit of a cop-out, surely?' Noel said.

'In a way,' Alice agreed. 'But you've got to remember that most people who came here were from London or other cities, here for a quick taste of arty-farty communal living – none of that hands-on self-sufficiency malarkey.' She pulled a face, remembering. 'It was as much as anyone could do to look at the food rota and sling any kind of meal together. Boiled socks. I remember boiled socks.'

'You ate *socks*?' Theo's face was scrunched up in disgust.

Alice laughed. 'No! But I remember coming into the kitchen one day and there was a saucepan steaming away on the Aga. It was nearly suppertime so I thought, oooh good, someone's remembered to cook. The smell wasn't great but then it often wasn't, especially if it involved pulses. Anyway I took the lid off and there they were. Socks. A big heap of horrible grey ones.'

'Rank.' Grace shuddered, appalled.

'What *did* you get for supper, then?' Theo asked.

'Oh the usual, I should think! Probably brown rice with leftover chicken stirred in, oh and there'd have been tinned peas. There were always tins of peas and usually half a cold chicken on a plate in the larder. We might have had a garden full of fresh vegetables but someone had to remember to pick and prepare them. Didn't always happen.'

'Makes the socks sound quite tempting,' Noel said. 'You should tell all this to Patrice – give him a view of the other side of paradise.'

'Alice! All of you! Come here darlings, you're needed!' Jocelyn's voice carried easily from the far end of the orchard, where she and the crew were gathered in a huddle.

'Ah. The Arthur moment,' Alice murmured as they made their way through the straggly dry grass. Grace, who knew what was coming, caught hold of her hand.

Katie was looking big-eyed and pale, as if she'd had a bad shock. Alice smiled at her but Katie – and Nick as well – just gazed back blankly. Patrice and Jocelyn were staring at the ground where a dense clump of aged rosemary was blooming prolifically.

'OK Nick, keep it running!' Patrice turned back to Jocelyn. 'So the illustrious sculptor Arthur Gillings is actually buried right *here* in the Penmorrow orchard?' He pointed to the ground, somewhere in the centre of the rosemary.

Noel breathed in sharply behind Alice. She nudged him to be quiet. Even the boys had fallen silent, though Sam was flicking at the end of his catapult as if he could hardly bring himself not to be loading and firing it at the birds that swooped between the trees.

'Oh yes, this is Arthur's grave,' Jocelyn said, in the kind of tone that suggested that surely all private gardens contained human graves. 'We marked it with rosemary for remembrance. He didn't approve of funeral furnishings. He died in Gosling cottage you see, simply fell asleep on the sofa in front of the fire. Look, you can still just see . . .' and she pointed up to the silver birch where high up a few scraps of fabric were blowing raggedly in the breeze. 'Prayer flags to help his spirit on its way. We hung the whole tree with them at the time, wonderful bright colours. They could be seen from parts of the village so of course everybody knew.'

'And so . . .' Patrice looked excited and flustered. 'Who conducted the service?'

'We all did. Milly was still here of course. That's Melissa Thorpe-Appleby, the painter, you know.'

'Gosh, yes of course!'

'Kelpie came back with her young family. We had a couple of songwriters and three young folks on their way to India. And Alice and Harry as well of course. Alice wrote a poem, didn't you darling?'

Nick swung the camera round to face her. 'I did, yes I remember. It wasn't terribly good. I remember thinking I'd rather have read some Keats or Byron, something much better than I could do.' Alice could feel Noel and Theo's boggling curiosity as if it was a dagger of heat. They were going to want to know details and why she hadn't mentioned before that there was a dead body lurking under the Penmorrow turf.

'And quite a few villagers and all Arthur's fishing and drinking friends came too,' Joss went on. 'Though he'd become reclusive over the last months and hadn't wanted to see people. We had a party, lots of booze out here where we'd put him. It was raining I remember, but it seemed such awfully bad manners to go indoors, it would have been like abandoning the guest of honour.'

'Um . . .' Patrice looked desperate. 'Was it strictly legal?'

'The party? Oh I'd have thought so, more or less,' Joss said. Alice couldn't help grinning. Joss being disingenuous was a rare sight.

'The burial,' Patrice said calmly. 'Don't you have to register deaths? And I thought . . .'

'All completely above board, darling, averse though I am to officialdom.' Joss reached forward, plucked a twig of the rosemary and sniffed it fondly. 'He was properly registered dead and this . . .' she waved her hand across the plants, 'became a lawful burial site. Just for Arthur – so far. Anyone can be buried on home ground, you know, as long as you have it all written down in your burial book as per legalities.' Patrice looked slightly disappointed. Presumably, Alice guessed, because he wasn't recording an admission of some kind of crime. He'd have enjoyed that, she realized, exposing this old eccentric as a shameless lawbreaker. Joss continued, loudly and clearly, 'Guinevere Partridge wove the coffin. Arthur had had it made months before – she'd kept it for him in her workshop. Now that was quite a shock, him having been so prepared.'

'*Wove?*' Noel's incredulous voice broke through. 'What's he in, a bloody rug?'

'Cut!' Patrice roared. 'We'll have to go again on that.' He turned to Noel. 'Do you mind? Sorry and all but we were on a roll here.' He moved past Joss and shoved his face close to Noel's. 'Did you think I was really going to let that pass? I know what I'm doing.'

'Sorry!' Noel called. 'But come on, it's just that . . .'

'OK, OK. But you guys know all this stuff already?' Katie tried to calm him down.

'Not me!' Noel put his hands up, backing away 'It's all news to me.'

'And me.' Theo stood next to his father, supportive. Alice and Grace exchanged mildly guilty glances.

'I mean most people just bury their dead pets, not their . . .'

'Right, on we go.' Patrice waved Noel aside. 'Just say the last bit again, Joss my love, about the Guinevere person.'

Jocelyn repeated her previous sentences without further interruption from Noel and continued, 'It was a wicker coffin. Arthur ordered it secretly. He'd been

193

measured up just as calmly as if it was for a suit and she'd made it for him. It was so beautiful, a true, loving art-piece and an awful shame to consign it to the ground.' Joss looked misty-eyed into the distance, remembering, then continued brightly, 'Of course it was rather unusual at the time to be buried in wicker, but it wouldn't be now, would it? Not in these days of cardboard coffins and burials in sustainable woodland.'

Patrice then called a halt to the filming and wrapped a cotton bandanna round his sweating head. Mo appeared at that moment, carrying a trayful of mugs and the biggest brown teapot to the lichen-tufted table at the top end of the orchard. Grace's cat Monty bounced around her feet threatening to trip her, and she gently toed him out of the way.

'Why did you never say anything about it? Why was it news to me that there's a . . . a rotting corpse under your mother's garden?' Noel hissed to Alice as they made their way towards the hugely welcome refreshments.

Alice shrugged. 'It never came up, did it? Penmorrow has never exactly been your favourite topic. Anyway, what else was Joss supposed to do with Arthur? He was scared about dying. She'd promised him he wouldn't ever have to leave.'

'He could have been cremated and then scattered here. That would be the choice of the rational, I'd have said, wouldn't you?'

Alice breathed evenly, remembering what Milly had taught her in the Penmorrow yoga sessions out on the front meadow.

'He was afraid of the flames. Joss had promised and she kept her promise. I don't see a problem. And neither should you – it was years ago.'

'Bloody bunch of old hippy lunatics. And prayer flags in the trees!'

'Oh big deal.' Alice laughed, trying to lighten Noel's mood. 'Down at Predannack there's a tree hung all over with teapots!' Noel ignored her, saying, 'And Grace knew, I could see by her face. She'll be getting ideas.'

'Is that such a bad thing?'

'What?' Noel almost barked the word.

'Ideas. I hope she does "get ideas". You make it sound like an unpleasant disease.'

Alice took a mug of tea from the tray and wandered away from the table towards the herb garden near the house. She wondered where Aidan was. He should really have been there to get Jocelyn's horse's-mouth description of Arthur's burial. She'd talk about that episode to him later, she decided, just to make sure he'd got it down. Jocelyn seemed to have assumed so much of her odd life was perfectly normal that it was possible it hadn't even come up. Thinking about it for the first time since Arthur's death, it now seemed rather a lovely ending, to be buried by and among those you most love. So much better than having your corpse wrapped in black plastic and hauled away by strangers, like an embarrassing spillage. As Joss had promised, Arthur hadn't had to leave the premises. Alice admired the way she'd stuck to that. She remembered Arthur lying in his wicker casing laid out on the big dining table. He was wrapped in his musty black velvet cloak and lay in a nest of cedarwood shavings and fronds of ivy. Eighty-two white candles, one for each year of his life, had burned, and when the last of them expired on the third day, Joss had decreed it was time for him to be buried.

Alice finished her tea and took the tray of mugs into the kitchen, then went out again through the front door. She found Aidan and Theo sitting on the front steps, talking, looking serious, talking intently. Theo was picking up scraps of gravel and aiming them at Big Shepherd's furthest sheep, the stones pinging off the bronze each time he scored a hit.

'Have they finished?' Aidan looked up and asked her. 'Did I miss much?' He looked, Alice thought, like a schoolboy who'd nipped out to the bike sheds for a cigarette. Why *wasn't* he there? she wondered. Surely if he was ghosting the complete life of Jocelyn he should take a thorough interest while he was actually on site, so to speak.

'Come and sit with us. Theo and I were just having a Tony Hawks moment,' Aidan explained as he shuffled along the step to make room for Alice and leaned back against the splintery wooden pillar that held up the verandah in front of the doorway. His hyper-chic glasses had gone dark from the sunlight.

Theo was looking completely awestruck, Alice recognized, which puzzled her: she hadn't had Theo down as a reader, and certainly hadn't seen him with a Tony Hawkes book.

'Aidan's got through all of game two and that's the best.' He could hardly get the words out for gasping admiration. 'He's gone into Spiderman, even into the secret levels, even the Helidrop and all of Skate Heaven. Jeez, that's just cool as.' Theo shook his head, overwhelmed by something about Aidan that Alice couldn't quite fathom. Tony Hawkes? This sounded like one of his books she hadn't read.

'Has Tony Hawkes got a new book out?' she asked. 'I've read the one about going round Ireland with a fridge, and – oh what's that other one – *Playing the Moldavians at Tennis*? Wasn't that it? I think he's excellent.'

Aidan took off his glasses and looked at her, smirking rather off-puttingly. 'Um – I think there's some wires that are crossing themselves here,' he said, slowly and precisely as if to a non-comprehending infant. 'We were actually talking about, um, Tony Hawks Pro-Skater? PlayStation games? One to three?' The questioning upward lilt didn't hold any hope at all, Alice was mortified to realize, of her being expected to understand what they were talking about.

'PlayStation Two? Games?' Theo was almost adding insult to injury by repeating. Oh good grief, Alice thought, completely tingling with the realization of her own middle-aged foolishness, Aidan was just so utterly, so remotely, young. How on earth could she have daydreamed away any kind of sexual energy on someone who still played with toys? She felt like getting up and flouncing indoors in an embarrassed huff. Quite why, she wasn't sure. Why on earth should it matter that at her age (or any age come to that) she knew lots about current books and absolutely nothing about daft computer games?

Chas and Sam had smeared their faces and much of their clothing with mud. It made their blue eyes, Grace thought, look overbright and scary. 'You'll have to do it too. And your hair. It's too yellow. We'll be seen,' Sam told her, leading her off the path into the gloom of the trees. The evening was damp and chilly and Grace shivered. Theo didn't seem bothered, he hunkered down by the rotting beech stump and rubbed earth into his face as if he was (and so unlikely this, Grace thought) giving it a good wash. His hair had got quite long now, she noticed, and he'd stopped bothering to get it to stick up in all the right places like he did at home. In fact at home, she thought, he was forever looking in mirrors, at shop-window reflections and other people's wing mirrors on the streets to tweak at his hair. Now he didn't seem to care at all, which was good. It crossed her mind that she wasn't obsessing about her appearance, either. Well you couldn't, she reasoned, when you spent half your time in the sea. Plus there was no Sophy to compete with, no crew of smart girly mates going for the Most Gorgeous stakes.

'Put this on over your hair.' Sam handed Grace a torn khaki baseball hat. She looked at it and he grouched, 'That's if you want to come with us. If you don't want to stay at home and paint your nails?'

'No, I'm coming.' She twisted her hair up, secured it with a piece of stick and crammed the hat on top of it. If only Sophy could see me now, she thought as she rubbed earth into her face, reminding herself at the same time that mud was supposed to be good for the skin.

'Heads down at the village,' Chas ordered, leading the way down the hill.

'Maybe we should have just applied the cammo when we got to the place?' Theo tentatively suggested. 'I mean suppose someone clocks us, that woman from the shop, people at the pub.'

'We're *going* round the *back* road.' Sam didn't even look at him, leaving Theo in no doubt that his ideas input was superfluous. Grace grinned at him, which made him feel better. She surely didn't take it seriously, all this fake SAS army-manoeuvres-type stuff? She looked like she was well into it, eyes shining, no whingeing about her shoes hurting, going along with whatever these mad cousins of hers said.

'Where's the stuff?' Grace asked as they crossed to the road at the bottom of the track and set off up the lane towards the back of the village and Hamilton Hall's main entrance.

'Under the hedge. We stashed it earlier,' Chas replied tersely.

They were fifty feet or so from the official entrance to Hamilton House and the coveted fishpond. Dusk was falling fast now, and through gaps in the high drystone wall Grace could see down to where the village lights were flicking on, and out to where freight liners and holiday yachts glittered on the sea. It was her favourite time of day at Penmorrow, when she could hear wildlife in the dense undergrowth stirring for a session of busy foraging. Monty would be out there, stalking mice and voles and doing all that lion-like cat stuff that he so loved. In Richmond, apart from a quick dash to dig holes in next door's garden, he mostly spent his evenings lying on the carpet under her bedroom radiator, sleeping and hiccuping as he digested his tinned dinner. Here, he indulged his wild side, hunting and chasing and lurking under bushes to see what could be ambushed. I'm being like him, Grace thought to herself as Sam and Chas pushed her and Theo into a thicket to avoid being caught in an approaching car's headlights. I'm being, she thought, a wild person, back to something more primitive. Catching food. She tried not to think of the theft aspect. That was where Monty came out top; he wouldn't end up in a Young Offenders place for what he was doing.

'OK, in here.' Sam pulled a piece of wire netting aside and climbed through a picket fence, disappearing almost instantly into Hamilton House's shrubbery.

'And try not to rustle too much,' Chas whispered to Theo. 'You don't want to scare roosting birds into flying up.'

'Is there a gamekeeper or anything?' Grace hugged her arms around her body, suddenly nervous.

'Gamekeeper?' Chas hissed. 'Don't be stupid! It's a garden, not a grouse moor! Now come on, keep close and keep up!'

Sam picked up a roll of binbags and a keep-net from where he'd hidden them earlier under a rhododendron. Chas was carrying a child's blue plastic beach bucket. In it, he boasted, there was enough stuff to kill a huge great lakeful of fish. 'It's the shells,' he'd explained to Grace and Theo up by the fire at the cave. 'You burn them really hot and they give off lime that poisons the fish.'

'But won't that poison us too? When we eat the fish?' Theo had asked.

'No. And if we don't put too much in, not all the fish either,' Sam had said. 'We only want about six. There's loads in the pond – they won't even notice these have gone.'

Grace wasn't so sure, now that they'd reached the pond's edge. She lay on her tummy looking down as the long gold and silver creatures slid back and forth lazily. It was hard to tell how many there were. The pond looked deep and further down only shimmery shapes could be seen in the half-dark. She wondered if they ever slept, properly sleeping with their eyes shut at the bottom of the pond, all curled up together. They looked like pet goldfish that a giant might keep, sleek and curvy and big-scaled and with horrible, huge gobbly mouths. Sam had scattered the lime on the top of the water and some of the fish had come up to grab it as if it was best fishfood. The twins looked uncertain, as if it was only now that they wondered if their plan would work. They all lay still for what seemed like ages, silently waiting. The moon rose behind massive oak trees and cast milky shadows on the grass beyond the pond site.

'Bad night for it,' Sam commented, shaking his head.

'No choice though,' Chas added.

Nothing was happening. The fish still ambled around and Grace was beginning to feel chilled and stiff. Then, just as she was about to ask if there was any point waiting any longer, there was a violent splashing in the water. She jumped out of the way as cold drops landed on her legs.

'Get down!' Sam ordered, looking past her anxiously.

'I'm getting *wet*,' she explained, watching horrified as the splashing died down and one by one a good dozen of the magnificent fish floated to the surface.

'Shit. Too many,' Chas muttered, reaching for the net. He leaned out and hauled in the first one. Theo helped him land it, shoving it quickly into a binbag.

'They're quite heavy too. How many shall we take?' Theo asked.

'Have to get all the dead ones out,' Chas told him, pulling another from the pond and letting it slither into the bag. 'Otherwise they'll know something's happened.'

'There's no way they're not going to know!' Grace pointed to the silvery corpses. 'There's loads of them!'

'It's probably not as many as it looks. We'll get what we can, chuck some in the bushes if there's too much and then the others will look like . . .'

'What?' Grace demanded furiously. 'Natural bloody causes?'

'Look, it's not a precise thing. We had to take a guess. Maybe they're not all dead, just a bit . . .' Sam started a snorting laugh.

Chas joined in, sniggering. 'A bit slightly ill. They might get better. If we leave them.'

201

Eventually they took ten fish divided between three bags. They were bulky and soft and Grace was glad she wasn't asked to carry one. Instead she accepted the net and the bucket. Only two dead fish remained floating in the middle of the pond, out of reach. So this was a true survival skill, she thought. Appalled as she was at the shocking shiny deaths, it had been quite exciting really. And if there was a war sometime she might need to know this kind of thing. All the same, if Mo ever really did cook these fish, Grace thought she might just opt for a cheese omelette.

Twelve

He was sure to collide with the wrath of Mo for this, but Harry was willing to take the chance. Needs must, he thought as he made his way to Cygnet, going the long way round past the polytunnels and keeping his head down. There was a mild but alluring scent of dope on the air from his crops which were now, triggered by the slight shortening of the day length, forming prolific, sticky flower heads. It was going to be a good year. A profitable year. Even so, that particular sideline wasn't going to wipe out their cash-flow problems all by its illegal little self. Whatever Mo said, holiday letting was still the business they were supposed to be running. Keeping the punters happy went with the territory. If they couldn't at least try to do that they'd soon be left with no territory at all. Flogging a few courgettes and lettuces to the organic farm shop, collecting the surf-shack rent and under-cutting the local dope dealers with a batch of quality home-grown wasn't going to keep the twins in trainers.

Alice was already there, waiting in Cygnet's open doorway with a notebook and pen in her hand. She was looking pretty much loosened up compared with how she'd been when she'd arrived at Penmorrow, he thought. She'd stopped doing that ridiculous thing with the collars of those horrible stripey shirts she seemed to like, turning them up high as if she was trying to keep a gale out of her ears. Instead she'd picked up some tight little tee shirts from the surf shops in St Ives and looked about five years younger. She wasn't wearing those navy tasselled deck shoes either that smart people from London always chose as appropriate seaside wear, and was roaming about everywhere either barefoot or in cheap little pink rubber flip-flops with glittery beads across the front.

'Have you had a look round yet?' Harry asked, peering back over his shoulder guiltily, half-expecting Mo to leap out of the bushes and pounce on him. Cygnet was a long, single-storey timber-framed cottage ('not unlike staying in a big garden shed' had been one of the sniffier visitors'-book comments): Mo could show up at any of the windows, glancing in and catching him and Alice colluding about lampshades.

'I have. It's actually not nearly as bad as Gosling was. At least everything in here works.'

Harry almost pushed her into the cottage and quickly shut the door after them both. Aware of Mo's hostility, Alice wasn't too surprised and continued, 'The bedroom windows haven't been leaking so the paint isn't all discoloured. All the way through you could get away with stripping out the carpets, polishing and staining the floorboards and hanging some unlined calico curtains. Those hideous old maroon Dralon things in the sitting room will have to go, and definitely the baggy-knicker blinds in the second bedroom. They're full of spider nests. I don't think anyone's touched them in years.'

'The furniture though. What about that? It all looks like something your granny might have thrown out.'

'If we'd ever *had* a granny. What's the opposite of "extended family"?' Alice laughed. Harry said nothing. Interpreting their upbringing wasn't his idea of time well spent. Silently, but with gloomy dread, he followed Alice past the bathroom and into the first of two bedrooms, where the tarnished brass bed took up much of the available space.

'There's just too much clutter in here,' Alice said, running her finger across the top of the chest of drawers. 'It looks musty and crowded – all those twiddly china ornaments and dusty little lace mats. Get rid of everything except the bed. There's plenty of shelf space in that huge alcove cupboard.' She looked round the walls. 'Put up some reading lights on the wall over the bed and they can put their glasses of water and their books on the window seats each side. In fact actually . . .' Alice opened the cupboard door and tapped the wall at the back.

'Actually what?'

'Hang on a minute . . .' Alice went into the next room, opened the corresponding wardrobe in the adjoining alcove, then returned to Harry. 'I thought so,' she said to him, 'this isn't really a wall at all, just a plasterboard partition thing. What I'd do, if I was in charge of this, would be to take out this whole wall, knock the two rooms into one big airy bedroom. You could easily do that in a couple of days, then paint the whole lot white, trade white though, not the brilliant one. It's softer. Forget about catering for a family and go for the urban-couple market.'

Harry laughed. 'And what are they, when they're at home?'

'When they're "at home" they are the folks with the cash. The empty-nesters, young pre-family pairs, gay couples, pensioners who like a bit of space, anyone who wants to come out of season and look at gardens and the Eden Project. They're everything but the bucket and spade brigade. You could do weekend breaks for that lot and charge almost as much as a full week. People who take their main holidays in hot places still like to do long weekends in this country.' Alice jotted down a few notes then went on, almost buzzing with enthusiasm, 'You could make this place look like a fabulous Long Island beach house. If cash was no limit I'd suggest you take the ceilings off, open it all up and line the roof with limed planks, put in tiny spotlights, all that. It could look truly gorgeous.'

Harry shoved his hands into his pockets and shifted about, looking uncomfortable. Unfortunately cash *was* a limiting factor. 'Sounds astronomically expensive. Mo reckons all this doing-up isn't worth it, in fact her words were "pissing in the wind".' He remembered that, it had been one of her new repertoire of astonishingly blunt phrases and had quite shocked him.

Alice sat down on the bed and shut her notebook. 'It would be worth it in the long run. It's more a question of chucking stuff out than buying anything in,' she said. 'But . . . I've got a feeling Mo isn't interested in Penmorrow as a "long run" any more. Am I right?'

'If we're talking long run then we'd go for Truro, Newquay, Penzance at a push, maybe St Ives. That's what Mo's hankering after. Sometimes I see her, looking through the business ads in the *West Briton*, checking out the B. & B.'s for sale. Manageable places, not like this,' Harry admitted, perching on the window seat and peeking out into the garden, sure that Mo must be within listening distance.

'But what about you?' Alice asked. 'And the boys? Surely you don't want to leave Penmorrow? You've been here all your lives.' That sounded patronizing, she realized as soon as the words were out. What better reason for wanting to move on, the fact that you'd never experienced the adventure of being somewhere else? Why ever shouldn't Mo and Harry want to do that?

In spite of this train of thought, it was still a surprise to Alice when Harry shrugged. She'd expected him to laugh and say something like, 'Don't be daft, where else would we go?' but instead he simply said, 'The boys would love to live in a town, especially now they're coming up to their teenage years. An out-of-the-way little village like this isn't going to be their idea of fun in a year or two. I wouldn't mind, but . . .' Harry grinned and gave her a sly look. 'I'd miss my polytunnels,' he admitted. 'And we're stuck really, while Joss is still around. We should have gone years ago but back then we didn't want to. Now we can't go anywhere because Joss won't be able to manage all this by herself. Having no choice is what really gets up Mo's nose.'

Well at least she wouldn't have to wonder what to cook. Mo stared at the unexpected bounty in the freezer and tried to count the fish that were bundled in untidily as if by someone in a hurry, each one wrapped neatly in clingfilm. Their eyes were still quite bright, so they must have been frozen immediately after being caught. Mo assumed Harry had put them there but was surprised he hadn't mentioned them. Usually when he came home with an edible bargain, courtesy of a villager in the pub, he was more than eager to let her know.

Mo pulled one of the fish out for a closer look. She could see it was some kind of carp. She'd been thinking about carp, too; she was sure she'd even mentioned it in passing, though not expecting to get any. She'd thought she'd have to make do with whatever the fish van in Chapel Creek had got left over. This was a fancy creature, just like a kid's pet goldfish but as big as, if not bigger than, a good-size bass. Bony things, these, she thought, and not what most people would choose. But they were tasty, if her memory from childhood didn't let her down. She remembered her mother cooking some that her father had caught, remembered the catchy reek of vinegar that had gone into the water she'd soaked them in to get rid of any lingering muddiness in the flesh. She'd got her mother's recipe somewhere among the old cookery books piled at the back of the larder. If Harry hadn't seen fit to tell her, then Mo wasn't going to ask where they'd come from, the same as she hadn't asked when she'd found three brace of pheasant hanging on the porch next to the wind chimes last October, or when Harry had brought home a ragged hunk of blood-soaked deer the night there'd been a new dent in the car's bumper. With these, she'd just have to consider their presence as a miracle. Not enough of a fish miracle to feed five thousand, but more than enough for this house full of Jocelyn's creepy-crawly disciples.

Mo could hear Jocelyn in the sitting room holding court with her film-crew people and getting over-excited, laughing too loudly at something Patrice was saying. The right and generous thing to hope would be that she wouldn't get too giddy and push her blood pressure up and out of control, but Mo, guiltily, could bring herself to hope for no such thing. It would be a handily quick and pain-free way (all round) for Joss to go, Mo thought, trying to square her wayward conscience. If Jocelyn simply dropped down dead, overcome by the delight of having so much squirmingly obsequious attention, then taken all round and looking back after the initial shock and sorrow of it, and after planting her in the orchard alongside Arthur, it mightn't be such a terrible tragedy.

I never used to think like this, Mo reminded herself as she pulled the rest of the fish out of the freezer, laid them on the draining board and counted them. She looked back at her young self as a grateful little mouse, only too willing to muck in and do Joss's bidding for the privilege of living with her and being part of this house. This house. Mo sighed as she began to unwrap the clingfilm from the fish. This house that wasn't her house. This house that was fast outstripping its owner in the race to be decrepit and demanding. The way things were going it would fall down long before Jocelyn did. She'd found four more roof tiles that had crashed to the back terrace this morning and it was barely even breezy. God only knew what ravages another stormy autumn would bring. There was a chimney that looked distinctly askew. Whether it was any worse than the year before, she really didn't like to guess. And the hot weather brought out the worst in the drains – well certainly a smell that didn't seem right, not if the septic tanks were functioning properly. When, oh when would she and Harry and the boys get to escape to live in a nice snug place somewhere on a milk round, a twice-an-hour bus route and only a short hop from Sainsbury's? Never, would be the answer to that one if Alice with her well-meaning arty-room makeovers got her way. She'd keep Penmorrow limping on till they and the collected sodding premises were all worn to dust and splinters.

'A beach barbecue! Oh yes, super idea. Such a lovely day for it,' Mo overheard Joss enthusing loudly to

Patrice. The voice was getting nearer, accompanied by the unctuous tones of Patrice himself as the two of them came into the kitchen.

'Mo – just the person.' Jocelyn came up beside her and squeezed her arm fondly. 'Oooh look at those beautiful fish! Are they for tonight's supper? How clever of you to find something so gorgeously glittery for us.'

Mo smiled and began washing the first of the fish, slicing it along its belly with expert speed and letting its insides flop out into the bowl in the sink, very close to Patrice.

'Ugh.' Patrice wrinkled his nose and stepped smartly backward.

'Shouldn't you be filming this, Patrice?' Mo asked, giving him a look of sly challenge. 'If you want the authentic Penmorrow experience, that is . . .'

'Well I suppose I might if Joss was doing it.' Patrice crept a little closer to take a cautious look, though making sure he stayed outside innards-splashing range. The stench from even the smallest drip would linger horribly in denim.

'Oh don't ask me, sweetie.' Jocelyn moved away, reaching for her cigarettes from the dresser shelf. 'Mo is the expert when it comes to cooking. I couldn't begin to compete.'

'No, really it's all right! If you want to do some of this I'll save you the last two. It's only a matter of slit and scoop.' Mo offered the bloodied knife to Patrice but, to his obvious relief, Joss's attention had skipped ahead.

'Mo, darling, will these fish be all right to barbecue?' she asked. 'Patrice wants us all on the beach later this afternoon for a few shots and a bit of a chat about the time we played cricket on the sand with the

Attenboroughs. He wants the whole family this time, at about five when the trippers have gone for their caravan teas and the light is still good.'

Mo decided that barbecuing seemed as good a way of cooking these fish as any. She would, she thought, adapt her mother's old recipe, wrap them whole in foil parcels with some of Harry's shallots, plenty of pepper and a splash or two of white wine. They weren't the type of fish you could even begin to fillet. It was only to be hoped that Jocelyn wouldn't be so busy being a star for Patrice that she forgot about being careful to avoid the bones.

Grace had lost her little gold watch. Noel had given it to her on her birthday two years before and although it wasn't what she'd have chosen for herself (she should have hinted for a purple Baby G or a chunky Animal one) she wouldn't want to hurt his feelings by having to admit she'd been careless enough to let it fall off.

Where the watch had fallen off was the big problem. Grace sat on the Gosling sofa with Monty purring on her lap while she bit the skin around her right thumbnail and worried about where it could be. She'd had it before the weekend, she was sure. She'd had it all the time she'd been reading *Angel's Choice* – she remembered looking at it late in the afternoon when she'd finished the book, and being surprised that it was nearly six o'clock and still so hot on the beach. She was almost certain she'd had it when they'd climbed up the rocks to Sam and Chas's cave and when they'd made the fire for the shells.

There was one scary possibility that she was going to have to think really hard about. Suppose, just suppose, it was up the hill in that garden by the fishpond? She wished she could remember exactly what she'd done there. She remembered putting her hand into the water to see if she could catch a fish the other way that Sam had been telling her about, 'tickling' he'd called it, by keeping really still till one of the fish sort of sat over her hand and then scooping it out. It would have been her right hand that she'd put in. She wore her watch on her left wrist. She couldn't at all remember if she'd put both hands in the water. All she recalled was that she'd given up very fast on trying to catch a fish that way – just in case the stuff the twins had put in the water was so toxic that she'd get gross skin blotches and some fatal foul disease.

Grace put Monty onto the cushions beside her and went upstairs to search through the clothes chaos on her room floor again. The watch must be somewhere. If it wasn't in the house this time, she decided, she'd go up to Hamilton House on a day when it was open to have a look round by the pond. If it *was* there, she wanted to be the one to find it. Otherwise, someone else might pick it up and hand it in to someone who'd decide it was evidence. They'd have no trouble finding her, her mother, of course, had had her full name, in accordance with school regulations, engraved on the back.

After hot days when holidaymakers had almost fought for space on the beach and trampled each other's territory with ball games and giant sandcastles, the shore became quiet again soon after five in the afternoon. The trippers folded the windbreaks, packed away the beach toys and left to bath and feed their tired and hungry children. This was the time the boy in the car park stopped charging for any car with a local number plate and a roof rack full of surfboards. The surf shack became busy with local custom, the bodyboarders and surfers arriving to catch the last of the afternoon's waves before the evening calm descended on the sea. Theo had taken to hanging out with them and joining in, well able to talk the surf talk even if his competence in the sea lacked their years of practice. Alice, walking down the path from Penmorrow with Mo and Aidan, could see him now, sitting on the café's front rail sipping something from a can and watching a couple of experts choosing the waves.

He was very tanned, she thought, contrasting him with his town-pallid father. He also looked unusually comfortable with his body for a change. Back at home he tended to slouch around as if he was too self-conscious to unfold himself properly. She'd commented on it once and Grace, more sensitive to a teen boy's feelings than she obviously was, had warned her not to do it again. Noel, lacking any sensitivity at all, had said loudly in front of Theo and a room full of their dinner-party guests, 'He shuffles about with his hands in his pockets and all hunched over so his trousers don't fall down.' Then he'd increased Theo's embarrassed misery by adding, with toe-curling jocularity, 'If they drop much further we'll all be able to see if he takes after his dad.'

Even Alice had winced at that one, but she'd suspected Noel might not be far wrong – Theo and all his friends went around with their trousers slung so far down they looked in danger of an imminent and calamitous debagging. Grace and her girly friends at least had hips, albeit skinny ones, to hold their clothes up. There was a girl quite close to Theo at the café now, Alice realized, perched a little way along the same rail, all long legs and bare brown middle. She couldn't see from that distance if he was actually talking to her. Probably not. Conversation was another of those things teenage boys didn't do a lot of, she'd discovered, along with getting up in the mornings without protest and remembering their games kit for school.

Noel and Harry had bagged a stretch of beach by the rocks against the sea wall which would be in the sun till the very last rays warmed the sand. They'd gone ahead of the others, loaded with coolboxes and picnic baskets and barbecues, and had joined forces to get a driftwood fire going. Noel had sunk bottles of wine deep into the chill damp sand and the two of them had had a chat about cricket and got a couple of beers down before everyone else joined them. Alice, Mo and Aidan could see them as they reached the lane that led towards the shop and the pub.

The shop looked busy – people were bustling in and out and a number of villagers had collected outside the door by the phone box for what looked like a pretty intense gossip. Who, Alice wondered idly, was their picked-over victim this time? It was a long time now since Penmorrow had been the main focus of collective curiosity, though Jocelyn's illness and the presence of Aidan had revived ripples of interest. In a brash (though futile) attempt at finding out what his role in the household was, Mrs Rice had cheerily ventured to suggest the term 'toy boy' to Harry but had had no luck there: unworldly Harry had simply come back to the house and asked Mo if the woman had been talking about some robot that was going to be that Christmas's must-have toy, and if so were the twins about to hanker after one.

'So you've been relegated to the second division

214

of Joss's favourites,' Alice teased Aidan as the two of them approached the gathering outside the shop.

Aidan sighed. 'Certainly looks like it. Just when the book was going well, she suddenly doesn't want to talk about herself – well not to me anyway; she doesn't have any trouble with Patrice. "Publishers can wait. Television can't," she said to me yesterday when I told her it was time we moved on towards the 1980s.'

'She's just revelling in the attention,' Alice reassured him. 'This time next week when they've gone she'll be all yours again, you'll see.'

'So what am I supposed to do? I've done as much as I can for now. I might as well go home for a few days, see if she's back down to earth after they've gone.'

Alice laughed. 'Down to earth is probably the last thing Joss will ever be.' She hoped he wouldn't go. Sometimes Aidan seemed to be the one sane link holding the household together. She'd told him as much that morning, as she'd sat on his bed, telling him what she remembered about Arthur's burial in the orchard, while he took notes at his desk by the window.

He'd frowned and looked a bit worried. 'It goes with the job,' he'd said, shrugging off her comment as if afraid that it would lead to her dragging him under his duvet. 'I'm just supposed to be normal and pleasant and nice to everyone concerned, like a sort of blank neutral thing – get them to trust me enough for complete hundred per cent confiding. You get told, well you sort of find out . . .' and here he'd hesitated, looking at the floor. 'Well you sometimes find out a lot more than is destined for the actual book.'

Alice, pretty sure that he was no longer talking about Joss, had left quickly after that, pleading urgent Cygnet-renovation ideas to note down before, as she

215

imagined he might, he backed so far out of what he might consider to be her lust-crazed grappling range that he fell out of the window. He'd sounded slightly unpleasantly calculating, as if he had no real interest in any of them beyond his professional capacity. Perhaps he hadn't. After all, as soon as the book was finished he could erase it and all of them from his mind, get started on whatever was next. Possibly he'd be moving on to a rock star with memory problems, a sportsman resentful of speedier upcomers. Who knew?

Still, she was glad he'd found the Arthur story really poignant. She'd been truly delighted that he'd not expressed the slightest hint that he considered it absurd to bury someone on home ground in a hand-woven willow coffin. If he went, she'd be left with Joss's fawning suitor Patrice and the steamy pouting Katie. Mo sulked and fumed, Harry was miles away, anaesthetized from reality by the effects of whatever crop he'd been sampling, and Noel was restless, jumpy and out of place. Only Grace, Theo and Aidan – and of course Jocelyn – seemed comfortably settled, perfectly contented and relaxed as if Penmorrow was an absolutely wonderful place to be. And it was. Or could be, a year's worth of building work permitting . . .

The attention of the small crowd by the phone box was suddenly diverted as two police cars squealed down the hill and whizzed up the dust as they swished into the pub car park.

'Murder at the vicarage?' Aidan suggested, laughing as four policemen, as if personally exhausted by the speed at which they'd driven, lumbered heavily out of the cars.

'Wouldn't surprise me,' Mo replied dourly. 'Everyone's off the vicar since he went all happy-clappy.'

'So the Sign of Peace is more of a battle cry here?' Aidan ventured.

'So they say,' Mo said, allowing herself a rare and, Alice thought, rather pretty smile.

The twins hadn't, as far as Alice could see, brought their catapults to the beach, so the Tremorwell seagulls should be safe for a while. She wasn't too surprised – Sam and Chas were hardly likely to misbehave so dreadfully on home territory. Even Jocelyn, who had encouraged the thrifty collecting and cooking of roadkill back in the commune days, wouldn't approve of pointless cruelty to inedible birds.

As Alice spread her trusty plastic-backed blanket on the sand she could see the boys watching her stealthily from the far side of Harry. They were quite unnerving, with their intense blue gazes and stolid expressionless faces. She wondered if she was the only one who imagined unknown thought processes going on in their heads and passing without speech between the two of them. It wouldn't be unusual with identical twins, but these two weren't identical and yet managed to give the impression that they shared a single, highly active, mischief-seeking spirit.

'Been a robbery in the village, Mo,' Harry called from the rock he was sitting on beside Noel. The two men were looking very companionable, Harry puffing deeply on something pungent from a small pipe and both of them drinking beers from cans. Alice guessed they were on at least their second, possibly third, for Noel was no longer looking as awkward as a catalogue model decked out in hyper-clean leisurewear. Patrice was fussing with Nick and the camera, muttering about sand getting everywhere, and Katie was sprawled with her eyes shut on a towel in a red bikini, oiled up to a mirror-like sheen against the weak late afternoon rays.

'Robbery? Where?' Mo called back to Harry.

'Up at Hamilton House, you know the one with the gardens?'

Grace slid silently down from her perch on a rock and went to make herself unobtrusively busy, pouring more wine for Joss who was sitting on a low, folding wicker chair and waving an empty glass in the direction of the coolboxes. Grace was very quiet today, Alice thought. Probably missing her friends. She'd talk to her about it later, see if she'd changed her mind about having Sophy down to stay for a few days.

'That'll be what they're all nattering about then, up at the shop. Well at least we know now,' Mo said, pulling her foil parcels out of their box. Alice had made a big bowl of salad in the Gosling kitchen, keeping well out of Mo's way. Couscous and herbs. She'd told Mo she'd got the recipe from Jamie Oliver's book. Mo wasn't sure about that young man – he seemed a bit flash and cocky on the telly, though the food looked good and tasty enough. As far as she was concerned you couldn't beat the old dignitaries: Elizabeth David and Robert Carrier or her special favourite, Jane Grigson. None of those did thrown-together things with couscous. Still, the herbs were from the Penmorrow garden and would be fresh and tasty. She just hoped the couscous stuff wouldn't get stuck in Harry's crumbling molars.

'We're going to be really informal with this, everybody. Just carry on as if we weren't here.' Patrice called them all to attention to talk about the shots he wanted. Katie had put on a sarong and was ready for duty. Nick and Dez were at last satisfied with the level of natural light.

'He shouldn't have said anything,' Aidan whispered to Alice. 'I think we'd forgotten he *was* here.'

'Now we'll all be looking sideways at the camera every time we say anything,' she giggled.

'Perfect!' Patrice called across to her. 'That's the kind of thing I want, just casual chatting amongst yourselves! I'll start with Noel and Harry attending the barbie. OK Harry? Let's roll!'

The foil parcels of fish were stacked around the edges of the barbecue, out of direct flames. Mo handed Noel a bunch of skewers on which were part-cooked pieces of corn on the cob. 'Give them something to chew on while they're waiting,' she told him, happy to hand over outdoor cooking to him. She didn't trust barbecues. They were unreliable and uncontrollable and nothing ever came out as perfect as it could if it had been put in an oven, even with an Aga as variable in temperament as the one at Penmorrow.

Joss was getting fidgety and quite hungry. Patrice was supposed to be talking to her about beach parties of old but instead was zapping about getting what he called 'background'. What did he need that for? He'd said the programme would end up only about forty minutes long. She'd got a lot more than forty minutes' worth she could tell him. Surely he could just sit with her and they could chat, as they did up in the hexagon window in the sitting room. He was a very good interviewer – he just had to remind her with a key word or two and her memory was off like a greyhound from a trap. Only that morning they'd talked about *Angel's Choice* as a potential contemporary West End stage revival, and whether Marianne Faithfull could offer anything new to the part of the mother. She'd be an excellent casting, having played Angel herself quite exquisitely in the first stage version. Joss had had some further thoughts on that, and she wouldn't mind airing them while they were fresh in her mind.

Harry didn't look comfortable being the focus of attention like this. He was a very private man and hadn't even been asked if he minded being centre stage in shots for this documentary. Joss was starting to feel a little like making something of a scene, just to rescue the poor chap. There he was, awkwardly poking at the coals with a knife that would probably start to melt in the heat any minute, while Noel wittered on and on about the sea view from the golf course over at Mullion.

'I think this lot is ready!' Noel called, brandishing a spatula on which rested a steaming foil parcel.

'Plates, Alice,' Mo said, directing Alice towards a frayed but once-grand picnic basket that was incongruously stacked with paper plates, paper napkins and plastic forks. Alice handed them round, noticing that Theo had chosen exactly the right moment to extricate himself from the surfers and join the party. He wasn't alone either: two of the bulky policemen were striding over the sand alongside him. They had a look of important purpose about them. Harry, catching sight, shoved sand quickly into his pipe and stowed it behind his rock.

'Evening everybody.' The first of them, who Alice thought resembled Fred Flintstone, removed his hat and greeted them all. Patrice looked flustered but signalled to Nick to keep the camera going as everyone mumbled a reluctant hello at the two men and Noel, ever polite, offered them a drink.

'Er, very kind but no, thank you,' the Flintstone said. 'Just wondered if you'd heard the news.'

'About the robbery at Hamilton House? My son just mentioned it,' Jocelyn said. 'Was much taken?'

'Only about fifteen thousand pounds' worth of koi carp, madam.' The two men were at an almost

220

caricature level of officiousness: arms folded, no hint of a smile, though Alice guessed they were finding it hard to suppress their delight at telling about a juicy, expensive crime in such a quiet holiday village. No-one said anything, but the twins started up into spluttery laughter. She sympathized with them; it was almost beyond a joke that anything living in a pond could be worth that much.

Mo had arranged hunks of fish, steaming and sumptuously wafting, on a large plate with lemons and wedges of bread that she'd baked that morning. Harry had freed them from the foil and given the skins a flaring at the end so they were crisp and slightly blackened, just enough. She was on the point of handing them round and obviously it would be courteous to begin with the unexpected guests.

'Nice piece of fish, gentlemen?' she offered to the two policemen. Alice handed them paper plates, forks and napkins and smiled as they gave in to their appetites and accepted eagerly.

'And do be careful of the bones, won't you?' Mo reminded them. 'We wouldn't want you to choke.'

Thirteen

'You could come back home now, couldn't you?' Noel suggested to Alice as they lay in bed in Gosling, listening to the owls hooting to each other up in the woods behind the village. Alice always wondered why the countryside was ever described as 'peaceful'. At night you could barely get to sleep for the sounds of wildlife murdering, mating or generally shambling about in the undergrowth. She turned her attention from the conversing owls back to Noel, who was saying, 'There doesn't seem to be much wrong with Jocelyn. I'd say she was pretty much on form again. Why don't we drive back together the day after tomorrow? You'll need time to get yourself together for Italy.'

Alice wasn't so sure. She murmured a non-committal 'Hmm' to show that she'd at least heard what he'd said and then lay silently staring at the blotchy ceiling, thinking about what 'home' involved. It seemed an incredibly long way away. It was as if the longer she spent at Penmorrow the more distant the house in Richmond became. At the moment it felt about as far away as Alaska. If she stayed much longer the idea of travelling back would be as mind-bending as a trip to a far planet. And what was there that she was missing so much?

She thought about London's traffic grime, tube strikes and bad-tempered drivers, about unexpected, scary shoutings in the streets at night. On the mornings after major rugby matches in nearby Twickenham every main street in the borough had its patches of dried-out vomit, shredded plastic glasses and drifts of fast-food litter. She thought about the school-run mothers in their massive (and very clean) off-roaders who scurried here and there for manicures and Pilates classes, courses on Container Planting for Colour and cliquey little reading groups. Did she really want to go back to those supper-party discussions that she'd had time and time again about whether it would be a wily move to send the children to a sixth-form college so that they'd be able to claim to be State-educated for the purpose of biased university entrance? And did she want to hear one more person loudly declaiming that Ikea's suede rag rug, Artist shelving unit and Pelto table were design classics to rival anything by Philippe Starck?

Alice also thought about her work. She could choose now, and it hadn't occurred to her till she left her routine behind at the far end of the M3 that she *had* the choice, whether to carry on with her Gulliver School books or simply stop and either write about something else or take up another occupation. Instead of writing a turgid boarding-school version of *East-Enders*, she could leave her fictional pupils exactly where she most loved them, forever suspended on the verge of the chaos of their teen years. Lately, she'd felt more sense of achievement in choosing the perfect shade of blue for Gosling's kitchen than she had from banking the cheque for her last lot of TV rights.

Overprivileged, that's what I am, she told herself, quite aware that if anyone else was whingeing this much to her she'd want to give them a good shake. How many people would almost kill to swop places with her?

'I wouldn't mind giving it a bit longer here, just to see if there's anything else I can do to help. Harry and I made some tentative plans for Cygnet that might be worth pursuing. He won't do anything unless I gee him up,' Alice said eventually. Beside her Noel sighed, out of a drift towards sleep in which he'd assumed he was going to be left unanswered. 'You could go back though,' she told him. 'If you want to, that is. I mean, what about work?'

'Work.' Noel sighed again, deeper this time. 'Oh yes, let me see, that's the thing I have to get up at six for every morning and travel to, crammed in with bun-munching, coffee-swigging hordes like a pig in an abattoir truck.'

Alice sat up abruptly and looked down at him. She'd never heard him express anything remotely resentful about his work routine. His face was staring up to the ceiling, expressionless, an eerie greeny-gold colour with the moonlight shining on him. He'll look like that when he's dead, she thought, with a vivid flashback to Arthur Gillings and the way she'd found him, lying stretched out on the Gosling sofa as if for an after-lunch doze, his velvet cloak around him and pulled up to his chin so only his pale, creased face was exposed. She'd sensed a lack of life as soon as she'd come into the room; there'd been something unnervingly tense and frozen about the air in the cottage, even though the log fire had been blazing away.

Alice had arrived to bring Arthur a lobster she'd been given down by the shore. It had a claw missing and so wasn't sellable and she'd thought, as he'd always loved lobster, that he might like her to cook it for him. He hadn't been eating very much for a long while but had dismissed any suggestion of doctors or treatment. Joss had moved into Gosling to be close to him and try to help him out of the depths of doomy depression that kept overtaking him, but even she, with enough energy for the pair of them, had had to admit that he had given in and seemed ready to be moved on, passively surrendering, from one world to whatever came next.

Alice, unable to wake him and perfectly aware why not, had nevertheless raced to the house and called an ambulance. Then she and Joss had gone back to Gosling and sat beside his body, all the windows and doors open so his soul had, as Joss put it, every choice of exits and no excuse to hang around resentfully haunting over the years. Smoke from the fire, caught up by the surfeit of draughts, had swirled around the room like Aladdin's lamp genie and made her wonder if it was only partly smoke and partly the mists of departing soul. When he'd been taken away, Alice, feeling in need of something to do, had plumped up the sofa cushions and handed Jocelyn the purple velvet one with the long silver fringes on which his head had been resting. It had been just slightly warm. It was still kept close to Jocelyn, in the peacock chair by the hexagon window, as if the last of Arthur's spirit had permeated into its fabric and feathers.

Noel was still staring at the ceiling, wide-eyed and now wide awake. It was way past midnight. Alice wondered what he was thinking about.

'Do you want to give it up? The job?' she asked.

'Only the commuting part,' he said after a pause. 'Only the mindless office banter and the greedy clients.'

'I'll take that as a yes then,' she said, lying down and snuggling into his shoulder. 'Can you think of something else to do instead?'

'Golf. A vineyard in Australia. Asking Catherine Zeta Jones if she'd like to swop her old man for another one the same age. Nothing that would make any cash. I can't collect on the pension for another couple of years and running those kids and our life isn't cheap. No, I'll just keep going. So what about you? Have you decided when you're coming back?'

Jocelyn woke up and sniffed the air. She could smell cannabis in the house. Harry must be having an early morning smoke up in the attic bedroom. She knew he indulged most mornings just to get himself mellowed out a bit to face the day. She realized her feelings were somewhat hypocritical, for over the years there wasn't much in the way of organic mind-enhancing substances that she hadn't made use of on occasions, but she rather wished he wouldn't, especially now those boys of his were getting to a tricky age. Times were different now. The twins were the type who'd be sure to try anything and everything and wouldn't stop at the more natural substances, especially if they knew that was the day-to-day potion of choice of their father. Teen years were for rebellion, for having something to get you to feel different from the generation before. Harry was making it hard for the boys to be anything less than dangerously extreme in the area of chemical experimentation.

Smoking the stuff also made Harry vague and dozy, so that he went through the day only half-finishing jobs that he'd started. If he wanted to smoke he'd do better to keep it till the end of the day, when there was time to relax. Things weren't getting done that needed to be done. Harry had made a start on fixing the boarding on the verandah months ago and seemed to have forgotten all about it, leaving a big hole where he'd removed the planks under the hexagon window. Small animals were living underneath and using the gap as a handy doorway. Jocelyn could hear them scurrying about at night. They were probably rabbits, the whole headland was overrun with them, but it could be foxes taking advantage of the unusually big space and digging themselves a cosy earth under the house. It would be impossible to get them out and before you knew it they'd be chewing their way up through the floorboards and into the house itself, biting through flimsy electricity cables and dislodging essential pipes as they tried to get to food supplies.

There were, she was sure, old rat traps in one of the sheds – they might be big enough for a fox. She would get the twins to put a couple down, see what turned up. They'd enjoy that and it would give them something useful to do for once. Perhaps they could then finish fixing the boarding – a sense of achievement might provide an incentive to help their parents a bit more – in the old days all Penmorrow children took on practical jobs. Even a toddler would understand which were the ripe tomatoes to pick and put in a bowl; Alice was in charge of growing mung beans and alfalfa at only five.

Jocelyn didn't feel right. She'd had fearsome fatigue ever since the barbecue on the beach. At first she'd assumed it was the effects of the sun and the wine and having to concentrate on what Patrice wanted from her. He kept urging her to talk about how much Penmorrow was a story of faded glamour, and had pushed her towards discussing its tatty present when she wanted to tell stories of its vibrant past.

What was it he wanted from her? Nobody wanted to watch a programme about an old run-down house. They wanted to know, surely, about the better times.

The exhaustion should have gone by now, after a few fairly restful days. She had talked Patrice through the final years of the commune and about how she rarely, these days, was called upon for opinions and comment. The last one had been a year or so ago, a piece for *The Times'* 'Been There, Done That' column, about being an artist's muse. All those years with Arthur had been reduced to eight hundred facile words and a telling-off from the features editor for mentioning only in passing the many other artists Joss had sat for and whom (in the editor's not-humble-enough opinion) the current readership would consider more fashionable and more amusing. 'You surely can't have meant to leave out any mention of the Thorpe-Appleby portrait?' had been said in a tone of whispered incredulity, as if hesitating to hint that Jocelyn must be losing a grasp of her memory. No, Joss had insisted, she *had* meant to leave it out. She did not want to give daft, mopy Milly the chance to think being painted by her had been some kind of life highlight, or that she was *in the least* impressed that Milly was now *Dame* (if you please) Melissa Thorpe-Appleby. Not so much as a Yule card for ten years, after all the help, support, nurturing, tear-mopping . . .

Jocelyn clambered slowly out of her bed and walked across the plaited rug (the chalk power circle hidden beneath it wasn't proving as effective as she'd hoped) to spend a few moments leaning on the window ledge and looking out across the bay to the far headland, waiting for the initial stiffness of her joints to stop throbbing. All those years of yoga and now, since her illness, she couldn't manage a proper sun salute without her balance giving out. Instead she greeted the day by watching it awaken from her window and taking in every tiny change.

Leaves on the beech and oak trees weren't quite changing colour yet, but had a dry look to them, as if they were becoming too tired to take in nourishment. She felt very much the same. Some vital energy was failing inside her but all her senses felt especially acute, as if she was an animal in the woods on full alert for a fatal predator. And that was just what she was, really. The predator was death, creeping ever closer. She could almost pick out footsteps padding on the ground as she and her maker cheated each other by turn. What she needed was another spell, one with a special ingredient, she thought as she opened the bedroom door and ran her fingers over the dried-out verbena wand on her way out. She would get Grace to help, so that she could add that elusive element of youth. It would also be an opportunity to pass on some useful tips to the girl. It might be best, perhaps, if Alice didn't know about it.

Patrice was pacing the orchard muttering urgently into his phone. Alice and Aidan sat on the bench by the table, drinking coffee and shelling undersized broad beans that Harry had brought in from his vegetable garden. Noel had gone off to Clowance to play golf with a retired accountant that he'd met in the Mullion clubhouse, where they'd made an impact on a bottle of Scotch and discussed the Ryder Cup.

'He's having trouble with the commissioning people,' Aidan whispered. 'I heard him complaining to Nick that they're talking about cutting these "Whatever Happened To . . ." programmes down to fifteen minutes a slot and that it'll now be late night.

The kind of very late night that only ancient insomniac intellectuals watch.'

'About three people then. Poor Joss, I think she was under the impression this would be a prime-time thing, something on a level with *The South Bank Show*. I could see her imagining that it would lead her on to things like *Start the Week*, so she could harangue Jeremy Paxman and tell him he had suburban morals.'

'Well lucky I'll be long gone by the time it's on, then. I wouldn't want to be around for a full-scale fury demonstration!'

'I'll be gone too, I expect,' Alice told him. 'We're supposd to be going to Italy.'

'Family holiday. Nice,' Aidan said, smiling. She wondered what he was really thinking. He'd sounded sardonic but it was hard to tell – his chic narrow glasses had photochromic lenses and as he was facing the sun they'd gone inscrutably dark.

'Nice? Is it? Which bit?' she asked.

'Nice family, nice holiday; you choose!' he teased, leaving her none the wiser.

'I don't actually want to go,' she said suddenly, surprising herself. She'd arranged it. Of course she wanted to go.

He shrugged and raised his glasses so she could see his eyes. He was definitely teasing her. 'Well don't. You're a grown-up, you choose.'

'It's not that simple. What about the others?'

'Just tell them . . . hey, I know, make it like school: tell them you can't go, you're feeling a bit icky and you've got a note from your mum!'

Alice punched his arm. 'Don't be ridiculous! I didn't go to school! I'll have to go. I don't do copping out. It's all fixed.'

Patrice flipped his phone shut and came to slump

onto the collapsing Lloyd Loom chair opposite Aidan and Alice. He crossed one long denim-clad leg over the other and his cream deck shoe dangled from his tanned foot. 'Bloody wankers,' he grunted, shaking a cigarette out of its pack, lighting it and inhaling impatiently. 'Nothing ever goes right in this fucking business. Nightmare.' He inhaled again, fast and furious. Alice noticed his hand was trembling.

'Work not going to plan?' she said, cheerily glib.

Patrice gave her a sharp look. 'Nothing I can't handle,' he said. 'You know what it's like. Or rather, of course,' he flashed her a superior grin, 'you don't.'

'You don't know that,' Aidan cut in.

'Don't know what?' Patrice challenged.

'You don't know that Alice doesn't know. You were being patronizing.'

'Aidan, man, it doesn't matter . . .'

'Alice might be an executive producer at Tiger Aspect for all you know. She might buy and sell people like you between lunch and a sundowner any old day.'

'Do you, Alice?' Patrice stubbed his cigarette out hard on the grass, leaned forward and stared intently into her face. It was almost possible to imagine, that for the sake of his programming schedule, he hoped her answer would be yes.

'No, but . . .' It wouldn't do him any harm to know that her work, if not his, rated mainstream TV slots and hugely healthy viewing figures.

He wasn't in a listening mood. 'Well there you are then.' He got up and strode away.

'That was naughty, Aidan.' Alice giggled. 'We wound him up.'

'He deserved it. He's a tosser. And worse, he's a creepy hypocrite.'

'Is he? In what way?'

Aidan hesitated. 'Just something I heard him saying to Katie down on the beach the other day. He . . . well he was a bit disparaging about Joss.'

Alice gathered up the empty bean pods and shoved them into their Tesco's bag. Her hands were muddy and her nails were green-grimed from the beans. She used to be, only weeks ago, the sort of person who'd either do this job in stout Marigolds or buy beans ready-prepared from M & S. 'So what did he say?' she asked. Aidan shrugged.

'You wish you hadn't mentioned it now, don't you?' she prompted. 'Go on, tell me. I'll get it out of you.' Regretfully, she recognized she now no longer wanted to do it by wrestling him to the floor so that they rolled together shrieking with giggles like grappling teenagers. The girlishly silly crush had vanished: it could be the last one she ever had. Rather sad.

'I know you will. OK. It wasn't much, just that he's not quite so fawningly devoted to Joss's great oeuvre as he pretends to be. He was telling Katie that she shouldn't bother reading *Angel's Choice*, that it was a dated little unimportant book and nothing special. And now I *really* wish I hadn't told you. Sorry.'

'Hmm. No don't worry about me, it's fine. I'm glad to have it confirmed that he's just a smarmy sod who got what he wanted by doing his homework. The old me would probably say good for him – he knows what it takes.'

'Does that mean there's a new you?' Aidan asked. 'Where did she come from? Did I meet the old one?'

Alice didn't even know where what she'd said had come from. She thought for a moment, then said, 'I think the old me came down here from London a few weeks ago but sort of decamped again after day one.

232

I've changed a bit. A lot. It's being here. I feel like *part* of Penmorrow again. This is the first time since I left at seventeen that I've felt like more than a swift visitor, and the place has got to me. I'd never ever normally think of cancelling a major family holiday.' Nor would she, she didn't add, think of passionately (though drunkenly) kissing a stranger in the woods and wishing that it (and more) would happen again. Poor Noel, it wasn't his fault, she thought guiltily.

'But when you go home you'll soon get back to your normal self, won't you?' Aidan asked.

Alice thought for a moment. 'Probably. But I'm not sure I want to. I quite like *this* being my normal self.'

She could hear the sound of her car tyres on the driveway, traced the swish of them as they rounded the bend past Big Shepherd's patch of meadow and then the silence as the engine was switched off. Noel was back from his golf. He'd be looking for her, looking for her decision about whether they were to pack up and leave the next day or not.

'Sam, can I ask you some things?' Grace found her cousin round at the back of Harry's polytunnels, attaching bits of wire to a long slim branch.

Sam looked up at her, suspicious. 'What things?'

'Nothing bad, just family things.'

Sam sighed and grinned at her. 'I thought you were going to ask me stuff I might have to keep quiet about,' he said. 'I'm good at lying but I think you might be good at knowing when I am.'

Grace laughed. 'I'm flattered! I think. Do you mean you thought I was going to ask you about what Harry's growing in there?' She pointed to the plastic tunnel where the elegant leafy plants had grown almost as high as the roof and the smell could have attracted nostalgic ex-hippies from miles around. 'Because I'm not stupid. You wouldn't have needed to lie. I wouldn't run off to the police.'

'No, s'pose you wouldn't. Specially after the carp . . .' He sniggered.

'Did you know they were worth that much?' Grace asked, watching carefully for signs of non-truth.

'Course not!' Sam looked indignant. 'They was *fish*! It's a bit like going out to catch a rabbit and then finding you've brought home the only solid silver bunny in the whole world! If we'd known, me and Chas would've just gone round to Chapel Creek and nicked a few lobsters from the tank at the back of the Mariners pub instead. What did you want to ask me?'

'Well . . . it might sound stupid but have you got any more family? Aunts, uncles, any other grandparents?'

Sam screwed up his eyes, concentrating. 'Yeah. Mo's got a dad over in Padstow. Sometimes we go and see him. We call him Grandad, not Jim. Joss said that was . . .'

'Commonplace.' Grace supplied the word for him.

'That's the one. Commonplace. So it is. For most people, just normal. Nothing wrong with normal.'

'She always says "commonplace" is the worst thing you can say about anyone. I was just asking, because I don't seem to have anyone else. My dad's folks are in America and Mum doesn't have any contact with them, so it's just Harry and Jocelyn and you and Sam. You're the whole of my family.'

'Aah! Bless!' Sam teased. 'You've got Theo and Noel,' he pointed out.

'Not really, we're not *related*. And they've got a whole fleet of relations of their own, enough to make a football match. You should see Theo's birthday

234

cards, all Aunty this, Aunty that. Mum says that Joss says that when you're born, *you're* the future. You shouldn't go looking back or sideways. Doesn't stop you wanting to know things about what you're coming from.'

'Suppose not.' Sam had gone back to his stick and wires now.

'Stopped Mum wanting to, though,' Grace continued, suspecting Sam had lost interest. 'She's not got the titchiest bit of curiosity about where she comes from.'

'That's because she comes from here,' Sam said, threading a piece of cord down the loops along his stick.

Grace laughed. 'Yeah, that'll be it. *Here* makes you weird. Er, Sam? What are you making exactly?'

He tied a slip knot in the end of the cord, leaving a loop about a foot deep. 'A running noose,' he told her, holding it up. 'You creep up to a place where the birds are roosting,' here he stood up and demonstrated on a nearby plum tree, 'at dusk, then you sneak this in through the leaves, get the loop round a bird's neck and PULL!' He tugged the cord and a plum fell to the grass. 'See?' he said, delighted with his handiwork.

'Ugh, horrible. But yes, I see,' Grace said.

Alice was dizzy from the stench of cleaning products. The kitchen and bathroom in Cygnet were now gleaming and sparkly and the stubborn turquoise marks in the bath, where deposits from the blue elvin rock that the spring water ran through had stained it, had at last been erased by an hour of determined scrubbing. Mo had stopped complaining that Alice seemed to be taking over, and had surrendered into simply being glad that there was another pair of hands helping to keep Penmorrow under control. It had taken some persuading: how many ways were there to tell someone that you weren't criticizing their housekeeping standards but merely sympathizing that there wasn't time to give it any extra attention? And what, Alice wondered, though sensibly did not say to Mo, would happen when she went back to Richmond? It wouldn't be long before the lack of enough domestic input became a problem again.

It was time now to take down the horrible maroon Dralon curtains. Mo had a sewing machine in working order, and Alice had bought twenty metres of cheap unbleached calico in Falmouth and intended to make some new, simple drapes for Cygnet's sitting room. She tested one of the dining chairs to ensure it would take her weight and climbed up to reach the wooden curtain pole and unhook the dusty fabric. It smelled musty, old like dead air and many years' worth of rotting insect carcasses.

The room itself was potentially fabulous – long and airy with huge windows on one side and French doors leading to a beach-view garden and the cliff path on the other. It was a pity, she thought, that there didn't seem to be any likelihood that the suggestions she'd made to Harry about updating this little house would ever happen. She caught herself thinking, 'If I lived here . . .' meaning Penmorrow, the whole of it, as she daydreamed just a bit about what she'd do to renovate and update the whole place. She felt deliciously excited at the prospect. She could make a difference here. Give or take a lottery win, of course.

Alice folded the first set of curtains and stuffed them in a binbag, trusting that Jocelyn wouldn't get weepy over this fabric as she had over the Gosling kitchen daisies. Then she crossed to the other side and climbed on her chair again. Through the window she saw Katie and Noel sitting at the orchard table, close to Penmorrow's kitchen door, heads bent together over a magazine. They'd found something in it that was funny and Katie's dark hair was shaking as she laughed and wriggled about. The strap of her little vest top slid down her shoulder and as Alice watched, Noel put out his hand and gently replaced it, leaning down at the same time to kiss Katie's arched neck. Katie's smile barely slipped, but, like the teenage girls at bus stops Alice saw daily joshing with trying-it-on boys, she gave Noel a small shove in the chest.

Alice stood rigid, clutching the loosed half of the curtain in one hand and steadying herself against the pole with the other. Noel wasn't giving up and took hold of both Katie's hands in his, leaning forward again to have another nuzzle at his prey. This time Katie stood up, still grinning but pointing a warning finger at Noel, before stalking off into the house, her short skirt flicking this way and that.

'God, he's an idiot,' Alice sighed to herself as she clambered down to the floor lugging the heavy fabric. She wasn't surprised. Nothing changed. He'd been seeing another woman for several months at the time Alice had met him, and only much later did Alice realize he'd been enjoying the thrill of a spot of two-timing for the first several of their dates. And then, she recalled, there'd been Theo's piano teacher on her weekly visits: a nervy, twenty-something ex-child-prodigy who'd accepted, with too much shining-eyed enthusiasm, a lift home from Noel the time that her car had broken down. Amazing, Alice had commented sardonically, how many times after that the car seemed to be mysteriously out of action for one reason or another.

This Katie though, well she'd be gone in a day or two. And Alice could just as easily have not seen what she did. She wouldn't, she thought, bother to mention it. She smiled as she thought of what her mother would say: 'Sexual jealousy, my dear? Oh how drearily *commonplace.*'

And there was the other thing Joss often said. She'd use that one if she then found out about Alice and Aidan in the woods. There'd be the knowing smile and the single, well-deserved checkmate word: 'Karma.'

Fourteen

Jocelyn had been keeping an eye on Grace from the hexagon window. She'd watched her sitting by herself, cross-legged on the meadow at the feet of Big Shepherd, idly picking daisies and threading some of them into her chakra bracelet. Grace looked as if she had things on her mind and didn't quite know what to do with herself. Perhaps she was bored, Joss thought at first, but Grace wasn't the sort to mope about with nothing to do. She was a reader, for one thing, and readers were never bored. Free time was a God-given chance to luxuriate in a book.

Joss picked up her sturdy stick, left the house and found Grace had moved to the pond on the far side of the track. The girl was peering into the murky, weed-strewn water as if looking for something she'd dropped. Jocelyn hadn't seen much of her in the past week. Even when they were all together at meal times, Grace was always at the far end of the table with Theo and the twins and didn't seem to want to get involved in talking with the adults. Who could blame her, Jocelyn thought, envying her granddaughter her careless youth, for what tedious things the adults chose to discuss. Patrice bragged about his past career successes as if he was trying to impress with his CV ('bigging himself up', as Chas had so acutely put it), Noel tried and failed to outdo him by boasting of his golf trophies and – surely unethical, this – famous clients. Alice talked of ghastly events (apparently the highlight of her afternoons) like anointing all the bathroom taps with lemon juice to get rid of limescale and about where to hire a sander for Cygnet's floorboards.

So dreary, this domestic obsession of hers, though she conceded Alice meant well enough. The floorboard idea was actually rather a good one; Joss had a trunk in the attic containing a stunning collection of kelims she'd been given by a poet who'd brought them back from India. They'd look wonderful on the polished boards. What a sweet man he'd been, she recalled now as she approached Grace, one of the few who understood that communal living meant just that: that you put something back into the household in return for hospitality. Some people, far too many of them really, had assumed that if they fetched a pint or two of milk from the shop and peeled a potato once during their stay, then everything else was theirs for the taking. There'd been occasional House Meetings about it when, say, the cooking rota had completely broken down, but that had resulted in the ludicrous sight of grown-up and otherwise successful people sobbing as they took their turn on the Beef Bag, expressing overdramatic devastation that their inadequate contributions to the household were criticized. That was artists for you; Joss had found it less hassle to give in. They had other things on their mind beside taking the garbage to the tip and putting bleach down the loo. It became her role to accommodate and facilitate. And she'd done it so well for so long.

Jocelyn was becoming bored by Patrice and his entourage. Patrice's phoney fawning over her was rather wearing. She especially wanted the Katie girl off the premises. Noel padded around after her like a dog scenting an in-season bitch. She'd seen what she'd seen, the two of them out on the verandah that first night, and much as she'd prefer Alice to have teamed up with a man less dull, she also didn't want her daughter to be put through a lot of pointless grief. As far as Joss was concerned, sexual adventuring was not in the slightest bit important – ironically, it seemed that Noel and she at last had something in common there – but Alice wouldn't see it that way and would make a rumpus if she caught him dipping into that particular honey jar.

'Grace? Have you lost something?' Joss was right next to her before the girl noticed her. Grace looked alarmed; her eyes were fierce and defensive.

'Goodness child, what on earth's the matter? You look as if you're seeing demons. Come and walk with me down to the woods and tell me what's wrong.'

'I was just looking to see if we had any fish in there. Are there some?'

'Oh I doubt it. We have frogs though. Only good for kissing and turning into princes. When you are a little older you must try.'

Grace felt trapped. She'd avoided being alone with Jocelyn ever since she'd finished reading *Angel's Choice*. There were things she wanted to ask, but at the same time didn't want to know. It was confusing. Lacking an excuse to refuse, Grace took her grand-mother's arm and the two walked slowly down the path into the shade of the trees. Jocelyn sniffed at the air, reminding Grace of Monty in the mornings when he trotted out through the Gosling cat flap to see what was what in his territory.

'There's been a good dew,' Jocelyn commented, poking her stick at the ground beside the path. 'Look how the leaves are damp and shiny on the top but dry beneath. Autumn isn't far away.' She sighed gently. 'We haven't even celebrated Lammas this year. That is the time to stop and do some blessing-counting. We all need to do more of that. I shall talk to Mo.'

Grace didn't know what to say. She knew a little about the year's festivals; her mother mentioned them as they came and went, even if she didn't always do anything fancy to mark them. Alice did make a bit of a thing about Yule though. She always brought plenty of holly into the house before the shortest day – but then most people did for Christmas. She also made a Yule log, which had to have the same number of candles on it as there were people in the house to eat it. Grace had brought Sophy home on the Yule-log afternoon the year before, and Alice had refused to let them eat any of it till she'd found and lit an extra candle to represent Sophy. Noel had been a bit snide about that, declaring it was all superstitious nonsense, but Alice had snapped back at him, saying, 'You didn't say that when the bishop blessed the new bar at the golf club. Don't pretend there's any difference.'

'I'll mention it to Mo,' Joss said again, almost talking to herself. 'Perhaps she can do something a bit special tomorrow night and we can have a bit of a ceremony. Patrice could put it in his silly film. Now Grace,' Jocelyn stopped at the foot of an oak tree and turned to face her granddaughter, 'there's something I want you to help me to do. But first, I want to know what is troubling you. Let's sit down here, on these dry leaves.' With the tree supporting her hand, Joss carefully sank

242

to the woodland floor and sat cross-legged opposite her granddaughter.

Grace felt caught out. How clever of Jocelyn to have noticed she wasn't entirely comfortable. Joss was difficult to fob off and Alice often commented that she was a great mind-reader.

'Let me guess.' Jocelyn put a hand each side of Grace's head, resting her fingers lightly on her temples. Grace could feel her cool rings against her skin.

'You like it here, don't you?' Joss smiled at her, knowing she didn't need an answer.

'I'd say you don't really want to leave. You don't want to go to Italy or back to London.'

Grace almost laughed. 'How did you know that? That's amazing!'

'It's not amazing at all, child.' Jocelyn removed her hands and took hold of Grace's. 'I can see you living here, it would suit you – you're a creature of nature and good, clean air. Look at these hands.' Here she turned Grace's hands palm upwards. 'You've too much gentleness in you for the tough ways of a city existence. Do you enjoy your school?'

Grace bit her lip and looked at the ground. 'A bit. I like Sophy and some of the others and some of the work but it's all so . . . *competitive*. Everything you do, everything you have, there's always someone sneering at you, just that little bit, you know? People look at your shoes. They look at how you have your hair. They look at your mum's car. And there's all the little in-crowds. There's the anorexia girls and the pony girls and the shopaholics and the witch girls . . .'

'Witch girls?'

Grace laughed. 'Oh they're no good. They don't do any of it right. They just do stuff to get boys and stick pins in Play-Doh models of girls they hate . . .'

'Dangerous,' Jocelyn commented, frowning. 'They'll find it'll backfire.'

'I told them that but they didn't believe me. I'm not one of their group so it's like I couldn't know,' Grace said, then went on, 'and there's the girls who ski at Christmas and come home showing off about it and the girls who go to Barbados and come home showing off about scuba-diving.'

'Apart from that, everything's fine then,' Jocelyn said, teasing her.

'Mmm! That's about it.'

'It mightn't be any different here, you know,' she warned.

'It's got to be. Nothing could be as up itself as the rich bits of London.' Grace felt exhausted. Where had all that come from? Jocelyn must have put a secret little spell on her when she touched her head. The spell had made her empty out all that she'd been feeling about school, all that build-up that had started on the day at the end of term when she just couldn't, wouldn't, face the gruesome ritual of sports day. She needed to talk about something else now though, before Joss started probing any further and making her ask questions about *Angel's Choice*.

'What was it you wanted me to do?' Grace remembered she'd been brought to the woods for a reason.

'Ah yes. I was going to ask you to help me with a small task but your need is the greater.' Jocelyn leaned heavily on her stick and rose to her feet. 'Come with me, I know just the place to find a big, fat, white mushroom. I can tell you just what you need to do to help get what you want.'

Her own charm-making would have to wait, Joss thought as she headed for the fallen beech where the best fungi grew. And besides, perhaps it was unfair

244

to involve Grace. Concocting a remedy for revived youthfulness shouldn't really involve stealing from one who already had it. As with Grace's school witch girls, things could backfire.

The scent of harvest was in the air around Tremorwell. Alice, driving round the headland to buy lobsters in Chapel Creek, watched a massive combine harvester working the big field at the top of the hill. There was no-one to be seen among the wheat, no-one to make any 'sacrifice' of the last of the crop to thank the land for its generosity. The combine resembled an alien space city moving across, but not really connecting with, the land. When she'd been a child, she and all the children of the village had been caught up in the excitement of harvest time; farmers then were still – just – doing their own combining, not yet booking in faceless contractors from miles away.

She remembered being allowed to ride with Sally and her schoolfriends on top of a truckload of hay as it was taken to be stored in the big Dutch barn at the side of the farm, just over the hill. And after the wheat harvest, back then, fields were set on fire to scorch away the last of the stubble which would then be ploughed back in to enrich the earth for the next crop. That had been thrilling, watching the lines of flames licking their way across the field, blackening the blond stumps, the last of the poppies and (best not thought of) a frantic collection of trapped wildlife. Soon after, it became illegal to burn stubble. Bales became industrial super-size, wrapped in green plastic like garden rubbish bags.

Mo had told Alice that Joss wanted a version of a Lammas harvest supper the next night, mostly for Patrice's benefit.

'We'll need a corn dolly or something, won't we? And shouldn't we have a cake made with the first of the flour? Not that we've got our own corn . . .' Alice had suggested, writing a shopping list at the Penmorrow kitchen table.

Mo had looked quite jolly for once, she'd thought. 'Don't worry about that,' Mo told her. 'I'll be making some chocolate fudge brownies; we can have them with clotted cream.'

'We always used to have gingerbread men,' Alice said, reminiscing. 'And do you remember . . .'

'The ones Milly and Kelpie made?' Mo started laughing. 'I do! They made sure we could see they were *men*!'

'Anatomically perfect! I remember all the men wincing when we bit them.'

Chapel Creek was packed with trippers and it was hard to find somewhere to park. Eventually she tucked the Galaxy in between a silver-blue Porsche and a big Audi estate. They reminded her of cars from back home. In fact it wouldn't surprise her if she ran into one or more of her London neighbours here, for Chapel Creek was almost entirely owned by affluent second-home yachties to the point where the place was virtually shut down in winter months. It boasted a gift shop and gallery and a busy little food store which sold all the delicatessen exotica that Tremorwell village post office couldn't begin to contemplate. There was an impressive cheese selection, frozen upmarket supper dishes for smart self-caterers, organic smoked garlic and other vegetables (some of them Harry's), but you would not find a can of Bob the Builder pasta shapes or aerosol-canned UHT cream brazening it out on the shelves.

The small harbour was crammed with gleaming,

white-hulled boats among which a small group of rusted old fishing vessels looked like an invasion of hard-core bikers at a society ball. Family groups ambled along the lane carrying oars and life jackets, fuel cans and ropes and other nautical essentials. Absolutely everyone seemed clean and affluent and well fed and as if, Alice was amused to note, they'd been dressed for a shoot for the Boden catalogue. It was exactly how she usually looked, it occurred to her, but somehow she'd lost her freshly ironed, slick, co-ordinated style over the last few weeks. For a moment she had to glance down at her own clothes, remind herself what she'd put on that morning.

She seemed to have acquired a peculiar assortment of not-Alice outfits and today was wearing Grace's candy-pink tee shirt with the word 'Doll' picked out on the front in purple sequins. This had teamed itself with grubby trainers and a full white skirt splodged with mauve and yellow roses that she'd found hanging in Gosling's wardrobe. She had no idea whose it had been, or how long it had been there. Presumably a holidaymaker had left it behind, possibly even abandoned it as either dated or simply a bad buy. It looked, now that she thought about it, like just a mad old skirt. But if she ran into friends from London who'd judge her outfit to be a sign of diminishing sanity, she'd only have to claim it was 'vintage' for the garment to be acclaimed with smiles, admiration and compliments on her cleverness at such a find.

The shellfish van was parked down at the end of the slipway beside the pub. Alice bought a dozen live lobsters and parted with an amount of cash that back home would have paid for only a quarter of what she now carried away in a polystyrene box.

'Are you intending to do the murdering yourself?'

Alice found Aidan waiting for her on the pub terrace at the top of the slipway, a pint of beer in his hand.

'Mo said she'd do that bit,' Alice told him. 'I think she suspects I'm likely to get squeamish and start thinking of them as pets. As it is, I'm sure Grace won't eat any, not if she hears them moving about in their box. We'll have to hide them in the larder.'

Aidan put his drink on a table and took the box from her. 'Have you got time for a drink?' he asked. 'I could do with the company.'

'Yes, OK, that would be good. Just a Coke though, I've got the car. Are you still feeling a bit of a spare part?'

Aidan laughed. 'Just holding out till that idiot Patrice has gone. He told me he's off after tomorrow, so perhaps I can persuade Jocelyn to sit down and get on with the book again. I've reworked what's already there. It's close to the end now.'

While Aidan was getting the drinks, Alice sat on the pub's low wall and watched a family on the pontoon loading up their dinghy and preparing to row out to their boat. Since she'd been grown-up, she hadn't really had much to do with boats, barely anything more than sunset trips round the bay in Antigua, a bit of rowing on the Serpentine with Grace and visits to a friend's barge for supper in Chelsea Harbour. Keeping a little day-boat on the Thames had never appealed – the river in summer was crowded and busy and was a tame version of sailing compared with how she remembered the sea expeditions in Arthur's old boat. Cornish weather changed fast and although they might leave the harbour on a fine warm day, they could easily end up sailing back on a spitefully choppy grey sea with leaden clouds threatening above and the wind scudding vicious gusts.

Aidan came back and sat beside her on the wall. Alice said, 'I'm glad they're going soon, Patrice and Katie.'

'Is it because of what I said? About what Patrice said about Jocelyn's book?'

'No. It's because of something I saw.' I shouldn't be telling him this, Alice thought to herself, but continued all the same. 'I saw Noel from the window in Cygnet. He was . . . well there's no better expression than the old cliché – he was making a pass at Katie.'

'Was he?' Aidan sounded genuinely surprised. 'Whatever for? He must be mad.'

Alice laughed. 'Why? She's incredibly attractive. Don't you think so?'

Aidan screwed up his face as if acting at hard thinking. 'Well in a mucky sort of way, I suppose so. How much did you mind? A lot? Or is that a stupid question?'

Alice considered for a moment. Did he really want to know, she wondered, or was he doing that professional thing he did of simply asking the right question so that you got the chance to confide all? Whichever it was, she didn't much mind. It gave her a chance to try out what she thought. After another moment or two she said, 'I think I mind Noel being so predictable. As soon as I saw Katie I knew he'd find it hard to resist having a bit of a go.' Even as she spoke she felt that perhaps she could have made more effort to keep Noel from being distracted. She'd been too distant. Too distracted herself. Mostly by Aidan. Ridiculous, and serve her right.

'I'm surprised she and Patrice aren't an item,' Aidan said.

'Perhaps they have been.'

'Nah – you can tell with exes, there's always a bit of

giveaway sniping from the hurt party, even if it's been over for years. No, I think it's an event waiting to happen. As my girlfriend always says, "I'd put folding money on it." '

Girlfriend? The word had slinked in smoothly like vodka over ice. Alice looked at him quickly. He was staring out at the boats, unfazed, watching the tripper-loaded ferry crossing the estuary. He hadn't mentioned a girlfriend before, or at least she thought he hadn't. In fact he hadn't mentioned anything personal about himself at all, as if he'd only brought his working self with him to Penmorrow. Well of course he had; what else should he do? He could hardly discuss all his own life baggage at every writing job he undertook. Of course he had a girlfriend – attractive young intelligent man like him, interested (or at least slickly excellent at making you feel he was interested) in everything: such an apparently selfless, well-practised listener. Alice revised her previous imagining about the interior of his Kentish Town flat. She replaced the squalor with gorgeously rich, toning fabrics, with a huge sofa meant for sex and sprawling. She mentally cleared up his kitchen and added a shelf-full of cookbooks by the current batch of TV chefs.

Alice sipped her drink and felt something in her brain whirring into action. It felt like a slow old computer trying to retrieve a long-deleted file. She could do a little something about Katie and Patrice – she'd done it before, long ago, with French Marcel and it had worked. All she needed were the right ingredients. That fancy Chapel Creek village shop was exactly the place to find them.

Harry opened the box of surgical gloves and pulled out the first pair. He chuckled to himself as he put them on, wondering if they counted as a legitimate business expense. For that, of course, you'd need a legitimate business.

The first of the crop was ready. The tiny white pistils on the flower buds of the upper stems had turned a sultry tobacco brown, and it was time to cut them down and get on with the harvest. The empty room next to his and Mo's up in the attic was all ready. He'd put up a dozen strings like washing lines along the length of the room and had rigged up a bit of old white cloth at the window, so that the sun wouldn't overheat the drying branches.

Just before he started, Harry rolled a fat joint with the crumbled bud from the first branch he was to cut. It wouldn't be the best smoke; it would be far too resinous and sharp, but it was a tradition he liked to keep up, to sample the very first of it as he worked. It made him feel the growing process was then complete.

Silently thanking the sun and the earth, the rain and the good Cornish air for the gift of this crop, Harry took his secateurs and started to cut down the branches from the first of his plants. He piled them up on the old trestle table in the middle of the polytunnel and, when he'd amassed a good-sized heap, sat on his old wooden stool and started the careful process of plucking off all the fan-shaped leaves, which he'd stack in binbags. It was a shame, he thought, as he faced this comfortably repetitive task, that he couldn't ask the boys to help him. Mo said they shouldn't be involved, for how could she expect them to stay on the straight and narrow if their own father recruited them into illegal goings-on. Perhaps in a few years . . . or perhaps not, perhaps they'd have all moved on to somewhere and something else. It would all turn out all right one way or another, he thought. Unless that was the smoke talking.

Well she could hardly have expected to get dried violet petals. Even considering the classy, urban tastes of the sophisticated Chapel Creek residents, the shop wasn't likely to be stocked with out-of-season flower heads. There had been packs of nasturtium, pansy and borage flowers, all ready to be mixed into salads. At a push the pansy would have done, but she didn't have time for the proper drying process. She didn't think it would matter too much though – Joss had always said the success or failure of these things was all in the level of sincerity. She couldn't be accused of lacking in that.

In the Gosling kitchen, Alice weighed out a pound of icing sugar and stirred in the ground almonds, then mixed in the violet cashews that she'd whizzed to powder in the spice grinder that had come from the Penmorrow kitchen. She hoped she'd given the grinder enough of a clean first – it wouldn't be any use if Patrice and Katie took one sniff of the sweets, scented a hint of ground cumin and didn't so much as take a bite. The mixture was looking a pleasing pale purple now, and Alice started to add small amounts of warm water. She hoped she'd remembered the recipe properly. She was using one for peppermint creams that she'd made when she was a child with Jocelyn and Milly. They'd used baking sessions to teach the household children about weights and measures, giving them sums to do based on the combined weights of all the ingredients and getting them to work out averages, while cakes and biscuits they'd made baked in the oven and warm delicious aromas filled the room.

When she'd finished rolling out the paste, Alice used a little heart-shaped candy-cutter that she'd been delighted to find in Mo's cluttered drawer full of ancient baking sundries, and cut out a couple of dozen shapes. Another thing that could do with a good clear-out, Alice had thought as she'd rummaged through broken birthday-cake candles, ancient icing syringes, flan tins and cake tins and crumpled baking parchment. Another lucky find in the drawer was a little packet containing small silver paper cases – perfect for sweets and almost as if, she thought, they were waiting there specially for this one occasion.

Alice lined a blue plastic food container with red card and laid the sweets neatly inside it, making four layers, each separated by more red card. That, she thought, should be plenty, even if everyone was feeling particularly greedy. Finally, she wrapped the box in silver tissue gift wrap (also clearly a must-have in Chapel Creek), tied a purple ribbon round the box and turned her attention to the sheet of red paper on which the names of her two targets were written. She cut the names out and placed them side by side on the worktop, then sat the silver package on top of them. An hour or so, Alice thought, that should be enough. After that it was only a matter of getting the inscribed slips of paper into their rooms and hidden somewhere in their beds. Hmm, she wondered, where did 'only' come into it?

Fifteen

Grace lit the scarlet candle that Joss had put on the desk by her bedroom window. Lighting candles represented the focusing of the sun's energies. It was early in the morning and there would have been plenty of natural light if Joss had opened the curtains, but she had insisted they must be sure all the ritual details were carried out. 'It doesn't do to be sloppy and cut corners,' Jocelyn said. 'Especially the first few times you do these things – later you can decide for yourself what to include and what to leave out.'

Grace felt exhilarated and gleeful. The school witch girls would be *so* jealous if they knew. They were so ignorant and just thought having candles was part of making a spooky atmosphere. Of course, if this worked, the witch girls would never get to hear about it anyway, that was the best, most brilliant thing, because she'd have got what she most wanted and would never see them or the school again. She'd miss Sophy, but then she could always come down and visit. Grace imagined Sophy tottering down the cliff path in the Prada boots she'd wangled away from her mother, simply by dropping one teeny, well-timed hint that her legs looked a bit *broad* in them. She hoped

Sophy would come; she'd tell her all about the surfer boys who hung out at the café. That should do the trick.

Grace, under Joss's scrutiny, painstakingly inscribed the short rhyme into the flesh of the soft pinky-brown mushroom that she and Joss had found in the woods, using the sharp end of an embroidery needle.

'Take it really carefully and slowly.' Jocelyn was looking over her shoulder, supervising. 'You need to get all the words on, as evenly as possible so they have equal importance.'

Grace concentrated hard. She felt as if she was engraving something incalculably precious.

'There!' she said when she had finished, admiring her work. 'Look, you can read it really easily. *Grant to me as this flesh tires, my dearest wish and heart's desires*. What do we do now?'

'Breathe on the words. A few times, just to make sure.'

Grace held the mushroom in front of her mouth and puffed gently onto it. She could smell woodland and damp and the delicate scent of the fragile fungus. She handled it with great tenderness, fearful that she'd damage it and wreck her charm. Only she and the mushroom knew her secret wish, though she suspected Joss had a pretty good idea.

'Now you need to chop up the mushroom into very tiny bits, put them on an oven tray and simply pop it in the bottom oven of the Aga to dry out,' Jocelyn told her.

Grace giggled. 'You sound like Delia Smith,' she said.

Jocelyn went to the vast old chest of drawers and started rummaging among brightly coloured fabrics till she found a piece of red silk.

'Can you sew?' She held out the fabric to Grace.

'A bit. Buttons and hems and stuff.'

'What you need to do is use this to make a tiny drawstring bag. I've got thread here . . .' Joss opened a drawer in the desk and pulled out a box of embroidery silks, selecting one that most closely matched the scarlet fabric. 'When the mushroom pieces are all dried out, you crumble them and put them into the bag and wear it next to your heart every night till your charm has worked.'

'Is that it?' Grace asked. It seemed so simple, seeing as she was asking for so much.

'That's it!' Jocelyn told her. 'It might take a while, so don't lose faith. Focus on what you've asked for and be patient.'

Suppose it didn't work for ages; she could end up at university still wearing a red bag round her neck every night. Or trying to explain it away to a boyfriend who complained it got in the way.

'Did . . . does Mum know all about this sort of stuff?' Grace asked. Her mother's Penmorrow life was something she didn't know nearly enough of. Mostly it was just something she'd grumbled about, like when she complained about having no education and that their lives were all so disorganized. It was weird to think that maybe when other kids her age were in school doing French verbs and the rainfall distribution of central Africa, her mother might have been learning all this stuff instead.

'She didn't take much interest, really,' was Jocelyn's disappointing response. 'Once when she was a teenager she said it was dangerous to "meddle with the occult" as she put it. That gave me hope at the time: I took it to mean she wasn't a complete non-believer. Anyway,' she said, brightening, 'you can keep the old traditions going instead. Now what comes next?'

'Er? Don't know?'

'You blow out the candle. Never forget that.'

Patrice, Nick and Katie were out. They'd gone to the shore for a few stock shots of the holidaymakers on the beach. Alice had watched from the Gosling kitchen window as they walked together down the cliff path. Nick and Katie were in front and Alice almost cricked her neck trying to see if Patrice, following, was watching Katie's swaying bottom (encased snugly in tight lilac trousers) with any particular interest.

Quickly, she took the two slips of scarlet paper with their names written on and ran up the lane to the main house. No-one seemed to be about. The front door stood wide open as it usually did and she slipped inside and ran fast and silently up the stairs. Someone was talking in Jocelyn's room – as she came closer she recognized Grace's voice. There was no time to speculate on what they were talking about. Perhaps Grace had at last decided to ask Joss about *Angel's Choice*. Possibly Grace would be the one person Joss entrusted with a full and honest reply.

Katie's room was at the end of the corridor. It was a small, rather dark space with walls painted in a murky shade of mauve, a shade the Victorians might have accepted as 'half-mourning', and was, Alice considered, thoroughly dismal. One of Mo's spidery blue and white dream-catchers hung at the window and in contrast to the gloom of the walls, the air was fragrant with the lightly floral scent of Katie's skincare products. She wasn't a tidy woman – lacy thongs were scattered across the floor and a pink and white polka dot bra hung from the inside door handle. Her small suitcase hadn't been properly unpacked and shoes and tee shirts spilled out from it. How can people do that, Alice wondered briefly, rather appalled. Wherever she stayed, even for a night, she always made a point of unfolding clothes, fluffing them out and hanging them up. She might have changed a bit in these few weeks, but she had some standards that she was sure would never slip.

Speedily, Alice took hold of the pillow and shoved the scrap of red paper inside the flap. That would have to do. The paper would fall out when Mo came to change the bedlinen and she'd probably guess what it meant, especially when she found the corresponding piece in Patrice's room. It didn't matter. Mo would assume that sensible, sceptical Alice would be the least likely person to have put it there.

Jocelyn had put out the orange tablecloth and the yellow candles for the Lammas supper. She arranged them on the table, spacing the five fat candles evenly along its length. She wasn't going to make a big ceremony out of it, even though Patrice was insisting on doing some filming during the meal. As he really seemed so keen to know how these things were done, she'd be sure to include the bit where he had to press his hand onto nettle leaves and get thoroughly stung. She was liking him less and less, somehow sure that he was, in some way, laughing at her and intending to make her look a fool. That wasn't comfortable and it meant that all the time he'd been cheating. It had started with her showing him Arthur's grave – she'd seen that cynically amused look. She could tell that in that moment he'd decided his take on her was going to be of a faded, failed, run-down minor icon who should never have become one in the first place. Soon he'd be gone – she wasn't going to waste her powers on dealing with him. Others were doing that for her: for what could he get across to viewers in a matter of only fifteen minutes?

In the meantime, while Mo worked her own form of magic in the kitchen, Jocelyn was going to ask Alice to show her what she had in mind for Cygnet. That way she could get in quickly with her own ideas before the place was turned inside out and filled with stainless steel walls, Perspex furniture and twinkly feature lighting.

Alice was waiting on the Cygnet front step. She watched her mother coming slowly along the path, leaning quite heavily on her stick, and she could see as Joss approached that she was breathing heavily. She wished she'd give up smoking – at this rate she would succumb to chronic bronchitis and wheeze away the rest of her life as a furious invalid. Joss was wearing ancient rust-brown cord trousers and an oversized ochre-yellow silk shirt. Harvest colours, Alice recognized, remembering how the household grown-ups used to enjoy dressing all the children of Penmorrow in outfits appropriate for whatever seasonal celebration was under way. Her favourite had been a silky dress she had when she was seven: the skirt was in layered petals of blue, the darkest underneath, overlaid with shades of paler colour. Three other little girls had been in the house at the time and Kelpie had made dresses for each of them, finished off by silver circlets for their hair, twined with crystal beads and forget-me-nots, violets and periwinkle. Alice had felt like a flower fairy. For the first time, it occurred to her that she had rather unkindly deprived Grace of these magical nature traditions over the years. Of everything that she'd rejected when she'd left Penmorrow and run off to a comfortably conventional life, these ancient pagan celebrations were possibly the things she should have hung onto. Grace's bit of tame maypole dancing at primary school, with no real comprehension of what it signified, and sterile, produce-free harvest festivals ('tinned contributions only please') didn't really come near to the close-to-the-earth excitement of the old festivals.

'What are you up to in here?' Joss peered past Alice into Cygnet as if she expected a team of designers to have stripped the place out already, and be busily measuring up for glass-brick partitions and more bathrooms than bedrooms.

'Nothing yet. The curtains are down and the carpet is up. That's all. Nothing irreplaceable – come in and see. Did Harry say anything about knocking the two bedrooms into one?'

Jocelyn frowned. Alice realized she was rushing her, and of course there was the question of cash. Even though Harry could do most of the work, he'd need professional help with relocating electricity sockets and relaying some of the flooring.

'Let me look. Don't talk for a moment, just let me get the feel of it.'

Joss slowly wandered from room to room, saying nothing but inspecting intently.

'Wonderful views,' she said, looking out through the French doors towards the shore. 'It's a good little house and I can feel a happy soul to it. My kelims would suit this floor too. I didn't know the boards were so dark – they'll polish up well. Arthur's Pan statue would settle happily over here by the fireplace.'

Alice was amazed – something she was doing seemed to be getting approval at last.

'I don't want paying renters stamping about on my rugs though,' Joss said, then looked at Alice intently as

260

she came out with her bombshell decision. 'I'd have to be the one who lives here.'

'*You?*' Alice exclaimed. 'Why?'

Joss sank down onto the crackled leather sofa. 'Stairs, in a word. Dilapidation in another; both Penmorrow's and mine. The house and me, we're falling together into a state of terminal disrepair. And there's Mo and Harry. I'm not a fool, Alice, I know they don't want to struggle along with all this any more. They do what they can but it's too much now and it's driving them insane. For them Penmorrow is a millstone.' She laughed briefly. 'Just as according to your Noel it's a goldmine.'

'But what would . . . would you sell it? Just keep Cygnet?'

Joss looked out of the window. Across the orchard was Penmorrow's back door, next to which more roof tiles had splintered on the path. 'Cygnet *and* Gosling, so you'll all have somewhere to stay. These are new thoughts. I haven't said anything to Harry yet. Now might be the time for a change. And this little house would suit me very well.'

The table was now a gloriously decadent post-prandial mess, piled high with discarded lobster shells and empty wine bottles, fat brown crumbs from the chocolate brownies and dollops of cream that had missed the plates as everyone got drunker. Joss had said it resembled the cover photo of *Beggars Banquet* and had claimed, truthfully or not, for who could say, that she'd been there at the time for that particular shoot.

Mo was pleased with herself. The cooking had gone well, everyone had had a jolly evening and no-one had picked a fight. That was the best thing about marijuana

261

– it blunted that edge of nastiness that made itself felt when people were drinking a bit too freely. Joss had been rather quiet – and later she'd be quieter still, having eaten three of the brownies. If she woke in the night with a panic attack, Mo thought, it would serve her right for being greedy. Even Noel had seemed quite jovial and had had only two tentative digs about the house falling to bits. He'd mentioned the chimney needing repointing (as if they hadn't noticed, it had been on the list for years), and had suggested the horror word 'subsidence' as the reason why the downstairs loo door wasn't shutting properly. Both comments had failed to get Jocelyn even mildly provoked. It was as if she'd given up. Only Patrice had seemed low-key and had an air of disappointment – Nick had kept the camera running for the entire meal, mostly, she could see, in the hope of a display of foul-mannered truculence. She was surprised there hadn't been a sneaky bit of whispering to Katie, telling her to stir things up by having a grope at Aidan or Noel, or to start flinging food about. In the event it could have been any old genteel dinner party of the sort (Mo imagined) that Alice and Noel were used to. Even the children had behaved well – they were still in the kitchen now, loading the dishwasher and clearing up, generously bribed by Alice.

Mo had hidden the rest of the special chocolate brownies at the back of the larder in the Princess Diana cake tin. She'd been careful to make sure that what the children had eaten did not contain any of the harvest – Chas and Sam were quite wild enough, and she didn't want to be the one responsible for giving Theo and Grace a taste for mind-altering substances. It was the sort of thing London parents might sue you for later, when they were trying to come up with the funds for expensive Arizona rehab clinics.

Mo went out onto the porch and helped herself, on the way, to another of the rather sickly violet and almond sweets that Alice had handed round with the coffee in the sitting room. They seemed a bit of a peculiar contribution, in her opinion. Why on earth hadn't she just bought some of the fancy overpriced chocolates from the shop in Chapel Creek when she'd been over there the day before? And so eleborately packaged, too. It was as if she was trying to pass them off as having been bought from some swanky specialist confectioner. If so, that was one hell of a failure. Perhaps she should warn her for another time: the Tupperware box was a bit of a giveaway.

In the kitchen, rinsing dregs of wine from the glasses before putting them in the dishwasher, Grace watched as Chas and Sam devoured yet another chocolate brownie each. She couldn't eat another thing. She was getting impatient – the boys had said they'd come out with her, sneak back into the garden of Hamilton House and look for her watch. She'd have preferred to go in the daytime, doing it the easy way by paying to get in, but the twins liked to turn everything into some kind of adventure. She didn't mind too much, just so long as they got it together soon. She wanted to be back quickly, to get into bed with her little red silk bag of dried-mushroom spell. The sooner she tried it, the sooner the charm could start to work.

'Go on, Grace, have one of these. They've got a special ingredient: Harry's Wholesome Harvest.' Sam giggled, crumbling cake on the table and picking up bits on a licked finger.

'I had some for pudding,' Grace said, 'and nothing's

happening to me.' She closed her eyes. Nothing was whirling about, nothing felt any calmer or spacier.

'She gave us the plain ones. I saw her hide these away where she thinks we won't know.'

'Go on then, I will.' Theo crammed a whole brownie into his mouth and spluttered out crumbs.

'Don't waste it!' Chas yelled at him.

'Why not?' Grace said. 'I've seen how much of the stuff he's grown in that tunnel. There's not what you'd call a shortage round here. You've got the European dope mountain out there. Your dad's got years inside if he's caught.'

Grace was feeling restless. Noel had commented that she'd got a pale band on the skin of her wrist where her watch had been. It just had to be in the garden of Hamilton House, down where she'd been lying by the pond. The more she thought about it, the more she was convinced she'd taken it off that night to put her hands in the water. She'd thought about it so much that she was no longer sure what was real and what she was inventing. The police had been in the village again. Noel had said he was amazed they hadn't got anything more serious to worry about, but Alice had gone all sensible and reminded him that theft was a major crime wherever it was and whatever was stolen. Noel, she'd said, was always the first to complain back home when the police got a bit casual about robberies and break-ins.

'Look, are we going to look for my watch or not? Because if not, I'm going back to Gosling to watch telly.' Grace headed for the back door.

'No, it's OK, we'll come,' Sam said, taking the Princess Diana tin back to its shelf in the larder. Theo dusted crumbs off his tee shirt and nodded. 'And me.'

It was a night that was too bright again. In the sky as

264

they walked Grace could easily pick out the Milky Way.

'There'll be shooting stars. It's that time of the year,' Chas said, gazing upwards and tripping over a stone on the path.

Grace didn't feel as scared this time, climbing quickly through the gap in the Hamilton House fence and half-crawling across to the shelter of the shrubs. They weren't going to do anything very illegal tonight, and you didn't get prison for a bit of trespassing. They hadn't even bothered to camouflage their faces. Silently, they followed the track to the pond, moving fast as if they were comfortably familiar with it now. Chas handed her his torch. 'I've turned it down so it only has a pencil beam. Point it down, where you think you dropped the watch. Don't wave it about.'

'I'm not stupid,' Grace hissed at him, crouching so the beam fell brightly on its tiny circle of focus. For a while the four of them crawled round by the pond's edge. Eerie pale shapes came and went on the surface of the water, the remaining fish apparently no worse for their brief poisoning. There was a low rumbling noise nearby. Grace, assuming it was a badger or fox, took no notice, but beside her she felt Sam's body go stiff and he clutched her wrist in a way that told her she had to keep rigid and silent.

The growling sound came closer, then turned to rustling and a ferocious barking.

'Run!' Chas yelled. Sam grabbed Grace's hand and hauled her after him as they raced through the garden, down past the children's playground towards the fence at the bottom of the hill. Some way behind them, Grace could hear the dog and the panting voice of its handler shouting, 'Hey you little bastards! Stop!'

Grace thought she was going to be sick. She'd never

run so hard or so fast in her life. Perhaps that was the way to get reluctant girls like her to excel on the school athletics field – set vicious guard dogs on them. Even when she and Sam scrambled over the fence and dropped down to the road, it wasn't over. She couldn't see Theo or Chas but was scared to slow down in case the dog and the man leapt over the fence. Sam kept running and so did she, panting and stumbling towards the village and the beach.

'Run into the waves a bit,' he shouted back to her. 'Put it off our scent.' They were on the sand now, racing towards the far cliff. Grace glanced back. She could see some movement under the lights outside the Blue Cockle pub but couldn't hang around to see if it was the man with the dog or not. They'd reached the rocks now and Sam wasn't stopping, so she followed. She would never know where her strength came from to haul herself up the slippery rocks after him, too close to the waves and dangerously near to being swept into the water as they crashed close by then ebbed, sucking back powerfully. At last they made it to the ledge and the twins' cave and collapsed inside, fighting for breath.

'Made it,' Sam gasped, flinging himself to the floor and reaching out to the back to retrieve a can of Coke. 'Grace? Fancy a drink?'

It had been hard enough to get to sleep. Mo had put too much stuff in those chocolate cakes and Jocelyn's brain had been racing with strange fancies. For what felt like hours she'd lain awake, thinking about past travels, past lovers. Far too much past, in fact. It was time to think about the future, while she still had one.

Eventually she'd managed to sleep, but too soon she was woken by the sounds from Patrice's room.

For a few moments she thought she was still dreaming, still reliving, deliciously vividly, one of her more passionate encounters from long ago. But the noises were on the far side of the wall: the all too clear sound of unconstrained passion. So, she thought, Alice's little charm (for she recognized that violet-candy ruse) had worked only too well. Patrice was evidently doing a thoroughly good job of pleasuring Katie in the bed that Joss had so recently deemed retired.

It wouldn't do to stay around and listen. It only led to regret that such times for herself were now in the past. Joss climbed carefully out of bed and wrapped herself in the long purple knitted coat (made from Tremorwell wool, all gathered from hedgerows and fences and supplemented by thefts from live sheep) that had been given to her by a grateful houseguest many years before. She would go, she decided, out into the garden and look at the sky. This was the season when the Meteors of Perseus could best be seen, and on a clear night like this she'd have a spectacular view of the shooting stars. The cannabis was still in effect; she could feel it softening her thoughts and she wanted to watch the universe's miracles in a state of mild hallucination.

Joss fumbled for the landing light switch but the bulb had blown again. She'd tell Harry in the morning, she thought, as, clutching her stick, she felt her way to the stairs. She was more than halfway down when the long, heavy coat tangled round her foot and tripped her. The noise she heard as she fell seemed oddly distant. With the protective mental detachment of one who is about to be horribly injured, she wondered: was it herself screaming? Or was it Katie yelping her way (at last) through an orgasm?

Sixteen

If he says what I think he's going to say, I'll bloody divorce him, Alice thought to herself as she watched Noel pouring brandy into the glasses lined up on the tray. This would be the moment, if he was going to say it. It was all too horribly likely that he wouldn't be able to wait, wouldn't be able to resist pointing out the obvious, as if it had only just crossed his mind, that Penmorrow was getting too much for Jocelyn – as if no-one else had noticed. She could just hear him being persuasive, reasonable. 'Staying here, you're only going to be a danger to yourself . . .' It would sound as if he was so very concerned. Joss wouldn't be fooled, she'd know quite well that he'd been on the point, ever since he'd first seen her using a stick to help her get around, of suggesting that she move into something more – how would he put it – secure. Sheltered housing was the phrase in his head – Alice could see it all brightly thought out, as if his mind was a fridge door covered in magnetic letters. She would tell him, very soon, that Joss had already made plans of her own.

'Medicinal purposes,' Noel said, fortunately for him, and very much surprising Alice, as he handed glasses to Mo, Katie, Aidan, Harry and Patrice. Alice didn't want one. She was still feeling a peculiar woolliness in her head from the stuff Mo had cooked into the chocolate brownies. She shouldn't have done that, she thought. It was dangerously irresponsible to let people unwittingly munch drugs, however tiny the amount. It was on the same risk level as spiking a drink by adding an extra shot or two of vodka. Suppose one of them had had to drive to Truro? Suppose the doctor had managed to persuade Joss that she needed a stay in the hospital? She could just imagine the scene. 'Sorry – it'll have to be a taxi or an ambulance, I'm completely (as Theo would put it) off me 'ead.'

Jocelyn lay on the sofa, quiet and dozy beneath her treasured silk patchwork quilt. Alice could see it was getting a bit tatty now; seams between some of the diamonds were coming adrift and thin, greyish wadding was poking through. It would be good to mend it. She had a clear picture of herself sitting on a sunny late afternoon in the hexagon window with the sun going down over the beach, sewing fine, strong little stitches into the silk. With some of the patches, the fabric itself was shredding and would need to be taken right out and replaced with something new. She'd take trouble to find the right colours, rich but muted ones, nothing too brash that would clash with the faded old shades. Except it wasn't going to happen. If Cygnet was to be revamped for Joss and if Harry and Mo were to escape to live as they chose, Penmorrow would certainly have to be sold.

Katie and Patrice were looking at each other as if they could barely wait to get back to bed. They kept touching lightly, just brushing hands, Patrice giving a small stroke to the back of Katie's neck. They were doing it as if trying to make sure nobody noticed, but as if they were equally sure everyone's eyes couldn't help but be on anyone but them. So it had worked then, Alice thought, her little foray into charm-making. The sensible, Home Counties wife in her told her not to be silly, that it was coincidence, but she was secretly delighted all the same.

Jocelyn wasn't badly hurt, only shaken up and bruised. When Aidan had found her on the floor at the bottom of the staircase she'd already been trying to get up. 'Go away, sweetie, I only tripped down a few steps,' she'd said, strenuously refusing to have anything to do with a hospital. The doctor on call from the village surgery was a reluctant compromise.

'Oh dear oh dear. So you've had a fall,' he said, misjudging Joss's tolerance of affability and unwittingly causing her to look as if she was thinking of the worst curse to put on him, and to reply, 'How clever of you. I'd better warn you that my brain cells didn't fall out in the process.'

Alice had groaned quietly. Whatever would Jocelyn be like in a hospital ward? She'd probably be thrown out for complete lack of co-operation.

'By mid-morning that Mrs Rice at the shop will have spread it around that I'm about to snuff it,' Joss grumbled after the doctor had checked her over and left, conceding only that she would lie on the sofa, although she'd been adamant she was quite capable of climbing the stairs back to her own bed.

'It was lucky,' she whispered to Alice while the others were getting stuck into the medicinal brandy, 'that I'm what Harry would call "completely out of it". Makes you so very relaxed.'

Alice wasn't so sure. Would Jocelyn have even contemplated wandering down to look at the stars if she'd been entirely in her right mind? She didn't think so.

And she'd feel worse in the morning when the bruises came up, however much arnica and paracetamol she'd had. Who'd be there for her when she was living alone in Cygnet, Penmorrow sold and Harry and Mo far away off the premises?

There was a loud scuffling from outside and Theo and Chas raced in looking frantic. Alice wondered where they'd been – probably down to the pub with the surfers, although it was now close to midnight. Chas and Sam weren't thirteen yet – had Mo and Harry even known they were out of the house? Was she, she then wondered guiltily, so much better – assuming but not checking that Grace was safely tucked up in her own bed with her cat, or camping, as she sometimes did, in Sam and Chas's den here in the main house?

'Where's Grace and Sam? Are they here?' Theo looked round as if expecting to see them emerge from under a chair. He didn't seem to notice Jocelyn, or that everyone – apart from Noel who'd been fast asleep fully clothed on Gosling's sofa when Mo came to tell them about Joss's accident – was dressed for sleeping.

'Aren't they with you?' Stupid thing to say, Alice realized as the words came out. '*Were* they with you? Where've you been?'

'Shit. They're not back.' Chas slumped into the peacock chair and stared out of the window. The wind was getting up and plump black clouds were now scudding across the moon.

'Theo – just tell me, where have you been and where did you leave Grace?' Noel cornered his son by Joss's statue. Theo stuffed his hands deep in his pocket and stared at the floor.

'We were being chased,' he admitted. 'Grace and Sam went one way, we went the other. We came back . . .'

271

'Back from *where*?'

'Um . . . she'd dropped her watch somewhere. We were just helping her find it. Then there was this man and the dog. I think the others must have . . .'

'They're in the cave. I just know they're in the cave.' Chas leapt out of the chair and went close to the window, leaning his forehead against the glass and peering into the darkness as if he could actually make out his twin and his cousin in the dank hole in the rocks. 'What time is it?'

'Twelve thirty, near enough,' Noel told him. 'Why on earth would they be in a cave? Why don't they just come home?' He moved close to the boy, looking, Alice thought, as if he wanted to shake information out of him. She stood next to Noel, frightened, taking his hand.

'Because they can't get out.' Chas said the few words in a chilling whisper. 'It's about an hour to high tide. It's a spring tide.'

'We're stuck, aren't we?' Grace looked down at the sea, watching the waves rise up close then pull far away again. In the dark the vast water looked like a huge creature that was trying to reach for her but couldn't quite get there. It didn't look as if it was going to give up trying, either.

Sam didn't say anything. He stood beside her on the ledge, pointing his torch up at the cliffs. She could see he was worried. She began to get scared.

'It's high tide now, isn't it? How long till it goes down enough for us to get home?'

Again, Sam said nothing. Why not?

'Sam? Are you listening to me? It's so cold.' She wrapped her arms round herself, wishing she was wearing more than a thin towelling hoodie and her

272

V-Dolls cut-offs. She pulled the hood up over her head and huddled her hands up her sleeves.

'It's not quite high tide.' He said it so quietly she could hardly hear, and it took her a few moments to realize what he meant.

'There must be another way out,' she said, frantically jumping up to see if there were handholds up on the cliff. 'We could climb up to the top.'

'Too dangerous, too slippery, too steep,' he told her. 'Come back inside, come and help me make a fire.'

'Oh great, so we'll die warm then.' Grace was close to terrified tears but followed Sam to his fuel pile at the back of the cave and started to help him carry kindling to heap up on the ledge.

'It's for a signal. Someone might see. And anyway Chas should guess where we are. We'll be OK.'

Grace wanted to scream, wanted to yell 'No we won't!' at him, but he was being so calm, so controlled, that she could only get on with what he told her to do.

'If we had room the best thing would be to have three fires. That's an international distress signal,' Sam told her as he carefully stacked the sticks. 'But we haven't got space or enough wood so it'll have to be one. Someone might see us. They must.'

It was the middle of the night. There were the red lights of a couple of helicopters moving across the sky out in the distance, miles and miles away on the horizon. Harry had said they were from the naval base, doing night manoeuvres. They weren't much use manoeuvring so very far away. Grace, close to panic, wanted to sit in the cave's mossy back corner and weep quietly with her thumb in her mouth, waiting for whatever fate decided. She could feel the little bag with the charm in it inside her top, and she reached under and touched the piece of silk. She'd wished she could stay in Cornwall, that she wouldn't have to go back to live in London. It looked as if she was about to be granted just what she'd wanted. She imagined her mother staring down at her sea-bloated body in a cold grey mortuary. Would she be in one of those big fridge drawers like they had on TV programmes? She and Sam would be stacked away like a pair of frozen pies.

The fire lit with the first match. Sam watched his little stack of dry leaves and kindling crackling into life. Grace wondered how long it would last before the sea spray killed it off again and then crept up the rocks to claim her and Sam as well.

Ropes. Harry knew exactly where to find them. He kept a collection of them at the back of the ruined shed where the little tractor was parked. They were neatly coiled and hung on a row of hooks, just in case. There hadn't actually been an emergency 'just in case' before, that he could think of, and he hoped the damp air hadn't rotted the fibres away to dangerous uselessness.

Even Patrice was coming with them. There'd be plenty of people to get the kids out. Noel knew about climbing techniques, or so he said: he'd done all his rock-climbing way back in his university days. Harry tried not to feel doubtful about this, telling himself that it might have been a long time ago but rocks and ropes don't change a lot over the years.

Alice ran on ahead with Theo, Aidan and Chas, racing down to the village and up the side of the far hill, fear and dread combining to give her the strength and speed to keep up with the young ones. She could see the glow from the small fire that Chas pointed out. At least it confirmed where Sam and Grace were, and, presumably, that one or both of them were still alive: if the fire kept burning the sea hadn't yet got to the ledge.

'No helicopter yet.' Chas looked disappointed. Alice had called the coastguard, concerned that they should be prepared with a back-up rescue route. It wasn't that she didn't think Noel could get to the children, but suppose they were injured? Suppose they were just too frozen with exhaustion and fear to be able to haul themselves up the rope?

They'd reached almost the top of the cliff, the best place, Noel was certain, for him to go down with a rope and collect Grace and Sam. Alice saw a flicker of something white on the grass beside a copse of trees and for a moment thought Grace had managed to get out, but it flashed away into the bushes. Grace's white rabbit. At least that had survived.

Noel was going down the rock by himself, secured at the top by the other six. Patrice was the last of them, the anchor if all the others mysteriously fell over or dropped into a dead faint. Noel hadn't been very keen on Patrice, but if he turned out to be the one person who kept him from falling into the heaving sea he'd probably feel like asking him to move in and set up home with the family.

'You have to go first. Noel's nearly here,' Sam said to Grace, looking up the rocks as Noel slithered his way down with the double rope.

'No you're the youngest, you go,' Grace argued. She didn't much want to go up the cliff. She was terrified but she also knew they had no choice. The sea had just started to lap at the lip of the ledge. The spray had put the fire out. She and Sam were both soaked and shivering.

'No you go first, really. I'll be OK.' Sam was grinning at her. She couldn't think why. What was there to smile about? Noel scrabbled down the last few feet and dropped onto the ledge beside Grace. On a tearful impulse she hugged Sam close to her. 'I'll see you at the top.'

'No you won't,' he said, still smiling. 'Look. I'm waiting for my lift.' He pointed across the bay. A helicopter was approaching, its sound almost drowned by the noise of the sea.

'Luck*eeee*,' Chas and Theo, hair blasted in the gale blown up by the helicopter's rotor blades, agreed as they lay on the top rock up by Grace's bench, the place from where they could best see Sam's dramatic rescue that was about to take place below. Grace was safe, tied to the double rope and half-hauled, half-climbed up to the top. Sam, though, that was something else.

'Hope he remembers about the static,' Chas said, half-expecting a big blue flash as Sam got hold of the winch sling. No flash came, but after a few moments, whirling up fast through the air, came the helicopter. The door was still open and they could just see, waving and grinning at them in the first sunlight of the day, the brazenly cheery face of Sam.

'Aidan gave me this last night just before that mad supper. I forgot to give it to Grace.' Noel, bringing a cup of tea up to Alice the next morning, put Grace's watch down on the window ledge. 'He found it lying on the verandah. The catch is broken. I'll see if I can fix it and then give it to her later, after she's had a chance to sleep off last night.'

He sat down on the bed beside Alice and handed her the tea.

'Thanks, Noel,' she said, taking a reviving sip. 'I should be the one bringing tea for you. Hero!' She leaned across and kissed him. She felt close to tears, remembering not only how close she'd come to losing

Grace, but how determinedly, selflessly, Noel had taken it on himself to get the girl to safety. It was what you did for your own flesh and blood, the sort of spontaneous bravery that you got in real families. Like theirs, if only she'd realized it.

'Look, Alice, I'm not bothered about Italy,' he said. 'We can go any old time. Some things are more important.'

'Would you really not mind? I'm sorry but I think I should stay with Joss for a bit. She's made some decisions.'

'No, it's fine. Do whatever you need to. Grace and Theo will be happy to stay on, they seem to love it here. And you, you're not the same as back home.'

'Which one do you prefer?' Me here or me there?'

'Either. Both.' He laughed and hugged her. 'Bring this version of you home as well when you come back!'

'Unless . . . unless I don't come back?' No, that sounded wrong. Noel looked as if she'd hit him with a brick. 'Not coming back? But why?'

'No, no I didn't mean it like that!' She slid her arms round him. 'I was just thinking, now that Joss has made the decision to sell Penmorrow. What's really so great to go back for? For any of us?'

Grace sat on the battered red leather beanbag beside Jocelyn's peacock chair. The beanbag was so dried out and faded, it looked like mummified skin that she'd seen in a museum on a school trip.

'Did you think you were going to die?' Jocelyn asked her.

Grace thought for a moment. 'A bit. Well no. Not really. Because Sam didn't. He was sure Chas would get something sorted.' Actually she hadn't thought

277

about the actual dying process. She'd thought about getting wet, about being in the sea and being tossed around on the rocks and about how it would hurt. She'd thought about being cold and sodden in her clothes and about the taste of too much salt, but drowning and what it would feel like hadn't crossed her mind at all. She didn't know whether that was a failure of imagination or not.

'You're young, you're still blessed with that certainty that you've got all the years you need. You stick with that.'

'What about you? Are you all right? I heard you fell down the stairs. Did *you* think you were going to die?'

'Heavens no! There wasn't time! My fall simply illustrates the dangers of overindulgence.' Joss sighed. 'Learn something from that. Though of course you probably won't, you'll make your own errors, as you should.'

'If you're going to overindulge, make sure you do it in a safe place.' Grace sounded as if she was reciting from a book. 'See, I did learn something.'

Grace was fidgety with excitement. She was not going back to London. Even Noel was excited about the idea. Alice was in full hyper-organization mode, doing her favourite thing with notebooks, making lists. There were builders to be talked to, schools to be checked out, agents found to handle the house sale in London. Penmorrow was going to be home. Mo was in a thoroughly happy mood. Some of the money from selling the Richmond house was going to buy them a bed and breakfast place in St Ives – something manageable, size-wise. Mo was going to have time to paint again – she could think of no better place to do it. Gosling Cottage would be hers and Harry's to visit whenever they wanted and so that Harry would carry on with his vegetable-growing. The home-grown cannabis movement would, he'd decided, have to carry on without him. Those long scarlet peppers were the thing, those and stripy yellow and green courgettes. Pretty food sold well. Arrange a multicoloured selection of those, with red and white onions and a long vine of cherry tomatoes, and punters would almost knock you over in the rush to hand over silly money.

'When I was in the cave,' Grace told Joss, 'I thought about that charm I'd made with the mushrooms. I'd asked it if I could somehow not go back to London. That was the only bit when I thought I *might* die – when I thought the charm had worked and that I was getting what I wanted but not *how* I wanted it.'

Joss shook her head and smiled. 'Ah, but that's the trick. It's just as well you're going to be staying close to me,' she said. 'You've a lot to learn yet. There's a knack to it. Lesson one is: be careful, very careful, what you wish for.'

Almost a year later Jocelyn's book (*Angel's Flightpath*) had made its way into the shops and onto the review pages in the smarter Sunday papers. It had only been out a couple of weeks but was reported to be doing well. Several journalists had ventured (on expenses, enjoying the May sunshine) to Penmorrow to interview Joss, and she was revelling in her new, though possibly brief, go at fame. Libby Purves had been gratifyingly sweet on *Midweek*. The *Sunday Times* 'Day in The Life' piece had been startlingly well received. It was only with reluctance she'd turned down Graham Norton on the grounds that it clashed with Grace's school play: *A Midsummer Night's Dream* in which, as Titania, she'd worn Joss's Ossie Clark rainbow elf outfit.

Jocelyn had a dozen copies of *Angel's Flightpath* lined up on the top bookshelf in Cygnet. Alice had caught her looking through each of them in turn, as if one might prove to have something different in it from the others, something that even Joss hadn't known about herself. Aidan's name featured in almost insultingly small print, she noticed. A hard, thankless job, ghosting, Alice had thought, seeing how little credit he'd got. No wonder he'd given so little of himself away. Why should he? No-one was paying him to spill out his personal life to strangers.

The family were all together now, gathered in the sitting room at Penmorrow waiting for Patrice's programme to begin. The roof had been the first priority and while the scaffolding was up the windows had been replaced with the perfect hardwood replicas that Alice had insisted on, much against the opinion of Mrs Rice and the other two dragons in the shop. 'You want nice polyurethane replacements,' she'd advised. 'You'll never need the painters in again.'

Alice had smiled and nodded politely, just managing not to point out that 'not painting' was fine if you were content only to live with white for evermore. She'd gone for a paler, subtler version of Joss's original purple and very fine it looked, in her and the family's opinion. What the village thought, she didn't much care. In the rest of the house, too, she'd been surprised at herself for not choosing her usual shades of putty and cream. One bathroom was to be John Oliver's vivid Kinky Pink, another was to be a Caribbean mix of turquoises. Penmorrow, the house, was almost making its own choices, and they were vibrant and exciting.

The builders had been on site for a good seven months now, for five of which and a damp cold winter,

Alice, Grace and Theo had stoically continued to live in Gosling while Noel worked out his notice and dealt with the sale of the Richmond house. On Penmorrow's middle floor, three bedrooms and one of the bathrooms were now finished enough to be habitable and the kitchen was a designer's wet dream, though with the revamped green Aga proudly reigning over the chic improvements, like an ancient dowager over a collection of frisky young debutantes.

'What time's it start?' Sam asked for the fourth time.

'It said eight thirty,' Theo told him, stretching his long self out on the floor in front of the new scarlet velvet chesterfield. Sam and Chas looked years older than in the previous summer. They'd grown inches and taken to a short-cut hairstyle, with the same Tintin flicked-up front bits that Aidan had had. Theo had lost his London flabby pallor, partly, Alice was sure, because he'd spent all winter careering about with his new schoolfriends on Tremorwell's hills risking his life on a skateboard, and as soon as the weather warmed up practically lived in the sea on a surfboard.

'A few bits of wood and polystyrene,' Noel had remarked one day. 'If only I'd known that's all it would take to keep him amused.'

'I've put the pasties in the Aga to warm up, Alice,' Mo said, bustling into the room with a tray of glasses. 'Where do you want the champagne?'

'Inside me, please,' Jocelyn demanded from her peacock chair. Alice had tried and tried, but Jocelyn had insisted that the ugly, unravelling cane chair stay in the hexagon where it had always lived. 'It fits there, sweetie. You keep it,' Joss had said, patting Alice fondly as if she was bestowing a priceless gift. Joss, of course, had treated herself to a stunning Matthew Hilton leather chair to take pride of place in the revamped Cygnet and spent her afternoons in that instead, peering down her new telescope at the beach and the opposite headland, and reporting back gleefully whenever she saw an adulterously active couple up to no good in the copse by Grace's favourite bench. Mo, well occupied with the new business in St Ives and recently converted to the delights of a nearby beauty parlour and hairdresser, commented that Joss should have better things to do than to go spying on villagers. 'Why doesn't she take up voluntary work?' she suggested. 'Or get on with another book?'

Alice poured champagne for everyone and turned up the volume as an advert for cat food faded away. Patrice, she hoped, had done right by Jocelyn in the editing of this life appreciation. It wouldn't, she thought, look good for him if he hadn't: Joss was, for the moment, something of a national treasure again, an admired survivor of mad times and excessive living. How long for, nobody knew. But then, Alice recalled, thinking of Grace and Sam trapped in the cave a year ago, who knew how long anyone had?

The programme started with the titles rolling across a view of Tremorwell Bay. Surfers bobbed on the water and there was the muffled sound of holidaymakers calling to each other and whooping through beach-cricket games.

'Oh look! Me and Big Shepherd!' Joss commented, pointing delightedly at the screen. Patrice loomed into shot, smiling at the view across the orchard, towards Arthur Gillings's grave. 'And here, for over forty years, an icon of her own, and succeeding generations . . . a muse, a symbol, a rebel, an inspiration . . .'

Alice caught Harry's eyes raised to the ceiling and smiled at him. 'She'll go all big-time after this,' he whispered to her.

'Yes, but what's new?' Alice said.

Grace watched the scenes of her new home as if it was another place and from another time. She lived here now – she was going to be the one who took over when Joss moved on. Exactly *what* she'd take over, she wasn't yet sure. All she knew was that she was now happy, at home and at her new school. And she was learning things here, things that the school witch girls wouldn't have the smallest clue about. Joss was a brilliant tutor, reading and instructing every weekend, sitting with Grace on the fabulous new rope swing chairs on the Cygnet terrace. Grace now knew the proper significance of each of the year's important festivals and about the part played by the gods and goddesses of the earth and planets and elements. Most importantly, she had her own special crystal that Joss had given her on her birthday. This Litha, Midsummer Day a few weeks from now, she would hang it up for the first time in the hexagon window and draw down the power from the sun for the protection and safe-keeping of all at Penmorrow.

THE END

NO PLACE FOR A MAN

Judy Astley

Jess has just waved goodbye to her darling son, off
backpacking to Oz. She's left with two teenage
daughters and husband Matt – all of whom find
themselves regularly featured in her popular and
lighthearted newspaper column in which she conveys
to her readers an enviably cheery muddle of
family life.

Things become less rosy when Matt, after twenty years
with the same firm, is made redundant. Only Jess sees
the potential calamity in this. Matt is delighted with
his new freedom and takes to hanging out at the local
bar with others of the male barely-employable
tendency, drinking and drifting and dreaming up
hopeless schemes to make them all rich. Daughter
no. 1, meanwhile, has taken up with a mysterious boy
living in an abandoned car on the allotment, and her
younger sister is over-burdened with a surfeit of
secrets. For Jess, trying to hold everything together
and missing her first-flown child, it becomes
ever-harder to maintain the carefree façade for
her readers. Of course she could just tell them
the truth . . .

'DELICIOUS DOMESTIC DISHARMONY'
Woman and Home

0 552 14764 8

BLACK SWAN

PLEASANT VICES

Judy Astley

'THIS DELICIOUSLY FUNNY NOVEL HAD ME
LAUGHING OUT LOUD'
Woman and Home

The residents of the Close were much concerned with crime
– preventing it, that is. With all those out-of-work teenagers
on the nearby council estate hanging around, stealing,
joyriding and goodness knows what else, it was just as well
that Paul Mathieson was setting up a Neighbourhood Watch
scheme.

Not that the inhabitants of the Close did not have their own
little activities, of course, but these were hardly the same
thing. If Jenny and Alan's daughter was caught travelling on
the underground without a ticket, and their son was doing a
little experimenting with certain substances, and Fiona didn't
see the need to declare her earnings from hiring out her
house to a film crew, and Jenny drove home only *just* over
the legal limit – well, these were quite different matters, not
to be compared with what went on in the Estate. And then
there was Jenny's discovery, when she advertised flute
lessons, that she could work up quite a nice little earner in a
rather unexpected way . . .

As the leafy London street resounded to the efforts of its
citizens to keep crime at bay, Jenny realized that it was her
marriage, rather than her property, that needed watching.

'LIGHT, FAST AND FUNNY . . . BY THE TIME YOU TURN
THE LAST PAGE, YOU'LL NEVER BE ABLE TO LOOK YOUR
NEXT-DOOR NEIGHBOUR IN THE EYE AGAIN'
Prima

0 552 99565 7

BLACK SWAN

JUST FOR THE SUMMER

Judy Astley

'OH, WHAT A FIND! A LOVELY, FUNNY BOOK'
Sarah Harrison

Every July, the lucky owners of Cornish holiday homes set off for their annual break. Loading their estate cars with dogs, cats, casefuls of wine, difficult adolescents and rebellious toddlers, they close up their desirable semis in smartish London suburbs – having turned off the Aga and turned on the burglar alarm – and look forward to a carefree, restful, somehow more *fulfilling* summer.

Clare is, this year, more than usually ready for her holiday. Her teenage daughter, Miranda, has been behaving strangely; her husband, Jack, is harbouring unsettling thoughts of a change in lifestyle; her small children are being particularly tiresome; and she herself is contemplating a bit of extra-marital adventure, possibly with Eliot, the successful – although undeniably heavy-drinking and overweight – author in the adjoining holiday property. Meanwhile Andrew, the only son of elderly parents, is determined that this will be the summer when he will seduce Jessica, Eliot's nubile daughter. But Jessica spends her time in girl-talk with Miranda, while Milo, her handsome brother with whom Andrew longs to be friends, seems more interested in going sailing with the young blonde son of the club commodore.

Unexpected disasters occur, revelations are made and, as the summer ends, real life will never be quite the same again.

'A SHARP SOCIAL COMEDY . . . SAILS ALONG VERY NICELY AND FULFILS ITS EARLY PROMISE'
John Mortimer, *Mail on Sunday*

'WICKEDLY FUNNY . . . A THOROUGHLY ENTERTAINING ROMP'
Val Hennessy, *Daily Mail*

0 552 99564 9

BLACK SWAN

UNCHAINED MELANIE

Judy Astley

Is there life after marriage?

Melanie finds herself single again after years of being
one half of a couple. Her friends predict loneliness,
frustration, disaster. Her parents are convinced she's
a failure in life. But Melanie is overwhelmingly
excited to be able to do her own thing – she plans a
programme of behaving badly, after a lifetime of
behaving properly. With her daughter off to university
and ex-husband Roger married off at last – to his
lamentably young girlfriend whom he accidentally
got pregnant at the office party – she has what a
teenager would call a Free House, and she intends
to make the most of it.

But is the single life quite all it's cracked up to be?

0 552 99950 4

BLACK SWAN

A SELECTED LIST OF FINE WRITING
AVAILABLE FROM BLACK SWAN